MURDEROU

CW00927045

DUOLCᴜᴛ

The Trans-Canada Killer

What Happened Next

Murderous Moves Duology

Lynda French

Published by Lynda French, 2023.

This is a work of fiction. Similarities to real people, places, or events are entirely coincidental.

MURDEROUS MOVES DUOLOGY

First edition. August 17, 2023.

Copyright © 2023 Lynda French.

ISBN: 978-1998074051

Written by Lynda French.

Sincere thanks to my Aunt **Nessa Mackenzie** in Scotland *(born Agnes Taylor in August 1927)* for inspiring me to complete the novel. I appreciate her encouragement so much, and have dedicated this book to her.

Lynda French

Published by Lynda French, 2023

THE **TRANS-CANADA** **KILLER**

a novel

Lynda French

The Trans-Canada Killer

Lynda French

Published by Lynda French, 2022

Chapter One

December 13, 1979

BANG! the skidding car sideswipes and knocks down the stop-sign dragging it into the intersection. Fortunately, there's no one around. The afternoon's freezing rain is over but few people have ventured out in this ice-misted night.

The driver pushes at her door, swinging back and forth until she's freed it from the wooden sign-post, and steps out triumphantly shouting "I didn't spill a drop – not a drop! The thirteenth is a lucky day for me!" She twirls around waving her glass at an audience of sentinel pines when suddenly her feet shoot out from under and she falls straight down into a sitting position.

"Whoopsie! I think I lost a bit so I better drink it up" she said and did. Hanging on to the door she pulled herself up and reaching inside the car announced "Time for a beer after the chaser, ain't that right kids? And maybe 'nother chaser after that."

There were no street lights but the wet metal guardrails reflected the little bit of light that came from the clouded sky. The car was on the highway but turned facing back towards the side road. The interior light faded out and since the woman hadn't bothered putting on her headlights it was only due to its pale colour that the car showed at all.

The semi didn't stand a chance of stopping but of course the driver tried. He spun the wheel and almost avoided colliding but instead caught the car's back bumper with his tractor and pushed it into the loaded trailer jack-knifing round.

The driver was thrown sideways smashing his head against the left-hand window hard enough to crack the glass but he wasn't cut so there was no blood.

He shouted, the drunk cheered, and from the car came a high-pitched scream ominously cut short.

The trucker jumped out of his vehicle yelling: "What did you do? Why's your car in the middle of the road? What have you done?" but when he reached the car and looked inside despite the dim light he saw more clearly than he wished and got his answer. Tiny bodies horribly torn and mutilated by glass and metal driven into the bloody upholstery.

The sight sent him reeling away to the side of the road where he vomited violently while the teary, beery woman shrieked: "Wha-what? What's going on, what, what's happening? Where are my babies! What happened? No, no, no, no, no, no, noooooo you killed them! You did it, it was you, your fault, you killed them. Killer, baby-killer, you did it, it's your fault, you're the killer, my babies, my babies, you killer, killer".

Coming up the road the policeman in the cruiser expertly drove into his skid and swerved around the collision but he couldn't avoid hitting the trucker who lurched into his path waving his arms. The cop radioed in for back-up and ambulances before checking the scene, securing his prisoner, and administering the first aid which saved the now-unconscious trucker's life.

The clouds had drifted and the moon shone down spotlighting the frigid, grisly scene but the policeman wasn't even aware of how cold it had become.

Afterwards there was plenty of talk of who was to blame:

The mother who chose to drink and drive?

The venue hired by her employer where the woman was over-served at an afternoon Christmas get-together – a poorly planned party because the company had waited too long to book?

Her colleagues who had joined her in the many, many toasts yet let her drive away?

The day-care worker who was already late having waited with the children for forty minutes, and, in a hurry to get home herself, pushed them out of her car since it was far too late and she was far too angry to have a word?

Even the ex-husband who had grabbed a last-minute offer to go skiing and begged off taking the children on the day of the staff party as planned?

The OPP officer had followed the tractor-trailer for about twenty miles and attested that Dale Terry, the driver, drove correctly and safely for the poor road conditions.

Despite being exonerated Dale, when he finally woke from his medically-induced coma, felt horribly, irrationally guilty. His recovery was slowed by the deep depression he fell into while mourning the tragic deaths of the two young children.

Chapter Two

Summer 2015

"Are any of those blueberries actually finding their way into your pail, pardner?"

Jake gave his grandfather a wide grin, showing off his blue-stained teeth, and proudly displayed his three-quarters full bucket of fruit. The two of them were picking wild blueberries on one of the hills by the highway near their homes.

Actually it was Jake's home only for the summer. He was staying with his grandparents while his parents had some 'alone time' to see if they could salvage their marriage.

Nova Scotia in August should have been an eleven-year-old's paradise but Jake was suffering through sullen, anxious, and angry moods. His grandparents were doing their best to distract, entertain, and hopefully, comfort the boy because they loved having him visit - despite the reason.

The blueberry-picking expedition was fun but it was just an excuse to get out of the house for some 'man time', and so Jake could hear more stories about the famous murders that he'd asked his grandfather about since Grandpa T had actually been there at the time.

"It was sooooo long ago!" exclaimed Jake.

"Well yeah I guess it was, I'm getting old, eh?"

"Yeah, you are."

"Hey don't sugarcoat it, kid!" laughed the old man in mock outrage. "And you're right, it happened half, well just about half, my lifetime ago. Close enough for Government work."

"You didn't work for the Government, did you?"

"Huh, no way. But I did fill out so many forms for the Government that it sometimes felt like I did."

"But you were just a truck driver, why did you have so much homework?"

"Nobody is 'just a truck driver', Jake. I mean I sincerely hope you'll get a good education with maybe even university but never look down on people in the service industry. They keep the country's businesses running. Remember the old slogan from the Ontario Trucking Association: *if you got it, a truck brought it*."

"Okay, I see what you mean. Now tell me some more about the murders."

They could only have these talks away from his grandmother because she thought Jake was too young to hear about such things, but actually it was Jake who first mentioned the killings. The sharing of secrets between the two males made the tales that much more thrilling.

"Tell me more about the highway murders, Grandpa T." asked the boy.

Grandpa cocked his head and smiled saying: "Hmmph, just like Mr. T, eh? Do I remind you of him?"

"Remind me of who? I've never met a Mr. T."

"Of course you haven't, he's the guy from that TV show, oh maybe that was before your time. It was called 'The A-Team', a group of mercenaries or something – good guys, I guess – and Mr. T was a big muscular black man with a Mohawk haircut and lots and lots of gold jewellery."

"Well that's dumb, why would I think that? You're not black and you sure don't remind me of this Mr. T guy because I haven't even ever heard about him. And what's a Mohawk haircut? And it's called 'bling', not jewellery. You're supposed to say bling." Jake added.

"Got it. First, tell me why you call me Grandpa T?"

"Because I've got another grandfather and I see him all the time since he lives near us and he told me to call him Grandpa C, for Cherwell since that used to be Mom's name, so it just feels right to call you Grandpa T."

"Good, I like it. Anyhow, a Mohawk haircut is supposed to look like an Indian haircut from way back when. It's a strip of hair, two-three inches high and sticking straight up, down the centre of your head here" he reached over to demonstrate on Jake's skull. "With the rest all shaved off."

"Ugh, that sounds awful. Why would a black man wear an Indian hairstyle?"

"I don't know but it suited him, I mean it went with his overall look, you know?"

"Sounds pretty dumb to me. Now, c'mon and tell me about the killings."

Grandpa leaned closer and lowered his voice in a confiding manner: "Well, so long as you understand that this has just got to be between you and me, nobody else, right?"

"For sure. I won't let on to my Gramma."

"*Especially* not to your Grammy-Pammy and don't tell any of the neighbours either".

Giggling, Jake interrupted saying "She isn't gonna like being called that."

"I know!" exclaimed the old man with an eyebrow waggle that made the boy laugh harder. "She never did like it, not even years ago, and I'm not the only one who ever called her that." He paused a moment, smiling at an old memory.

"OK, here goes. In the first few months of 1980 Canada had a series of murders especially brutal in their violence.. this isn't going to scare you or anything, is it?"

"Noooo." breathed Jake in a wide-eyed whisper. "Tell me about the famous policeman."

"What famous policeman?"

"There's always a famous policeman. I don't know his name but there's always some guy."

"Hmm, well I don't remember that. I do remember an Inspector Lund of the Winnipeg police department. I didn't like him, which is probably why I remembered his name. I met him a couple of times, in Winnipeg and in Edmonton. He got the ball rolling on the investigation and kept at it, but he always said that the connections were made by Cam Stillwell. Funny, I still remember that name, too. She was a lady with the Royal Canadian Mounted Police but not a police officer because they didn't have women RCMP then. At least, I don't think they did."

"A lady detective!" exclaimed Jake, his eyes now bugging out in surprise.

"They say she didn't actually become involved in the investigation until the fourth murder but perhaps it was really the fifth, or even the six because not all so-called unlawful killings come under the jurisdiction of the RCMP and the murderer may have killed earlier in the new year and nobody found out. There was really no way to ever know for sure.

I do remember some politicians complaining that the Government didn't take the murders seriously or it would never have put a civilian in charge – and a woman, at that! There was also some talk that she was going to write a book about the investigation but couldn't because of RCMP confidentiality except she wasn't a member of the force... I don't recall much about that part."

As he spoke he realized that he could remember parts of that year with extreme clarity. Not that he had ever thought much about the murders. So much had happened that year – it was a big year for sports and an eventful time in the world and in his own life too. In fact, every time Willie Nelson came on the radio singing his version of 'Help Me Make It Through The Night' it was just like going back in time.

"That was the year that the Winter Olympics were held in Lake Placid, New York."

"Have you ever been to New York, Grandpa T?"

"Once. And once was enough for me. I don't really like Americans, they're a different breed altogether. No stranger is ever really safe around those people, and you never really feel comfortable among them."

"I've seen a lot of cars with American licence plates since I've been here."

"That's true, we do get plenty of tourists and I'm sure the town needs their money. I'm just getting sidetracked onto one of my pet gripes. OK, back to the murders.

Seven women were, as the newspapers put it 'bludgeoned to death' but connecting the crimes almost didn't happen, you know. It was Mrs. Stillwell who put everything together and even then not until it was almost over. And still some questions have never been answered. You know all about Playboy Magazine, don't you?"

Jake frowned at the sudden change of subject and looked away. He didn't even like listening to sex talk with his friends. What he thought about having such a conversation with his elderly grandfather was evident from his expression.

"See, in 1980 there was a beautiful blonde from Vancouver called Dorothy Stratten and she was chosen 'Playmate of the Year' which was a really big deal back then and still is now, I guess. Mostly that title goes to an American girl. Anyhow, it was the murder of Dorothy Stratten, by her husband by the way, that finally bumped the mystery of the Trans-Canada killings out of the newspaper headlines.

Up until then the papers were full of speculation with specialists chiming in because FBI profiling was still fairly new and nobody knew about DNA evidence back then, I don't think we had DNA in courtrooms until the 90s or something. So although all the details like the whys and hows, and all the facts were never actually spelled out the crimes were no longer news. See these victims weren't famous or glamourous. Their horrible deaths were the only thing about them that was newsworthy. They were just regular women who had got themselves killed."

Chapter Three

The door to the Dispatch office of Big Sky Moving was already open although it wasn't quite seven o'clock when Pamela arrived this morning. Arnie, the warehouseman, had, as usual, gotten in ahead of her. She could hear his radio playing.

Pamela was still on winter hours, meaning she could leave at 3:30 in the afternoon, but not for much longer. The busy season hadn't started yet – that wouldn't really kick-off until the kids were out of school. Already the bookings were coming in for a busier-than-usual Spring.

Corporations were trying to move as many employees as possible ahead of the summer rush. The Summer months were a busy time for everyone from real estate agents to carpet cleaners - even to small plumbing contractors hired to disconnect and secure the appliances for moving.

In addition, a lot of work was coming from companies who were relocating their businesses out of Quebec because of the language issue. Most were going to mid-sized communities in Ontario. Not Toronto, because the cost of housing was so high there.

It was standard policy for corporations to offer top management and executive staff low- or no-interest mortgages for the difference between their selling and buying prices when transferred to a higher-value real estate market. A lot of corporations decided to come to Alberta to enjoy all the advantages offered to businesses here such as less bureaucracy – meaning cheaper set-up and licensing costs – and no provincial sales tax which reduced spending.

Most of their fellow van line agencies chose Big Sky as their destination agent because of its reputation for good service. Since household furniture isn't built to be moved claims for damages happen and Big Sky handled the job with quick efficiency. It had a good name for keeping everyone happy.

The destination agent also stored shipments until the owners arrived and new homes were ready. It provided set-up and unpacking services, often making a second trip at a later date to pick up the unwanted boxes.

Once the season got going Pamela would be working long hours over six and even seven days a week. Sundays were a wash-out with no shopping allowed, so Pamela tried to get groceries in on Saturdays. The end-of-day was a good time to buy perishables. On Sundays only entertainment facilities such as theatres, bowling alleys, and restaurants were open.

Contracts couldn't be signed and money couldn't be banked. Trucks couldn't be on the road unless they were headed home and that had to be within a certain distance, statutes varied across the country. But it all meant Pamela would have a chance to get caught up with the invoicing, reporting, and other assorted paperwork requirements. Roughly two-and-a-half months of being crazy-busy when the company would earn the bulk of it's annual income.

Meanwhile, working winter hours was good.

There was never much traffic at this time of day so it was always a quick drive in but it was leaving early that made a real difference to the drive. Her little Honda Civic was no longer the novelty car it had been in 1976 when she bought it but it still felt so teeny-tiny when driving down the freeway surrounded by tractor-trailers. They blocked out the sun!

Of course her co-workers always seemed to urgently need her attention when she was packing up for the day. Usually it was Fiona, head of the Sales department.

"Why do you have to leave now, where on earth do you go this early?" complained Fiona one afternoon.

"Actually to the office of one of your biggest clients." Pamela retorted. "On Mondays and Thursdays I play in a bridge club that Craig Macallan told me about. His company provides the venue and coffee and it's great. We play contract bridge and draw for partners from whoever shows up."

"I didn't know you played bridge! And what a sly dog Craig is, he never told me he'd been chatting you up."

"He hasn't been – he knows I know he's married – but if he calls with a question about one of their moves and you're not here then he asks for me and we get talking. He loves a gossip, doesn't he?"

"Oh he's an old woman and I love it, he keeps me up-to-date with all the goings-on which are plenty! He goes to the bathroom and hides in a stall so when there's a particularly juicy story to tell. Well, it's a big office, isn't it? Lots of staff and lots of stories. So tell me, have you met any cute guys there?"

"No, there are plenty of nice folks but competitive card games don't bring out the best in people. Afterwards sometimes the winners will take the losers out for a drink but I usually don't go because it always seems to turn into a re-hash of what hands were played poorly. Sometimes the blaming and shaming gets awkward.

There are a few people I enjoy going out with because they're always a laugh but otherwise I don't. Besides, I'm usually starving by time we finish and all I want to do is hit Harvey's for a cheeseburger and fries."

"Fast food isn't good for you but I guess you never cook living on your own."

"Of course I cook! In fact I'll be roasting a turkey and a ham come Easter."

"Really? But that's so much food!"

"There's a lot you can do with leftovers and I'll make up meals and freeze them."

Recalling this conversation made Pamela think again about inviting some friends to share her Easter meal but she really didn't have any friends here except for co-workers. The truth was she was thinking about was inviting Dale – and Gerry too, of course – if they were in town.

She hung up her coat and went through to the office kitchen carrying the two coffee carafes which she rinsed before filling them with water. She loaded up a couple of filters with coffee and brought everything back to the coffee-maker in the Dispatch office.

She was busy thinking her thoughts while tidying up the coffee counter. She tossed out yesterday's detritus of stir sticks, crumpled napkins, and a plastic spoon with a nasty coating of coffee whitener. She opened a new box of sugar cubes and added to it the few remaining from the old one. Pamela didn't take any kind of sweetener herself but discovered that most of the men did and the office went through a lot of sugar.

The Easter holiday was still a ways away, the first weekend in April, but it was getting closer and she couldn't make up her mind whether she wanted to host a dinner after all. And what day would she choose? Probably the Saturday, because Easter Sunday or even Easter Monday were reserved for family. But of course lots of people made plans for Saturday nights.

Good Friday might work out, pretty much everything was closed that day, but would it be in bad taste – she smirked to herself at the pun – to have a meal? Were any of her guests Catholic and if so were they staunch Catholics who fasted or didn't eat any kind of meat that day? This was getting complicated.

What if only one of the guys was in town: would he get the wrong idea? She could ask Suzi and her boyfriend to come too but would that look like she was trying to make a date? So much for a fun, casual get-together! She was getting into knots about it. "I'll probably end up doing nothing at all and calling myself a coward." she thought.

Meanwhile, this quiet time in the office was her chance to get started on the paperwork. Arnie would be coming in any minute now that the coffee was ready. She poured her own cup and was soon immersed in her job scheduling trucks and crews to handle the upcoming moves.

Chapter Four

Monday February 18 to Wednesday February 20, 1980

"Dispatch, Pamela Wright speaking."

"♫ I'm back in the saddle again. Back where a friend is a friend.. ♫" sang Gerry Tanner before Pamela's laughter interrupted him.

"Well isn't it good to hear from you out there on the road singing your fool head off."

"It's good to be back at work. I miss being on the road and I really missed you, Perfect Pammy."

"Don't call me Pammy." she replied automatically. "How are you feeling? Where are you now, what are you doing, and where are you going?"

"Sometimes I get a bit headache-y but otherwise all good. I'm in Trenton, I just delivered on the Base. Then I'm taking my Cold Lake load straight through to Halifax. I think Van Line Dispatch must have been feeling sorry for me because they've given me a really great trip in and out."

"Hey, you're a hero and we're all glad you're healed up and back to work."

"No big deal, I've got a hard head and that's not all..."

"Give it a rest. Listen Dale's heading East too, he filled out with a load from Grande Prairie for Proctor and Gamble. He was still in Ontario when he called yesterday but said he should be in Halifax tonight or tomorrow."

"I'll catch up with him late tomorrow. I haven't heard from him but that's because the CB is jammed up with everybody talking about the murder just outside Kingston. I should get a phone in the truck."

"What murder?"

"They just discovered this body near the road, a woman. Somebody beat the hell out of her then dumped her on the side of the highway. Traffic's being diverted where they can and down to one lane where they can't so they're backed up for miles. I'm parking it till the road's fully open again. Hopefully just a couple of hours or so."

"Was she a hitchhiker?" Pamela asked.

"Nobody knows but everyone on the air's got a theory: she's a hitchhiker, she's an American who sneaked across the border, she's some trucker's wife, she's some trucker's girlfriend, she was running away from someone or she was chasing after someone. She was naked, she was fully clothed, she's young, she'd old, she's Native or White or Black – take your pick 'cause everybody's got something to say."

"And you're right in there saying your bit too, right?"

"I'm having a blast telling them how I just spoke to a guy at the gas station who's brother-in-law's with the OPP and he gave me the inside scoop and I'm making it up as I go along and everybody's listening like it's gospel."

"Well you sure do tell a good story." Pamela couldn't help laughing as she reprimanded Gerry saying: "It's really not a laughing matter, some poor woman is dead and it sounds like she died badly."

"That's true but nobody's really thinking much about her they're all bitching about the cops shutting down the Trans-Canada and how their schedules are getting all screwed up.

It's only the very beginning of the season and yet there are lots of familiar voices on the radio, and plenty of pals in the truck stops, too. It's good to see folks again. Actually I enjoy the chit-chat on the radio so maybe I wouldn't use a phone much."

"Gerry vehicle phones are a huge cost, I mean they're such a new thing and you'd probably need to re-wire – they have long antennas, right? So for the minimal added convenience do you really think it would be worth the cost?"

"I guess not, it's just I was listening to Bell..."

Pamela interrupted saying "Oh you hate him, why would you listen to a word Marshall Bell says?"

"Yeah you're right I can't stand him but he was talking about how he calls up his girlfriend when he's out on the road late at night and they talk and the talk turns sexy and Pammy I could call you and we'd sure burn up the phone lines."

"Seriously stop calling my Pammy, everyone's started doing that and I don't like it. And if you think you're going to phone me late at night for steamy sex chats you couldn't be more wrong!"

"I know you really want me but feel you have to hide your longing while we're at work and I understand, it's cool." Even Gerry chuckled at what he was saying.

"Oh just stop, you're such a goofy guy. Anyhow, if it turns out this killing is a real mystery maybe there will be something on tonight's news?"

"I'll let you know what I hear, it might just be a local story."

Chapter Five

Monday February 18 to Wednesday February 20, 1980

Being handed a hot cup of Tim Horton's coffee brought a delighted smile to Constable Jenny Renwick's face. The cold had given her a rosy glow and she radiated the cliched 'picture of health' of a mother-to-be.

Sgt Zadravec smiled fondly at the young woman. Although she herself had raised her family and finished with marriage years ago she could still enjoy Jenny's infectious happiness. And it wasn't like her family life had been a grim ordeal or anything.

Noreen had already joined the OPP when she met her husband, a Croatian from Yugoslavia, and continued to work throughout their marriage. He liked to cook which was a huge plus since her shifts often overran her scheduled work hours. The overtime money always came in handy when it came to outfitting two growing boys in sports gear, especially since the financial burden usually fell on her.

Unfortunately both parents missed attending games too many times. Noreen because of her job and her husband because of his gambling. Racetrack staff saw more of him than his family did. The result was that the brothers relied only on each other and grew independent of their parents. There had been good family times but just not enough to hold the four of them together.

Young Jenny and her husband will do things very differently, thought Noreen.

Peter Renwick was an earnest young man who attended the pre-natal classes with his wife and even went on his own when she couldn't make it.

He planned to be an active part of the child-rearing from diaper duty to bedtime stories to endless loads of laundry – starting in the delivery room. While having Dads alongside was becoming more common the majority of men weren't in there holding their wives' hands and encouraging them to push.

Noreen was certain Peter would be apologizing to Jenny each time she cried out in pain. She had strongly recommended having the epidural needle despite the current trend for delivering mothers to forego the drug.

She encouraged his enthusiasm for shared parenting since it would help Jenny achieve a good position in the Provincial Police force. With Peter's support she'd be able to go away on training courses and sign up for the many seminars that were necessary to those officers who were serious about advancing in their careers. There were still too few females in today's police force.

Meanwhile Jenny was stuck out here on the Trans-Canada this chilly afternoon maintaining a perimeter to preserve a crime scene. This is where the victim's body was discovered.

Two lanes were closed which reduced traffic to a crawl. None of the westbound highway lanes were barricaded but drivers slowing down for a look caused significant delays in both directions.

There was nothing to see since the fatal beating hadn't happened at the side of the busy road but curiosity is an integral part of human nature. When people heard how the woman died they'd be back rubbernecking in the hopes of spotting blood.

"Too bad some of these Lookie-Loos couldn't see some of the gore we've had to deal with, eh Sarge? That would cure them of being so curious and excited about somebody's violent death."

"You're just grumpy because you're cold, Jenny. Otherwise you would never wish something like that on the public."

Being reminded of the cold made Jenny stamp her feet, trying to ease the numbness. It seemed like her big pregnant stomach was the only part of her body that was warm. The dead woman was in her thoughts and she wondered if the victim had been a mother.

"Do we know who she was yet?"

Noreen untangled Jenny's poor grammar and answered: "The victim had identification in her purse, at least in the purse that was found a couple of metres from her body and assumed to be her purse, but the address is Saskatchewan. So we don't know for sure if it is her purse. And if it is we don't know if she's a visitor or if she moved here awhile back and hasn't gotten an Ontario licence yet or what."

"Maybe she just moved here? like now. If so, that might explain why nobody's looking for her because they don't know she hasn't arrived. That didn't come out right, I mean, no one knows she's not where she's supposed to be. Or at least, no one knows yet because if there was solid information they'd give us the word to wrap up this crime scene and move on, right?"

"Yeah, maybe she was in the middle of a move. Sure was one hell of a welcoming committee – as if moving house isn't bad enough!"

Chapter Six

The killer was thinking about the Kingston murder too.

The whole Morin family had been there when he arrived to deliver but the man took off when a couple of guys came by to pick him up. That gave the wife something else to gripe about.

"I don't get any help and it's not like I even wanted to move. I was nicely settled in where I was, even thinking about going after a part-time job to earn a bit of my own, but no, he puts in for the transfer and before I know it here we are. Right back where we started from."

Meanwhile the kids ran from room to room checking out their new home their shrill voices calling to each other to come see this or that. Their ever-increasing level of excitement meant pretty soon they'd be fighting or crying or both.

Their mother screamed at them to shut up and slapped the biggest kid, a girl, on the side of the head. Tears stood in her eyes but she didn't cry – instead one of the younger ones started wailing until Mom threatened to give her something to cry about.

Into this scene walked a woman saying "Is this any way to greet your Auntie Dorrie? Come and give me a kiss." And as the children clustered round her she smiled at their mother saying, "Hey Stacey, I know how crazy the whole moving thing is so I thought I'd take the kids out of your hair until these guys are finished. Afterwards you're all coming to our place for dinner."

"Your husband's already been by to steal mine away."

"Brian was here? Oh, well you know what brothers are like. He is so thrilled that you guys have moved back here. And I am too, of course, and so are your cousins," she said to the children, "so let's go meet up with them, OK?" To a chorus of noisy agreement she shooed the kids out before turning back and saying to the movers "Will a couple of hours do it?"

"I'll walk out with you." said Stacey Morin.

She was back again a few minutes later saying: "She means well but she does not think.I mean, what I need is a couple of jugs of milk, some juice, and bread. But the last thing I want to do is go to the store with hyperactive kids – this whole moving thing is really unsettling for them too – so I guess I'll have to wait for my husband to show up and God only knows when that'll be. No doubt that brother of his has taken him to the bar so he's only thinking about beer for himself not milk for his kids which is typical."

The driver turned to the crew he'd hired asking if they could get a ride back to their warehouse with the crew that came to unpack.

"Then I could give the lady a lift to the grocery store if you know where one is near here."

"Sure, it's only a couple of blocks remember where we turned left to come into this subdivision? Well if we'd turned right we'd have come to a big IGA."

"Oh that's not far at all so I can drive you if you like."

"Oh would you? That would be great. You'd only have to drop me off and I'll remember the route and can walk back. I'm only buying stuff for breakfast."

"Sure thing. As soon as we get the rest of the furniture in then you and I will go while these guys set up and unpack."

He couldn't say why he'd made the offer. He didn't mind helping people out but he didn't much like this woman. He didn't like her complaining and he wasn't happy about the way she treated her kids or spoke about her husband or her sister-in-law. She seemed the type to always find fault and nag about it. So why on earth had he said he'd take her grocery shopping?

Afterwards he still didn't know the answer.

He'd dropped the lady at the front of the store then waited in the parking lot till she finished. He knew that when a woman said she was going to pick up two or three things it always ended up being two or three bags' worth. So he was going to drive her back except... well things inside his head got all tangled up in blackness, blackness that turned red.

It gets dark while it's still afternoon in February. The killer was able to push her body, along with the two bags of food she'd bought, out of the truck with no one noticing a thing.

Since there was no car left in the grocery store's parking lot, or disabled on the side of the road, the police concluded that the victim had accepted a lift from a stranger while walking home with her shopping.

Chapter Seven

Pamela was trying to think objectively about Dale Terry but without much success. He was the only person she'd ever met whose surname could have been his Christian name. She'd only noticed that the other day when writing out a list alphabetizing the employees by last name, first name. She knew of some famous people with names like that - John Wayne, for example, and Terry Thomas. Also the author Jacqueline Susann. She smiled to herself wondering if it was possible that someday the name Dale Terry would be famous.

She wondered where he was – Gerry said he hadn't heard yet – and then she wondered when she'd hear from him herself. She couldn't deny she found Dale attractive, but she was determined to keep her feelings secret.

A relationship with one of her drivers, even though as a broker he was a contractor rather than an employee, wouldn't be appropriate. It would undermine her authority. Females in this job were rare and there were already enough men walking into the dispatch office with a chip on their shoulders ready to argue or complain about the arrangements she'd made for their work.

She couldn't stop anyone from talking behind her back but she preferred to leave them speculating about her personal life instead of giving them facts. Even friendly fellows sometimes tried to embarrass her if they had an audience.

"Pamela, how come you're so secretive about your private life?"

"Because it wouldn't be private otherwise."

"Well, you're not married, right?"

"Why do you ask?"

"No reason, just making conversation."

"I see. Is this the kind of conversation the guys at your wife's office have with her?"

"My wife works in a store at the mall."

And by time Pamela had replied with a comment like: "Oh, so she really gets to meet lots of new people all the time, hmm?" the rest of the workers had already joined in to tease the man which enabled her to end her participation.

But the questions and remarks continued and none of that changed the fact that whenever she was talking to Dale on the phone she couldn't help but notice how deep his voice was, or how happy he sounded – except that time he was angry after an argument with van line dispatch and called her 'Baby'. She figured he didn't even notice what he'd said.

Sometimes there would be a lengthy pause making it clear that neither one of them was ready to end the call yet and she'd catch herself holding her breath but... she always made sure she was the one to say goodbye first.

He'd asked her out for a drink once, not long after they'd first met, and although she'd said no – she'd already gotten into her car to head home – she had hoped he'd ask her out again.

Chapter Eight

Thursday February 21 – Sunday February 24, 1980

Christie Baird looked down at her sister's body and something inside her snapped, something that said: "I just can't take any more, and I won't deal with this".

There had simply been too much in too little a time. She couldn't absorb anything new, she was beyond handling another crisis. There had been too much upset, too much stress, too much falling on to her shoulders to deal with and she'd had enough.

First that awful phone-call from Alberta about the fire that destroyed the cabin the Bluetts had rented for the holidays: her nieces dead, her brother-in-law dead, her sister in hospital – burned and in shock.

Then the long flight with three plane changes from Halifax to Grande Prairie.

Then dealing with everyone and everything: the move, the pulp mill where her brother-in-law had worked, the real estate agent, the bank, the insurance company, and the movers.

Accomplishing all of this to shelter Tammy while struggling with her own shock, and grief and exhaustion. Somehow Christie got through all of that.

Next, getting Tammy out of the hospital in an almost zombie-like state then travelling the lengthy journey back home with her, not knowing what to say or how to fix the mess because it was impossible to make things better.

Once they were back in Halifax Robin had helped tremendously. It wasn't easy living these past three weeks with Tammy and the ghosts of her family. Robin had found her a place to rent and finally, when the moving truck full of Tammy's furniture arrived, Tammy was at last showing an interest in something. Eager, in fact, to reunite with her possessions, the tangible reminders of her loved ones.

They knew she there was no way to fit everything into her apartment but now wasn't the time to sort out what they should sell, discard, or store. Instead they had crammed the rooms full and would deal with the next step when Tammy was ready.

Although Christie knew they had a long ways to go at least they'd left the nightmare landscape of the previous weeks behind. Tammy was now able to begin the long slow process of coming to terms with the tragedy. Finally, it looked like they might be able to start patching up the holes that had been left in their lives with the tragic deaths of their dear family.

That was yesterday. The relief and release had lasted for only one day.

Today Tammy herself was dead, her face black with bruises and blue with asphyxiation. Tammy hadn't killed herself. Tammy had been murdered and Christie's mind simply refused to deal with one more thing. She covered the confusion of thoughts by screaming.

A neighbour heard the screams and, knowing nothing about the new people who'd moved in next-door, called the police to report an assault of some kind. By this time Christie had been with her sister's battered body for almost half-an-hour.

When the police arrived Christie's voice was almost gone.

Chapter Nine

Thursday February 21 – Sunday February 24, 1980

Dale sat behind the wheel of his truck feeling restless, unsettled, and not knowing why.

He was a bit headache-y but that wasn't anything new, not since getting out of the hospital. The doctors all said it was to be expected, he'd taken a violent blow and it would take time to heal fully. But months had passed and the headaches weren't fading. If anything, they were becoming stronger and, well, not more frequent because the pain had never stopped, but more intense. Sometimes black-out strong. Was he getting migraines?

A real pressure behind his eyes, at the top of his skull, at the base of his skull, in fact all over. He could live with it, and had started getting used to it, but he looked forward to the time when the constant ache was gone.

The bitter cold was a distraction from the pain. The temperatures in Alberta had been much colder but the dryness there makes a difference. Here in the Maritimes the wind off the ocean was numbing and it felt so much colder.

He'd just finished his daily call to Pamela Wright, his dispatcher, and as always it was good to hear her voice. She was pleased to have him back at work again and that made him feel good.

He'd asked her out for a drink when she first started working at Big Sky Moving but she'd turned him down, claiming she already had plans, That might have been true since it was a last-minute offer. At the time he figured she wasn't interested but he thought he should ask again when he got back to Edmonton.

She was a pretty girl and smart too. In most moving companies her job was done by a man but Pamela handled the work with ease and efficiency. She was well-liked and respected and Dale felt respectful towards her.

It might be that she was that friendly and warm with every guy who phoned but he didn't think so. He felt there might be something more. He smiled at the thought that maybe she could cure his headaches.

Thinking of the headaches brought his thoughts back to the accident, never far from his conscious mind since it had happened less than three months ago.

He was grateful to the doctors who operated on him, the nurses who looked after him, and the physiotherapists who got him back on his feet. He'd been helpless in the hands of strangers who had treated him with care and compassion.

His head had taken a hard blow in the accident but he was lucid and talking so being sent to hospital was just a precaution until discovering he couldn't get off the stretcher when the ambulance arrived. He couldn't walk. Turned out he'd damaged his spine but it was an injury that could heal and through the good efforts of a lot of medical professionals he was back on his feet again.

His struggle with depression, guilt, and blame – after all, two innocent children were dead – was almost as difficult to overcome as his physical rehabilitation. But the social workers on the hospital staff had helped him and yes, he was thankful to have encountered such genuinely kind people and that gratitude definitely shaped his attitude and aided his recovery.

Those were good thoughts but still his head ached.

The usual dull reminder was now an insistent throb pounding away. He put his hand up to shade his eyes, the light (although twilight, already) was bothering him. He couldn't shake the pain. You can't close your eyes, even briefly, when driving a tractor-trailer unit in a city the size of Halifax but all of a sudden that's what he wanted more than anything: to close his eyes and close his mind and drift off into peaceful, unknowing sleep.

Something shifted inside his brain and switched him into auto-pilot mode away from any consciousness of the pain and the horror of the memory.

Chapter Ten

Thursday February 21 – Sunday February 24, 1980

Suzi looked a little dazed when she came from the boss's office into dispatch to fetch herself a coffee. Pamela smiled remembering how long she herself had taken to get used to Eddie Ferragamo's intense personality.

He was relatively young to have built up such a big business. His wife had held a surprise party at the office for his fortieth a few years back and he was a trim, fit man.

He had unusual looks for an Italian, Pamela thought, until she learned that his sandy-coloured hair and blue eyes were common in the northern part of the country where his parents were born.

But by far the most unusual thing about Eddie was his focus and concentration on whomever he was speaking with. He'd stare right into your eyes, leaning in close, making you feel you had to choose your words with care because he was so interested and he was listening so intently.

Those blue eyes sparked while his gaze darted across your face. He leaned in and would lightly touch your hand or shoulder or arm as if strengthening the connection. It was intense.

Generally it took females awhile to realize that Eddie wasn't coming on to them and that his manner was the same with men or women. Pretty soon they found his demeanour comforting enough to confide, even to flirt with him, and he was popular with the guys, too.

Once she'd gotten over the discomfort his intense scrutiny had caused Pamela at first she found that Eddie was one of her favourite people to talk to. He chatted openly about his family and their experiences, co-workers, friends and competitors in the industry – Pamela knew he

must talk about her too but also knew his words would be kindly.

When Dale had that horrible accident Eddie hurried straight to the hospital, even though it was very close to Christmas and meant he'd miss out on a number of get-togethers with his extended family. He'd phoned Pamela a couple of times each day with progress reports, sharing her concern, which she very much appreciated.

Of course Dale's medical treatment was covered since he was in a Canadian hospital but Pamela knew Eddie had deposited a generous 'bonus' into Dale's bank account to cover costs while he was unable to work. The independent drivers had to pay their own Workers' Compensation premiums and always wanted to keep costs down as much as they could. Of course in this case the lawyers for Workers Comp would be busy chasing down any possible repayment through the insurance companies of the vehicles involved.

Eddie Ferragamo was a great boss and an extremely nice man, Pamela felt very lucky to work for him. She knew Suzi would come to feel that way as well in time.

Meanwhile the girl looked shell-shocked and no doubt she had half-a-dozen or more commissions ("phone so-and-so and say...", "go thank the Sales Manager for...", "tell Arnie to get sandwiches or pizza or something for the men working in the warehouse...", "call the florist and order a nice colourful bouquet to brighten us all up in this gloomy gray weather...") so Pamela gave a reassuring smile and let the girl get on with it.

Chapter Eleven

Thursday February 21 – Sunday February 24, 1980

Constable Yardley knocked on the Inspector's door and entered, file in hand, at his shouted, 'Come in'. She'd worn her police-issue parka out at the scene but had spent most of her time indoors and the heat had reddened her face.

Inspector Chalifoux noticed that as well as how stressed and worn-out she was looking as he motioned her to a seat. It was obvious that the interview with Christie Baird had been an ordeal: for Mrs. Baird who had needed treatment from the police doctor; and also for Constable Yardley who was drained and exhausted by the lengthy, difficult questioning.

The Inspector hid his sympathy because Annie Yardley was prickly and saw sexism in the most casual of gestures or comments. He indicated she could proceed. For her part, Constable Yardley saw Denis Chalifoux's coldness as disapproval and decided she was getting a little tired of having to prove herself yet again.

"Christie Baird, Mrs. Robin Baird, is still suffering from shock but was able to participate in the preliminary interview and we've received the following information:

"Her sister, Tammy Bluett, Mrs. Roger Bluett, recently lost her family in a fire at a cabin they'd rented for a winter break. A propane storage tank exploded (with charges of negligence filed against the time-share company that rented out the property) and Roger Bluett and the two young daughters, twins, Michelle and Rochelle, were killed. Tammy Bluett was having a bath at the time and suffered smoke inhalation and burns while trying to pick her way through the collapsed building, plus hypothermia and frostbite once she got outside. This happened in northern Alberta.

"Tammy Bluett was originally from Halifax and met her husband when he was here on a training course. They married and re-located to Grande Prairie where they've lived for the past six years and where their daughters were born.

"After the accident, Tammy Bluett was sent to hospital and the RCMP contacted Christie Baird to give her the news. The only other family is the women's mother but she's in a nursing home here in Halifax suffering from Alzheimer's disease."

When Constable Yardley paused, the Inspector commented that Christie Baird had a lot to contend with.

"She's looked after everything." continued Annie. "Christie Baird flew to Grande Prairie and made the arrangements for her sister's effects to be moved back here. he husband's company has something called a 'final move' policy where an employee is covered for moving costs to any Canadian city they choose after leaving the company. I doubt if this sort of circumstance ever crossed anybody's mind in the Personnel Department when they established policy but it was certainly an immense help to Tammy Bluett.

"Settling the estate, or at least the preliminary settlement, took about a week and the two sisters returned to Halifax. Tammy Bluett had been staying at the home of her sister and brother-in-law these past three weeks until the moving truck arrived yesterday.

"Tammy Bluett wanted to be at the new place to supervise the moving in, an apartment suite in a house the Bairds had rented in Rockingham for her, and when Christie Baird went over yesterday evening she said her sister had decided to keep working at the unpacking and setting-up and was going to stay the night. The other half of the house is rented out as a holiday home so it's empty at this time of year.

"The sisters arranged that Mrs. Baird would come by in the morning, after she'd driven her kids to school, and they'd go out for some breakfast.

When Christie Baird arrived about 9:00 this morning the front-door wasn't locked so she walked right in and discovered her sister's body. Tammy Bluett had been severely beaten and it's a gruesome sight. The Medical Examiner will know more after the autopsy but said the killer used some sort of weighty implement that caused enormous damage smashing bones that then broke through the skin leaving bloody, lacerated flesh.

According to Christie Baird very few people knew Tammy was moving back to the city and they were all friends of the women from years back. For now, it appears that the Alberta accident doesn't have any connection with the murder here.

"Prior to the training course of some..." Yardley flipped through her notes to get the exact information. "Eight-plus years ago, Roger Bluett had never been in the Maritimes. He didn't keep in contact with his family or, if he did, this was never told to Christie Baird who was very vague when questioned about the Bluett relations.

"The rental has been empty for some time so it doesn't look like a case of the victim being mistaken for someone else.

"At this point the only person of interest is Christie Baird herself and she's small and very much overweight. I don't think she could have administered the beating her sister was given. Tammy Bluett was younger, taller and in better physical condition then her sister. Of course, she was weakened by her tragic experience and because of that she could be easy to overpower but I think that when you talk to

Christie Baird yourself you'll agree with my findings. Which leaves us with absolutely nothing at all."

Inspector Chalifoux felt the tragic events that had occurred in the Baird and Bluett households in such a short time was appalling. He knew that moving away from a tragedy wouldn't lessen the impact but getting away from many of the daily reminders would have been a way to help start the healing process. Such sadness for everyone.

He told Annie to finish up for the day and said he'd speak to her further in the morning. "Good report, Constable. You handled a difficult interview very well, and did a good job."

He was rewarded by a smile which briefly softened some of the tension showing in his officer's face. It made him wonder why he'd been told she was a difficult person to work with. But he put his musings aside because despite making a good start there was a lot of work to do if they were going to bring this killer to justice.

Chapter Twelve

Thursday February 21 – Sunday February 24, 1980

"Yes, Operator, I'll accept the charge." said Pamela and once connected asked her driver Gerry Tanner for his number so she could call him right back.

"Hello darlin', sorry about the collect call but I'm in a phone booth here at the Wayfarer. I can't check into my room yet."

"You gave me the Nova Scotia area code, are you in Halifax already?"

"Yeah and I'm looking for Dale, did you say he's heading here or is he here already?"

"He's there, staying at the um, Regency I think. Hang on, I've got a phone number and his room number. How fast are you travelling? You shouldn't be there already."

"My customer's a bigwig and he doesn't want his stuff unloaded into a warehouse so when I heard I'd be getting paid waiting time I hauled ass to get here. Delivered my small shipment and now I'm getting paid for doin' nuthin'. So this is me checking in with my favourite dispatcher."

"Well if you're killing time make sure you behave yourself. You'll be in strange bars so don't go poking your nose into someone else's business, don't get pass-out drunk, and no fighting."

"Yes, ma'am. You know I don't go looking for trouble, I told you before like it says in the commercial I'm a lover not a fighter, and besides what kind of guy can just sit quietly by when a lady's honour is at stake?"

"You mean Our Lady of Lapdancers? Gerry, just how drunk do you have to be not to know that any girls working the audience in a strip club aren't worried about their so-called honour?"

"When-when-when-when-whennnnn am I going to get a chance with you? I know that if I had a girl like you Pammy I could really turn things around 'cause you'd fix up my life just fine."

"Easy to say when your 3,000 miles away and don't call me Pammy. But seriously, no matter where you are you're no good to me if you're in hospital so I mean it, no more fights or black-outs, OK?"

"It was just a concussion and I've had enough of those to know what they feel like. I didn't even have to go to the hospital. Not like the time before when I was laid up for so long. Anyways, getting knocked out cold meant I missed the real fun. I heard the whole place got into it. The real problem is I heard that now everybody's barred, which doesn't sound too likely so I figure by the time I'm heading back it'll all have been forgotten. It's the best peeler bar in the country, they can't keep me out of there!"

"It wasn't fun, it was criminal. You need to get over your fatal attraction for blonde bimbos. That reminds me you've got a message, it's from 'Dee-Dee', who says you've got to call her and it's really, really, really impor.. oh wait, I forgot the fourth 'really', important. Something about her car payment is overdue."

"You can be a cold-hearted woman, Pammy. But you know, it's a good idea for me to keep on the move this leap year otherwise I might get caught by a Sadie Hawkins proposal."

"Hah! what makes you think they actually want to marry you? Anyhow stay sober and I think you'll be fine."

"I promise that if I feel I'm getting too drunk I'll do a line to sober up, OK?"

"I didn't hear that, seriously – don't say stuff like that to me – goodbye now."

Gerry was smiling when he hung up the phone. It seemed like it was easy to get Pamela going but he knew mock outrage when he heard it.

A woman like Pamela was great fun to banter with, especially over the phone, but she wasn't his type at all. Too serious, too smart, too buttoned-down, and although the possibilities were interesting... but no, if he was a different type of man, or if he'd reached a place in his life where he'd be willing to work hard at a relationship he'd have stayed married. Actually, he would have stayed married anyway but, sadly for him, the choice wasn't his to make.

The big 4-0 was looming and somehow that had caught Gerry by surprise. He wouldn't admit to a mid-life crisis because he wasn't ready to admit to a mid-life anything but he couldn't stop chasing the chicks. Of course chasing wasn't the problem, it was catching them and then getting caught himself.

Sometimes he felt lonely and a bit sorry for himself, and he missed his daughters a lot, but most of the time he was thoroughly enjoying the single life. Dale, he thought, didn't seem to know how to enjoy himself.

Gerry figured Dale and Pamela should get together but he would love to see Dale cut loose first. He knew Dale could be a hard-drinking man who could hold his own in a fight, but he never spent much time in the bar and he never spent any time with the girls in the bar.

Gerry was happy to notice that his headache had disappeared. Feeling better, he decided to cab over to the Regency to find Dale to see if he couldn't make a bad influence out of himself.

Chapter Thirteen

Thursday February 21 – Sunday, February 24, 1980

"Uh-oh, somebody musta been asking for trouble because it just walked in the door" shouted Murray, interrupting the story that Johnny, a local driver was telling, as Gerry walked into the lounge at the Regency. He spotted the crew and headed over to their table after taking a bow.

"Oh never you mind Murray, Tanner's a goddamn hero and I'm gonna buy him a beer."

"Well thanks for that Ken but it was only a bar fight and as I was just telling my dispatcher I missed most of the action." laughed Gerry.

"I'm not talkin' about that nonsense. Jeez. I meant you breaking up the fight when those goons tried to hijack Alex McKay's rig and darn near killed him. He told me so too. I haven't seen you since but he said 'if it wasn't for Gerry stepping in when he did I'd be dead and all over a load of stupid electronics' so yes, boy you are a hero."

"You would have done the same."

"I don't know about that, I'm not as stupid as you are. Hijackings are seriously dangerous business."

"It was dumb luck for sure. Talk about being in the wrong place at the wrong time, eh? for me I mean. I ended up in hospital after the kicking I took but I survived and Alex survived and we gotta hope those guys learned to leave the truckers alone."

The police didn't catch anybody for that, did they?"

"Huh, as if. They only make arrests when somebody rats somebody else out."

"Yeah like that new thing they've got called Crime Stoppers where you phone in..."

"Hey! never mind that I didn't finish my story. Gerry, you're gonna love this." said Johnny, taking the floor once again.

"So it's a big move with state-of-the-art computers coming into a whole new wing of the hospital where everything is spick-and-span. All these suits are hanging around bragging to each other about how great these computers are and since they're only telling each other what they already know all this computer-computer-computer talk is just for the dumb moving guys. Apparently the computers will take up three walls of this one big room and the movers are only bringing in a modular shelving/cabinet arrangement. Movers aren't skilled enough for the computers, right? So they're listening to all this talk about seamless walls and air-conditioning and an earthquake floor – like that's a really big concern here, hah! – and humidity control and then the installer for the cabinets gets there, pulls out this fancy new drill and looks around and says 'where's the plug?'"

"No fucking way!" exclaimed Ken.

"Swear to God but the funniest part was when Al Gauvin said.."

"Cape Breton Al? is he still around?"

"You didn't hear? he was supposed to retire, right? he bought a motor-home for him and his wife to go travelling.."

"Wait, you mean he wanted to spend his retirement driving all over the place after just spending his whole working life driving around all over the place?"

"Ha-ha, I never thought of that but yeah, you're right that's exactly what he'd planned to do. Crazy, huh? But then the interest rates went sky-high. See he borrowed to buy the motor-home thinking he'd sell his truck and pay off the loan but nobody's buying anything because of the interest. So he did manage to sell his K-Whopper but for way less then he'd planned, still has a loan on the motor-home, so now he's working for wages for probably another year or so and even more miserable than ever!"

"That sucks. Not that I like the guy, I mean who could like him? The mouth on him: swears non-stop while complaining about everything under the sun."

"Well, he was on this part of the hospital move" continued Johnny, "and into the dead silence that follows the installer guy asking about a plug Al says 'I'm guessing all this ee-leck-trickle, pronouncing it like a real rube, equipment is gonna need an outlet. Probably more 'n one, probably need a power bar. Maybe more than one. Guess you could run an extension cord into the hallway but then you'd have to leave the door open' and all the suits start blaming each other and hurrying away shouting for the specs while all the movers are about to piss themselves and old Al is actually smiling."

Everyone laughed at that. Drinks were drunk, new orders called out, and then Gerry asked: "Has anybody seen Dale since he got back on the road? I keep missing him although we should be able to meet up here. Any idea how's he doing? His accident and hospital stay was worse than mine."

"I talked to him in Quebec," said Murray "and he seems to be doing okay. He's never been a big talker but we chatted some while we were in range of each other. Helluva thing he went through. Hey what's up with you guys from Big Sky? are you cursed or something?"

"Oh we're definitely something" replied Gerry with a leer that got big laugh from the company of men.

Chapter Fourteen

Monday February 25, 1980

"Pick one." said Suzi.

Pamela smiled at the secretary saying: "Pick one what? it sounds like a card trick."

"I mean, choose a guy. Everybody around here is flirting with everybody else but you need to move forward, you need to make a choice. It looks like you've narrowed it down to Dale or Gerry so now it's time to choose which one of those two."

Suzi Wendell was the latest hire at Big Sky Moving. Her official title was Sales Secretary but she did the typing for Dispatch as well. The sales staff were rarely in their office and Suzi was a lively girl who liked company.

She had always lingered for a chat when she came into Dispatch to drop off the bills of lading she had finished. One day she moved her IBM Selectric to one of the empty desks used by visiting truck drivers and made it her own.

Pamela enjoyed having Suzi share the office. She enjoyed the younger woman's chatty company. Suzi was very much the 'thinking out loud' type, about herself and everyone around her, and she showed a real interest in the trucking business. Plus, Pam could tell to shut up and Suzi wouldn't take offence.

Suzi had a boyfriend whose white '77 Corvette was the envy of the younger male staff. They got to see it a lot since Derek dropped Suzi off each morning and picked her up at the end of the work day. Every entry and exit from the trucking company's parking lot came with a squeal of brakes and a gunned motor. It had a sweet sound.

Suzi had decided that her position as cherished girlfriend gave her the right, or at least the credentials, to lecture Pamela on her love-life. Pamela chose to be amused, saying: "Everybody always acts like they're coming on to you because that's the nature of the business. These guys spend long hours behind the wheel and it's standing jokes, flirtations, and gossip that keeps the loneliness away. The majority of them are married with families so they're just kidding around – believe me."

"That may be true with most of the guys who come through here but it's different with Dale and Gerry, admit it."

"Well of course it is – they're ours, the long-distance owner-operators for Big Sky Moving. They bring in really good money and we'll probably be adding another broker now that our sales numbers are at the level necessary to qualify for three."

"Yeah, but they phone you all the time."

Pamela explained: "Dale and Gerry have to let me know where they'll be and that often means them phoning in daily. They call because it's their job, it's not personal."

"Have either of them ever asked you out?"

"Both have."

"Did you go?"

"No."

"Why not? You're not seeing anybody else."

"No, but Gerry is a hound – he's a smooth-talker with girls in every city. I'm sure he'd show a girl a good time but I'm also a hundred percent certain a date with him would be like fighting off an octopus."

"But he's so good-looking! Why would you fight?"

"Also who's to say his marriage really is over?"

"I'm not saying you should marry him, in fact he's obviously not marriage material, but he's funny and really nice and any woman would enjoy yourself in his company."

"Fine, you go out with him."

"No way he's too old."

"Gerry's only 37."

"My Dad's 38."

"Really? and you're 19, right?"

"My parents were high-school sweethearts. They're still like really good friends even though they've been divorced since I was little."

"That's unusual, but lucky for you."

"They were the lucky ones, they inherited a lot of money from Mom's great-aunt who'd married rich and had no kids of her own. My parents married way too young but they got the inheritance just when they realized it was a mistake and having the money helped them make the split. They say it's money, or rather lack of money, that makes most divorced people bitter and resentful. And then, Dad won $50,000 on the Western Express."

"Hmm, your Dad is divorced and well-off, eh? When do I get to meet him?"

"Forget it. Dad is totally under the thumb of Serious Sylvia, that's what Mom and I call his 'lady friend'. She's all about money and building up their business and accounting for every penny and she's just no fun at all. Besides you've already got one too many men to worry about. So, OK you figure Gerry isn't serious but Dale's a pretty serious guy so why didn't you go out with him?"

"Why don't you and I get back to work and leave the personal chat for some other time?" and then, seeing a stubborn look on Suzi's face and feeling somewhat guilty since she'd allowed the talk to go on, added: "If you like we can go out for lunch about 1:00 and talk some more then."

Pamela was determined not to discuss her feelings for Dale. She was aware that he'd been very much on her mind from the moment she heard about the accident and the thoughts she had now, now that he had recovered and back to work, had changed. Sure, she was interested in him but felt it wasn't a great situation.

When he'd asked her to go for a drink after work she'd said no because that was her natural reaction to a last-minute invitation but there was more to it than following 'the rules'. She realized Dale was a grown man, even a bit of a tough man, who would expect to end the evening with more than a goodnight kiss. He was a widower after all, so he'd expect more than she was prepared to give. Pamela wasn't a virgin but she wasn't going to hop into his bed.

She wanted to start dating again but... she wasn't sure if she could handle someone like Dale right now.

She decided it'd be better to not get started on something that could turn awkward but she figured Suzi would call her a chicken if she explained. She was saved from saying anything more when a stentorian blast signalled the arrival of the Lunch Truck. The warehouse door crashed open with a group of men jostling their way into the dispatch room.

"Ah Christ, who farted?"

"Jeez, how can you stink that bad even before you eat off the E-Coli Trolley?"

"Don't look at me, it was Roger."

"Like Hell it was, you're just trying to cover up."

"Nothing could cover up that.." the voices trailed off as the men continued out the side door.

"Eeewww, they're disgusting."

"See it's easy for guys to be great guys when you're not around them too much and don't have to listen to their stupid talk. For me that's a big part of why the long-distance drivers are likeable."

"True, these guys speak idiot like it's their mother tongue."

"Actually E-Coli Trolley is a new one, they're getting quite inventive."

"I suppose, but isn't it pronounced ee-koh-lye?"

"Yeah, but that doesn't rhyme with trolley. Anyhow at least it's a change from maggot wagon and ptomaine truck."

"I'm so glad I never eat off that thing! but I am running out to get a pack of smokes so do you want anything?"

"No thanks, I can wait till lunch. But hey, their cigarettes cost too much you can have some of mine till we go out.""Oh Pam please, I hate menthol. I mean, thanks for the offer but really no thanks!"

Chapter Fifteen

Monday February 25, 1980

Jasmine Brown wandered through the rooms of her new apartment – not that there were many – feeling the strangeness of living alone in her own place for the first time in her 38 years.

She'd been still living with her parents when she met and married Alfonso eighteen years ago. When he wanted a separation she'd expected to go on living in the family home with their son Antony but it was Al who insisted on staying and Jasmine who was pushed out on her own.

Yet once she got over her anger and resentment she had to admit that it felt good. A little scary... but Jasmine was frightened by most aspects of day-to-day living. As far back as she could remember she'd always been anxious and worried all the time. Even crazy stuff that she knew couldn't possibly come true but she worried anyhow. She could never get the 'what ifs' out of her head and she sure was imaginative.

She'd been a nervous child with a weak stomach that knotted into sickness under the mildest stress. Such as exams, though she always scored well; sports competitions, though she was naturally athletic; and music recitals, though she never fumbled a note when performing on the piano in public. The family doctor referred Jasmine to a therapist who reported back that since the results were always fine the vomiting shouldn't be a concern and recommended a light breakfast of plain crackers and ginger-ale to get the retching over with as soon as possible.

The fact of 'Jasmine's nerves' became part of her family lore. Al couldn't understand it and was determined to fix Jasmine's problem.

He believed that once his bride understood how well-able he was to protect and take care of her she'd soon be able to relax. Unfortunately the issues wouldn't fade away because there as no simple cure and Al's frustration turned to impatient resentment.

The trouble got worse when Antony came along. Even before his birth, which was astonishingly easy, Jasmine worried frantically about every possible thing that could go wrong. As Antony grew so did her anxiety. She went with Antony to Play Group and interfered in all his interactions with the other toddlers; at the park she objected to the swings, the slides, and the sandbox; all dogs were suspected biters; all water was labelled dangerous; all toilets were germ-infested.

Jasmine was over-protective to an embarrassing degree and soon the family doctor, the staff hospital Emergency, the school teachers, and all secretaries and receptionists hated to hear the sound of her voice – they were fed up hearing from her.

Antony wanted to join in the games at recess, he wanted to go with his class to the zoo, he wanted to cross the road without having his hand clutched within his mother's. He rebelled and Al back him up.

Balked in her efforts to protect only exacerbated Jasmine's fears. She couldn't find any peace. She became more energetic and was constantly on the go, always busy doing something, never resting, getting by on a few hours of sleep, and never sitting down to a meal but instead nibbling all day, burning off the calories with nervous energy. She made sure she never had time to stop and think... and worry herself sick. Her menfolk were irritated by her fidgets and fussing, exasperated by her nagging and nonsense, and fed up with the non-stop arguing.

When Antony entered his teens he and Al forced Jasmine to leave. Despite loving her they couldn't live with her the way she was and she wouldn't get professional help because she'd been told since childhood that her problems weren't problems at all so she didn't believe she needed help.

At first she'd gone back to her parents full of tears and indignation but they'd bought a condo where the spare bedroom was actually their den. The couch was a hide-a-bed but its purpose was to provide one or two nights' accommodation to welcome visitors, not a permanent home to an unhappy and neurotic adult child. This living arrangement was untenable from the start but the older folks were happy to furnish their daughter's small apartment from the items they'd stored after selling their home. They even hired a moving company to save numerous trips back and forth.

Running two households on Al's income wasn't an option so Jasmine got a job in a small real estate office, answering the phones and typing Purchase Agreements, where her meticulous attention to detail was well-appreciated.

She'd found a bachelor apartment within walking distance and now here she was, getting accustomed to her new place. She'd heard it would take about three months before it felt like home and was pleased to discover that she was looking forward to that. She had no idea what her future held but for a change she felt upbeat anticipation instead of the usual doom-and-gloom. Jasmine figured this was because she was finally 100% in charge of her own life and she wouldn't have to rely on anyone else to take care of her. True, if there were failures they would be her own but she confidently accepted that.

Then she heard a knock at her door. All good feelings fled in an instant and she froze in fear. Who could it be? Why would someone come here? No one knew she was here! The knock-knock came again – not too loud or sounding angry but steady and patient. Jasmine tiptoed her way to the door certain she wouldn't be opening it but overcome with an urgent need to see who was there.

With great daring she peeked through the peep-hole and saw that it was one of the men from the moving company. She was holding her breath so he couldn't have heard her but he must have sensed her presence because he said:

"Ms Brown? Sorry but I've got some papers that need to be signed. Look, I know it's getting late and I don't want to bother you so how about if I just leave them outside the door here for you to pick up when I'm gone and maybe you could mail them when you're done. It's entirely my fault this didn't get taken care of sooner and I'm sorry about that. Anyhow, I really appreciate it because I don't get paid until you sign off on the job. So thanks, and I'll get out of your way now. And I really am sorry about this."

While Jasmine watched he disappeared from view and she heard the rustle of papers against the bottom of the door. Then he straightened up and gave a little wave before turning away. Immediately she felt foolish and opened the door calling: "Hi, I'm here and if you'll just wait I'll sign these right way. You shouldn't have to wait to get paid, you all did a great job and.." but her words were cut off when his hand closed over her mouth and his body forced her back into her apartment.

She needn't have been concerned over his pay since his involvement in her move was him repaying a favour – no money changed hands and no names were written down.

Jasmine's Brown short-lasting future turned out to be doomed and gloomy after all, and her surviving relatives inherited tremendous feelings of guilt.

Chapter Sixteen

Monday February 25. 1980

It wasn't unusual for Gerry Tanner to wake up disoriented in a strange room since he was a heavy drinker who partied at every opportunity on the road but this morning's headache felt like much more than a hangover. He figured he must have blacked out. Again.

He also had no idea who was in bed with him.

Gerry's taste generally ran to busty, bleached blondes but when he turned towards the naked flesh pressing up against his back he saw a very slender girl with short brown hair and a boyish figure wearing nothing but a chain with a tiny gold crucifix. She opened her big brown eyes and smiled at him with crooked teeth. Definitely not his type but she sure had a pretty face.

"Morning Yuri."

"Gerry."

"Yah, Yuri."

"And where are you from, beautiful?"

"The bar, you pick me up last night remember?"

"Well no honey, and that's not exactly what I meant but..oh" her hands got busy under the sheet and distracted him. "I can see why I did."

"You call me 'Beautiful' and 'Honey', means you forget my name, right?"

"I drank too much."

"Not too too much. We had fun. I tell you my real name: I am Floriana. My stage name is Carling."

"Carling O'Keefe?"

"Yes! How come everyone knows my name? I've only been here for three months. I am just Estonian girl and not famous dancer. Not yet."

"You're a dancer?"

"Yes, I dance and take off my clothes. All my clothes, not like back home where we have to keep on a little bit – what you call 'g-string'. And men give me tips and you gave me lots of tips and you smiled nice at me. Most men aren't nice to me although they do give me tips mostly the green dollars, but also brown two dollar bills and sometimes blue five dollar bills."

"You're an exotic dancer, a stripper."

"Yes, everyone likes to watch me. I am pretty girl."

"You certainly are and apparently you are my type after all."

"Type?"

"Yes, a fun girl. That's the kind I like to spend time with. Usually they've got blonde hair and big.. uh.."

"Ta-tas, you like big ta-tas. Is OK, I'm earning money to buy some and the owner of the Club he says he will pay half."

"Career advancement, well isn't that something."

"Enough talk, time for fun again."

"Again, hmm so that means I didn't blackout until after?"

"Yes, you get out of bed to look for cigarettes you pick up blue jeans and fall down. I have to really pull to get you back on to the bed and you don't wake up at all although I keep calling your name. But you snore loud so I know you're still alive. Finally I go to sleep too. Is OK?"

"Sure darling, Floriana, that's a pretty name by the way. I had a kind of accident awhile back and sometimes I pass out and don't remember what happened."

"Oh we had good time. We smoke cigarettes and little skinny cigarettes and I dance for you and then you dance with me. You show me something called two-step. And we have drinks and we make sex."

"I don't remember any of that."

"Is OK, we do sex again and then you remember."

That brought a smile to his face and he felt a rush of affection for this uncomplicated young woman. He'd always loved the ladies and Floriana was delightful.

Then, from out of the blue, he saw in his minds-eye his own two girls. He felt a real wrench at the thought of Julie and Jody, realizing that he missed them very much. At 15 and 16 no doubt they were already involved with boys and their father would be the last person they were thinking about.

He wasn't sure what their mother had been telling them either. Jan was usually a very fair woman and he was pretty sure she wouldn't air bitter hurt-wife feelings to their daughters but who could say for sure? She was always so perfect, so right, so long-suffering... She should realize that a bad husband didn't necessarily mean a bad father but Gerry knew he wasn't a great dad. He was lazy about keeping in touch and he didn't call the girls often enough and didn't see them as much as he should. Especially at the ages they were at now.

Today he had his hands full, literally, with Floriana but he resolved to phone his girls tonight for sure, tomorrow at the latest. If possible.

Chapter Seventeen

Monday February 25, 1980

"So I called 9-1-1 and said 'somebody better come to 828 Olympique right away because it sounds like the new neighbours are killing each other', I mean they just moved in and OK so it's quiet now but you shoulda heard them then! Banging about like they were throwing the furniture around, and shrieks and crying out and we're not putting up with that. We just got rid of a bunch of noisy students, there were at least half-a-dozen living there, and now this."

"Right, well it was good of you to call us Mrs. Garbel, as you know there's been a death."

"I saw the ambulance men carrying out the body, I knew it was a body because they didn't bother putting the siren on." She looked expectantly at the Inspector adding: "Well, they wouldn't would they?" as if she expected an answer before carrying on to say: "The landlady told me a woman, a coloured woman, was going to be the new tenant so I know it was her who was killed. I don't know her name but she wasn't a Jamaican-coloured, she was an Indian-coloured. I think. Doesn't matter to me one way or the other so long as the tenant shows some consideration to the neighbours when it comes to making noise. And it was murder you know, not just a death, I know because I heard it."

"Yes, and that's what I'd like to hear more about. What time was it when you first heard the noise from upstairs?"

"Well I can't say exactly but it was about 10 minutes after 8:00. I know that much because I'd just settled in to watch a movie, that "Kramer vs Kramer" that was such a big hit last year? all week long they've been advertising the TV premiere and I was looking forward to seeing it. Guess I'm not going to get another chance to watch it for quite some time but isn't that just typical? Still, a murder is an awful thing to happen."

"OK, so you're saying it was about 20:10? and how long did it last?"

"Longer than the darn commercials do and there were plenty of those let me tell you! They usually play about 10 or 15 minutes of the show before the commercials start. Three or four had already played and by then I was more than ready to get back to watching the movie so I was pretty fed up when the noise started up."

"So maybe 7 minutes or so?"

"Could of been but I think it was longer than that. See first I heard a scream like a loud yelping sound and right away I thought "they've got a dog in there" because it sounded just like a dog does if you step on its tail, you know? and this is a no-pets building. Well, it's supposed to be but I know somebody's got a cat because I've seen the bits of kitty litter spilled around the garbage chute, and down the hall's got a bird that really squawks but pretty much just in the mornings so that doesn't bother me much.

My husband complains because he works a few nights a week, the darn pension isn't enough with the price of everything always going up, so he likes a lie-in next day and if that parrot or whatever it is is making a racket then my Joseph starts making a racket too. I get no peace. Not even on a night like tonight with Joseph out at work and me all happy to sit down with my mending and watch a good programme on the TV for a change. And then this happens. Poor soul, no matter where she came from or whoever she is."

"So you didn't know the woman who lives upstairs but is there anything you can tell us about her?"

"Yeah, she didn't live upstairs for long. In fact, she just moved in today. That's why I phoned the emergency number, I figured if I don't nip this in the bud it's never gonna stop. Day One and already there's loud carryings-on. That's not right. Me and Joseph are old now and we can't be doing with stuff like that."

Inspector Eden interrupted to say: "Had you ever actually seen the woman?" in an effort to get some concrete facts but Mrs Garbel wasn't to be silenced or sidetracked.

"Domestic violence is what they call it nowadays. Generally it's just too much drinking by him or too much nagging by her. Oh yes, I heard plenty tonight. First off was the movers stomping around. They've got a freight elevator they can use so they don't inconvenience the rest of the tenants but they've still got their truck blocking half the parking-lot and the doors propped open so anybody could get in and this isn't the nicest of neighbourhoods, not anymore although it was nothing to be ashamed of when we first moved here back in... but ah, you don't want to be hearing that old story.

So, OK the movers left just before Joseph went out to work. He'd been fretting about 'how was he gonna get his car out?' and it turned out he'd worried for nothing. So that woulda been 'round about 7:20 or so. He's only got a 15-minute drive but he likes to leave early in case traffic is bad or he hits all the red lights or something. That something being him being a fussy worrier, that's what. Anyhow, he starts at 8:00 and works till 2:00. They've got four six-hour shifts because as long as it's all part-timers they don't have to pay any benefits or anything.

The movers must have quit making noise upstairs by quarter-past and then it was nice and quiet until I sat down in front of the TV. Well, actually until 10 or 15 minutes after that. It started with the scream I told you about then there was a thud and a couple of crashes, like something breakable – maybe a lamp – got knocked off when a table fell over although if they just moved in she'd hardly have had time to unpack the lamps and set them out, would she?"

"You said 'they', Mrs. Garbel. The landlady only mentioned one tenant, a woman, so did you see a man with her?"

"No, but it stands to reason she didn't beat herself up! There was a man up there all right but whether or not the landlord knows anything about it I couldn't say. She lives here so she should know what's going on but who can say?"

"So you didn't actually hear a man's voice?"

Mrs Garbel screwed up her face and looked upwards, as if she was trying to see through to the rooms up above, before carefully answering: "No. I heard a shout that sounded like a man but I couldn't say it was, not to swear to that is. After the crashing about there was a steady pounding noise just bang, bang, bang against the wall and I got out my broom handle that we keep under the couch here and I banged the ceiling right back at them. It got real quiet after that for a couple of minutes, just long enough for me to think 'good, that's stopped them' when I heard the loudest crash ever. I swear to God Almighty I jumped half-a-foot out of my chair it was that loud. Well that was the final straw so to speak and that's when I dialled 9-1-1 and got that first lot of policemen over here but by then he'd already left."

Inspector Eden sat thinking over what the witness had said and calculated that the actual death-blow, which they all figured happened when the hutch was dragged down off the buffet and onto the victim with its glass doors slicing through her neck, would have occurred at about 20:20 or 20:25.

Mrs Garbel's call to the emergency service was logged in at 20:27. She was an elderly woman and she'd had a scare so say it took her a minute or two to get herself together before she got up to phone. Would she call immediately or think about it for a bit, wondering if she should call her husband first? But no, she wasn't the type who would interrupt him at work and besides, it sounded like she would make up her own mind – and her husband's too if given the chance. No, 20:20 to 20:25 would be right and that was the time-frame they'd be checking out.

"So just to re-cap Mrs Garbel, you heard movers delivering furniture upstairs but you never saw the tenant herself, or possibly it was tenants plural."

The neighbour interrupted him to say "But I did see her, earlier in the day. I was checking the mailboxes but it was too early for our lazy mailman – oh excuse me: 'letter-carrier' to have come by. She was in the lobby and I said hello. She looked a nervous type but pretty with kinda delicate features. She didn't have one of those red marks on her forehead, though."

The Inspector absorbed all of this without commenting and continued:

"Then, about an hour after the movers left, which was just before your husband left for his job at 19:20, you heard sounds of a physical fight, a scream, and possibly a man's voice. Once you knocked on your ceiling to signal the neighbours to quiet down it seemed like this altercation stopped for a minute or so only to finish with one extremely loud crash and then nothing else was heard. That's when you called 9-1-1. Does that accurately sum it up?"

"Yes, that's very good. I see you wrote it down in shorthand, not so many people know shorthand nowadays and I bet you could get yourself a good paying job as an Executive Secretary and wear nice clothes – maybe even marry the boss!"

Inspector Eden felt her smile freeze but looking closely at the older woman she saw that no, Mrs Garbel wasn't joking – she really meant what she said. The Inspector, who was used to fighting against the sexism of her male co-workers, was simply at a loss for words.

The lift of the old lady's eyebrow made the young policewoman think it wasn't an innocent or uninformed remark at all.

Chapter Eighteen

Summer 2015

"Granpa T you must know the Trans-Canada Highway really well, right?"

"I certainly do. I even remember what it was like driving across Canada before the highway was completed. It wasn't even fully paved until 1971.

That highway transformed the cross-country trucking industry. It really is a marvel of a thing. 5,000 miles, give or take a bit, that goes from Newfoundland in the Atlantic to Vancouver Island in the Pacific.

Both St. John's, NFLD and Victoria, BC claim to be the Mile 0 that begins the journey – but it really just depends on whether you're travelling East or West.

Back in the early 1960s you couldn't get through the mountains but once the Rogers Pass was opened up we drivers saved hours of travelling by crossing through instead of routing south through the States. The same in Northern Ontario where miles were cut through the dense forest around Lake Superior.

You know this country is a truly 'a sight worth seeing' as they say, and I hope you'll make a trip across it someday. I realize that right now you're more interested in the big machines, the earth-movers and steam-shovellers and mile-high cranes.."

"They're not a MILE high!" laughed Jake.

"Well, they're way higher than anything I ever want to climb up in, that's for sure. But what I was saying is maybe you'll change your mind about the construction trucks and think about long-distance trucking. It isn't the life for everyone but for me it was the greatest job I could ever have.

Anyhow, less than 20 miles southeast of Winnipeg, you know that's the capital of Manitoba, eh?, there's a sign marking that spot on the Trans-Canada as 'The Longitudinal Centre of Canada'.

"Longitudinal." repeated Jake, lovingly sounding out the word.

"Yeah, that's a 10-dollar word, as they used to say when I was a kid. Anyhow, I am one of the truckers, and there aren't all that many of us, who can actually say, well brag I guess, that they've driven every mile of the TCH. Of course since it starts and ends on islands it means it cost me several hundred dollars in ferry fees – each way – to take my rig across the water at either end."

"We saw those big ferries when we went to North Sydney."

"That's right. They're all owned by Marine Atlantic now but it was CN Marine back when I was trucking. Oh well, things are always changing. The highway holds good, bad, and mad memories from all of the countless people who have travelled over some or even all of its route.

When there was all that publicity about the killing spree back in the late spring of 1980 the newspapers got a lot of mileage out of the Trans-Canada connection writing headlines of "Cross-Country Killer", "Coast-to-Coast Killfest", and "Trans-Canada Terror" although truth be told the terrorizing was over and done with before the media ever knew anything about it."

"You were actually there, reading all about it and watching it on the news and listening to what everybody had to say, so tell me what you heard."

Chapter Nineteen

"Suzi can you please type envelopes for the addresses on this list? I've got to get these Fuel Reports done and into the mail."

"What are those reports, anyways?"

"They're a headache, that's what they are. Every month I have to fill in a report for each province showing the miles driven and the fuel purchased by each of our brokers."

"Why?"

"So the provinces can be sure they're getting enough taxes. See, in a province like Quebec the fuel costs a lot so drivers will fill up just before they leave Ontario and not have to buy in La Belle Province at all. The calculations in the monthly fuel report show if the drivers have purchased enough diesel for the miles they've travelled and if not, and usually they haven't, we have to pay the difference to cover the tax."

"That's so sneaky!"

"Well they have actually driven on Quebec's highways so the province really is entitled to its share of road tax, or whatever they call it, that's normally collected at the pumps."

"No, what's sneaky is that Quebec doesn't care about the sales, it just cares about getting its taxes. Probably it's because of the taxes that the cost of fuel is so high but the province doesn't care that the gas station owners aren't making any sales."

"Our driver's don't care much either. In fact, they prefer to do as little business as possible in Quebec because of the whole language thing."

"Well it's been a few years now, everybody should have gotten used to Quebec being bilingual."

"Quebec isn't bilingual, New Brunswick is our only bilingual province. Quebec is French-only so that makes it unilingual."

"Why is New Brunswick bilingual?"

"I guess it has a large French-speaking population. It's been bilingual for a long time, way before the whole thing started in Quebec."

"Well I think, as Canadians, we should all speak French. It is one of our national languages."

"Do you speak it?"

"Mais oui."

"Well like everybody else I learned it in school but I was taught Parisian French which is different from what they speak in Quebec. Personally, I can recite 'Le Renard et Le Corbeau' and that's about it."

"You learned Aesop's Fables in French class?"

"Yeah, not something useful like how to book a hotel room or give a destination to a cab-driver. Of course it was Grade Four so I guess they figured it made sense to teach something interesting to a child. It doesn't matter anyhow because apparently if you don't speak Quebecois the people pretend they can't understand you."

"Maybe they're not pretending. Especially if they're from small communities."

"You know that could be true, after all we have some small French-only communities here in Alberta."

"Where?"

"Girouxville, Bluesky, plus others up north of Grande Prairie and in the Peace region. Anyhow, enough chit-chat – I've got to get there reports done and if you do the envelopes that will save me some time. Deciphering some of the stuff these guys send in is a headache all on its own! But not this month at least."

"Why not?"

"Because both Gerry and Dale have just gotten back out on the road so there are no logs. Of course I still have to send in the paperwork even when there's nothing to report. And then there's the year-to-date comparison over last year to be calculated – such fun.

Normally the guys send or drop off their daily logs which detail their trips and expenses with receipts if they're Dale's, because his logs are a work of art, whereas Gerry's are a dog's breakfast."

"Hey, if they buy too much fuel in a province do they get a refund for the extra tax they paid?"

"Hardly."

"That's not fair."

"Oh wow, somebody should alert the media."

"Ha ha. Show me next time you get some, OK?"

"OK, now just type up those envelopes please. I need one for each provincial capital."

Pamela got busy on her calculator and for the next while the only other sound was Suzi rolling envelopes into her typewriter and pounding away at the keys until Suzi asked:

"Did you know the capital of British Columbia is Victoria, not Vancouver?"

"Uh, yeah."

And a minute later:

"Hey, this address is Toronto but isn't Ottawa the capital?"

"No, Ottawa is the capital of Canada and Toronto is the capital of Ontario. You did go to school, right?"

"We learned French, we didn't learn about stuff like this."

"Well you should have. Other than French what did you learn?"

"Well for starters we had Sex Ed so we learned stuff like..." but a look from Pamela was enough to shut Suzi up until she finished her task.

"What other work do you do for the brokers?"

"I calculate their pay statements which I make up every month. That means figuring out their share of the hauling revenues minus expenses like the Workers Comp we pay on their behalf, cash advances, fuel taxes, that sort of thing. Actually I developed the monthly statement process and the guys really like it."

"How did they get paid before?"

"Almost exclusively by cash advances. When the guys got back to the office it meant a nightmare of paperwork to sort out. While they were on the road they'd courier completed bills of lading so we could invoice the van lines who in turn invoiced the client and that would give us a rough idea of the driver's earnings. But for someone like Gerry cash issued to him while on the road too often got spent on the road instead of going to his family who needed a regular income for groceries and mortgage payments.

Jan told me the monthly statement was a godsend. She has a part-time job that helps out but raising two girls, basically on her own, is a full-time job really. Having an accurate forecast of what Gerry's earnings will be helped her budget, and knowing there would be a payment every month instead of six weeks, then three weeks, then eight weeks, etc.. made a difference."

"So it was a problem over money that caused their marriage to break up?"

"That was a factor but I think Gerry's serial infidelity was the main reason."

"Serial infidelity, I love that expression!"

"I guess any criminal activity can be done in a series."

"You think infidelity is a crime?"

"Betrayal is the worst crime that can occur in a relationship."

"So if you were married and your husband had an affair, or even just a one-night stand, would it better – in your opinion – if he confessed or would you rather not know ever?"

"I wouldn't like to be made a fool of, to have other people know and maybe be feeling sorry for me or something, but whether he told me right away or I found out years later it would still be unforgivable."

"Really? Even if you'd built up this great life together and you found out something from years before, something that didn't mean anything to him?"

"I think that would make it worse. I mean, there are so many things beyond our control that we just have to accept and live with day after day that when it's something we can control 100% then I really believe it's vital that we make the right choice. If I'm living in some fairy-tale belief that my husband has always been faithful then my happiness has been based on a lie. I've been foolish and naive and stupid, and the man I've loved has actually been a liar and a cheat."

"Wow, that's heavy stuff. No forgive-and-forget for you, eh?"

"Well as I once heard somebody say: 'I'm not Jesus and I don't have Alzheimer's'"

"This betrayal thing, are you speaking of a personal experience?"

"If I am it's something from my past and that's where it should stay."

"So you wouldn't even consider dating Gerry?"

"A few dates maybe, so long as it was just for good times, but a serious relationship? Absolutely no way. I guess I have trust issues as the pop psychologists say."

Chapter Twenty

Tuesday February 26 – Thursday February 28, 1980

When the doorbell rang Angelica – but call me Angie – Posani was elbow-deep in a carton that seemed to be empty except for crumpled balls of kraft paper. She'd already discovered the movers used lots of wadded paper inside every box but she had to check each ball to make sure it wasn't wrapping some small item like the lid of the sugar-bowl or a crystal knick-knack.

Considering how many moves she'd accomplished in her thirty years of life Angie was again surprised at herself for the quantity of acquisitions she'd made. Oh well, she loved to shop and each new city she'd learned to call home housed a wealth of stores to explore and unique, sometimes quirky, objects to acquire. She couldn't pretend every purchase was an objet d'art but it was something she found attractive.

Now, hopefully, the moving days were over and could invest in some decent furniture. She'd been tipped off years ago that frequent relocations were tough on furniture – after all, it's built to be sat on or slept on, not moved around on a truck – and so she'd never spent much money on her stuff. Things should be different now, now that she'd made it to Toronto, the company's headquarters.

All those other moves had been promotions, each time to a bigger centre than before, all leading towards Head Office. All roads lead to Rome? Finally, after eight years of moving around the country, most recently Halifax, she'd found her Rome.

It's funny that her hard work had only resulted in a slow ascent whereas her tumultuous office romance with a married boss heaved her into the higher ranks. It was a huge relief to know that Steve wasn't going to be hanging around her office or parked outside her home. He might still phone to hear her say hello thirty or more times a day but she felt that absence would work favourably.

She'd always preferred to have relationships with married men. Angelica was an ambitious woman who didn't want the complication of romance or settling into traditional male/female roles. Determined to get ahead in her job she knew she wouldn't marry for years, if at all. She never wanted to fall head-over-heels in love – just pleasurable lust.

She marvelled that not too many years ago a lifestyle like hers would have been impossible due to the likelihood of pregnancy. Hard to believe that free and easy access to birth control was still something of a novelty even though it was now 1980. A woman she'd gone to college with told how all four of her children had been conceived while she was taking black market birth control pills. She remembered the woman saying "All I did was get high – and pregnant!"

Even recently, a co-worker had complained that his family's GP wouldn't prescribe birth control to his wife saying 'There was no reason for her not to have a baby since she was healthy and married' and it didn't matter that neither she nor her husband wanted a child. Some doctors seemed to think people wanted their opinions and not their services. Angie had encountered one doctor who wanted to interfere in her life so she'd found someone else instead. She knew she couldn't take The Pill forever – deadly complications were a risk for older users – but it worked well for her now and with no side-effects.

Another reason for choosing partners who were already spoken-for was that she'd discovered secret sex was electrifying. Sneaking around for a tryst, or meticulously planning a rendezvous, was way more exciting then a mere date. And having to act normal around the watchful eyes of co-workers added to the fun. Brushing up against each other – accidentally, of course – innocent-sounding entendres, playing footsie under the desk... dozens of seductive ploys to keep the arousal levels high and enliven the daily routine of office work.

Flirtation, imagination, anticipation, and finally satiation. Fun, fun, fun!

Steve, disastrously, fell possessively in love. As Angie was distancing herself he was wrecking his marriage by confessing to his wife. He didn't mind when his wife threw him out of their home until he realized that Angie was no longer welcoming him into hers. Steve turned ugly and the higher-ups intervened.

Usually it was the female half of an office affair who suffered the consequence of corporate discipline – often termination – when private lives disrupted work but both Angie and Steve were valued employees. Steve was allowed to stay where he was or accept a higher position, but at a much smaller office, in PEI with or without his wife. Angelica got her desired promotion to Toronto.

A previous short-lived but enjoyable fling with a senior VP had contributed to that decision. Angie couldn't care less knowing she was qualified to do the job and her personal life was her business.

Today was moving-in-day. It was a hassle, as always, but especially exciting this time. Her second-last location, Vancouver, was big but it's a city that's composed of communities, self-contained areas that even had their own phone-books, whereas Toronto was cosmopolitan urban, an international-class city, that represented the big-time for Angie.

At first she'd been worried when the company sent her to Halifax, thinking that working in the Maritimes was a step down after

Vancouver, but instead she'd joined a vibrant young team in a brand-new division and had learned so much and done so well. She looked forward to good future prospects.

And if, as seemed likely, she was settling down into one place long-term then now she could start building some friendships, start putting down some roots and developing the personal side of her life that she'd put aside, willingly enough, in order to concentrate on her career. She could join a golfing Ladies League, sign up for some cooking courses in foreign cuisine, go on a singles vacation... she was looking forward to new adventure plus there would be lots of good shopping venues to discover and explore.

The only people she'd seen today were the Real Estate Agent, who'd met her this morning with the house-keys and a house-warming gift of a fire extinguisher, and the three movers. When the doorbell rang she knew exactly who it was and why.

She was half right.

Chapter Twenty-One

Tuesday February 26 – Thursday February 28, 1980

Ted Eberhart, Director of Personnel, dialled Karen Seannachie's line and asked her to come into his office. It was important to Ted that his employee came to him, as important as phoning Karen despite the fact that he could easily have called out since only a partition separated their offices. But in Ted's opinion that kind of behaviour lacked decorum and was unseemly. Ted was big on the look of things.

He wasn't happy about his office but then there weren't many things in life that did please him. Ted's personal characteristics were completely against him ever holding a job in Personnel, never mind heading the department, but as a stickler for detail he'd worked his way up to his present position through conscientious effort.

He also wasn't happy about the new transfer-in because Angelica Posani came to Toronto as the result of an office scandal. That information was being kept under wraps, of course, and Ted Eberhart was determined to keep a watchful eye on Ms Posani to ensure nothing untoward happened in his domain. He often thought in cliches.

The move to Head Office was actually a big step up for Ms. Posani and Ted knew he'd better do his best to welcome her to this location, no matter what his personal feelings about the young woman might be. That's why he'd called on Karen to deputize for him.

Karen Seannachie, who was open and friendly, pretty and well-groomed, presented an ideal "Personnel Department" image.

"Ah, Karen, you can take a seat. I have here the Personnel Record of our latest transferee, Ms Angelica Posani, and I would like you to handle the personal greeting." He studied the contents of the folder a moment then handed the file over to Karen, continuing: "Ms Posani is regarded very favourably, very favourably, by our superiors and I think it would be appropriate to extend our personal greeting to Ms Posani at her new residence. I think a plant is called for, perhaps a poinsettia? although no, the season has passed and it wouldn't do to look like we bought something marked down. So a selection of the latest blooms, don't you think?" Ted worded it as a question but only agreement would be an acceptable response.

Karen responded as required.

"Good, then that will be all for now. You may leave the office an hour early in order to pick up the bouquet and deliver it to Ms Posani at her new home."

Karen answered that she'd phone the company florist to make the arrangements right away and left Ted's office leaving him thinking, magnanimously, that Ms Seannachie, despite her youth that had caused him his earlier misgivings, appeared to be shaping up well under his tutelage.

He wasn't happy about how the spelling of her surname differed so much from its pronunciation but dealt with that issue by ignoring it. Karen dealt with Ted by rolling her eyes a lot – but only in her mind because she was a good employee who enjoyed her job in personnel.

Chapter Twenty-Two

Tuesday February 26 – Thursday February 28, 1980

Pamela sat in her car thinking. She was looking at a 'Do Not Back In' sign without seeing it. The townhouses in her complex had their own garages but the apartments shared an area outdoors and the signs were a safety reminder. Exhaust fumes from cars left running to warm up in the cold weather could seep into the windows of lower level suites spreading deadly carbon monoxide fumes.

Pamela was musing about her last phone call from Gerry. In the midst of his usual banter he'd let slip that "Dale has a thing about you" and when she'd asked him to explain he'd covered up saying 'no more than I do'. Pamela wanted to know more but couldn't ask without showing her interest. Gerry was an awful tease and a gossip too. She didn't mind him saying that Dale was interested but she'd be mortified if he told Dale the same about her.

"Although I don't see any way the information is going to get passed on if it's left just to the two of us. Dale's always so gentlemanly, like he's holding back or something. It's just his way." she told herself. "I can't make the first move. Well, it would be the second move since he did ask me out once already but I can hardly say right out of the blue 'yes, now I'm free to accept that drink you offered.' I mean, I guess I could but I can't, I'd like to, I'd like to be the kind of woman who can just say stuff like that to a man but I'm not so there it is."

She recalled a hot summer's day when she'd gone into the warehouse to tell Dale the mechanic called to advise his trailer was repaired and ready for pick-up. He'd been helping Arnie load a storage box and they were both sweating in the heat. Dale had quickly buttoned up his shirt when she approached. Arnie noticed this and said "What?

Are you shy or something?" but Pamela pretended not to hear. She'd forgotten about that incident. Yes, he was quite gentlemanly and considerate.

She hadn't forgotten the time when Dale called her 'Baby' on the phone but she'd ignored it at the time. She figured the attraction was only on her side but maybe...

When a neighbour pulled into the next parking-space Pamela woke from her reverie and gave a smile and wave. She lived in a friendly complex. Her home was part of a co-operative housing project gone awry but in such a way that worked out favourably.

Her apartment was in an eight-plex within a townhouse complex, and the second floor of the building was reached by a long, uncarpeted stair. The eight-plex was designed for fixed-income seniors but none were interested in the top-floor units after seeing such deep risers on the steep stairs.

Pamela was able to live in a large, new unit at a very reasonable rent. When asked what duties she could perform on behalf of the complex as part of the co-op model her offer to type notices, and the like, was accepted but so far she had never actually called upon to do any work.

This was her first place on her own and she found she liked it. Once she'd had a scare after an obscene phone-caller claimed he was watching her. That turned out to be a long, long night. She kept telling herself no one could see in her windows and she was quite safe up on the second floor but then she noticed a trap door in the ceiling - to a shared attic space? - and got nervous and worried all over again.

The next day her night frights felt foolish and she was never troubled again with fearful thoughts. Of course it helped that the caller had probably dialled her number at random because he never called back.

Now Pamela was trying to picture her place through Dale's eyes, and soon she was trying to picture Dale in her place and imagining a conversation and further events.

She realized that yes, she was very definitely interested in him but how did he feel about her?

Chapter Twenty-Three

Tuesday February 26 – Thursday February 28, 1980

The killer checked through the rooms one last time. He'd been careful. He knew it was important to be careful but he didn't like to think about why too much. Some thoughts were better pushed aside. Like trying to remember that feeling of urgency he'd experienced before. Now it was gone and even the memory of it seemed unbelievable but he didn't know why and he didn't think he wanted to know why.

The townhouse was an end-unit with the front door turned away from the common area and parking-lot. It was a curvy, fancy-built place (evidence of yet another architect who hated movers) and it worked in his favour that the homes were positioned for privacy.

He'd taken a cab to a garage. The driver, a woman, had asked if he wanted her to wait while he checked if his vehicle was ready. Only a woman would ask something like that, he'd sighed to himself. It sounded like a nice gesture but it was just another way of poking their nose in and getting involved in your life. Out loud he'd said thanks but no, he'd already talked to the shop and had even made a deal for cash which is why he was carrying such a wad. Because, of course, she'd noticed. Women noticed so much; rarely were they paying attention to what was important but any stupid little detail and they'd be onto it like a shot.

The last thing he wanted was a nosy woman waiting for him to come out of the garage when he had, in fact, no intention of ever going in.

The garage was handy to where he wanted to be tonight. A trucker going to a garage was a trip no cabbie was likely to wonder about or comment on. He only had a couple of blocks to walk and then he'd be seeing Ms Angelica Posani. He'd have to see other people afterwards but Ms Posani wouldn't ever be seeing anyone again.

So now he was done. The place was a mess of cleaning supplies and movers' cartons, some, knocked over in the struggle, now spilling their contents over the freshly-washed carpets. Not that there had been much of a struggle: that fire-extinguisher was still sitting at the front-door and once he'd cracked her across the face with that most of the fight had been knocked out of her. The carpet, in the current fashionable shade of gray that's supposed to to make rooms look larger was stained with blood where the fire-extinguisher had rolled after he'd dropped it. He doubted very much if those stains could be easily washed away.

Of course she'd still struggled, and even tried to run as they had the bad habit of doing, so a trail of blood marked their progress from the hall to the living-room to the bedroom. His knuckles were raw from the punching he'd had to do.

He left Ms Posani's body on the bed. She was sprawled across it diagonally and, even in death, her skin was still purpling with bruises.

She had said that she'd never lived in Toronto before and wasn't due to start work until the Monday so he wondered how long she'd lie here in her own mess before someone discovered the killing. Utility hook-ups, cable TV company, meter-readers, were all expected over the next couple of days but they couldn't let themselves in and hewasn't going to leave the door invitingly open.

The longer it took for Ms Posani's murder to be discovered the better. He'd be miles and miles away. That was his job. Perform a service for the customers, talk to them (or rather listen while they talked to you, a stranger they'd never see again), and get a picture of their lives. A picture substantiated by their personal belongings which you got to see and appraise and formulate your own ideas about.

Some of the stuff they found – nudie photos galore, video cameras attached to headboards, hash pipes, rolling papers – revealed a different kind of truth behind the facade of modern décor furnishings.

Ms Posani had been quite a talker. Very excited about her move and her new position and very full of herself and her plans. She'd told him everything he needed to know. Enough to mark her as his victim. Before he left the townhouse he'd made sure the four-wheel dolly was half-hidden under the bed. A place where she'd be sure to find it but not before the truck had pulled away from the complex. She couldn't phone the company because she didn't have her phone installed yet. She'd have no objection to letting him in when he came back later to pick up his equipment.

It had all gone according to his plan.

He found himself wondering, again, about the blood from her mouth and if it was internal bleeding or if it had, in fact, come from her tongue. He didn't know if tongues bled much. Having these kind of thoughts was frightening, he needed to let go of the memory.

He never knew exactly what his hands and feet were doing when the pain in his head turned his brain into a tangle of black but he thought that he was getting angrier, and more violent, and he was surprised, dismayed, and a little scared to discover his cheeks wet with tears. There was no reason for him to be crying, he was the.. the... man who did what had to be done. Someone had to do it. It was a man's job with no regrets allowed.

Chapter Twenty-Four

Tuesday February 26 – Thursday February 28, 1980

It was almost three o'clock and Lou Lysincek figured he could swing by Castleview Downs (where there was no castle, no downs and little view), see Angelica Posani, pick up his kids from day-care, then pick up the babysitter from her place, and take them all home leaving himself plenty of time to clean up and still make it to the restaurant in Streetsville on time. He left his agenda with Marie, the receptionist, before leaving the office to head east on the 401.

Lou was pleased with his scheduling. It had taken quite a while and a lot of hit-and-miss efforts before finding his groove. Ever since his ex-wife decided he should try maintaining a household for children while meeting the commitments of a full-time career instead of her being burdened with it Lou had been at a loss but he'd learned quickly.

It was a never-ending chore of scheduling: grocery shopping, cooking, laundry, school and after-school activities, day-care and after-school care, evening and weekend babysitting. Although they were his own children Lou refused to consider it anything but babysitting when he was the one looking after them. He loved his children and since he'd been spending so much more time in their company he discovered that he also liked his children but he still believed it wasn't his job to be looking after them.

In addition, as a Real Estate salesman he felt his job wasn't suited to the routine of children, whereas a nine-to-five routine like Joanne's was. But he'd accepted the challenge and demanded she pay him child support. He suspected his ex-wife was delighted to exchange a cheque for her free time and had resolved to demand a better arrangement before school was out come summer. He'd got over the Winter Break panic by taking his family to Disney World in Orlando, Florida although he'd have vastly preferred the Bahamas without the kids.

His thoughts carried him through the drive. He'd reached the point of hoping Joanne's maternal instincts would get the better of her – and soon! when he arrived at the town-house complex. He was pleased to see a woman standing at Angelica Posani's door, holding a florist's bundle of green tissue and silver foil, figuring if she had company, even if was only Welcome Wagon, he wouldn't get drawn into a lengthy conversation.

Not that he would have minded spending more time with Ms Posani, an attractive and upbeat young woman he'd enjoyed meeting when he came by with the house keys and a fire-extinguisher house-warming gift. She was also a VIP at a major account of his so he'd stay for a bit of a chat but not too long because his schedule was nagging at him.

He hurried out of the car and introduced himself to the attractive blonde who said she was Karen Seannachie from the personnel department of the company. A good contact for future reference. He hoped he was scoring some brownie points for his personalized attention.

"I've been knocking and knocking and I'm sure Ms Posani isn't home and I can't really wait much longer, I'm afraid."

"She's not home?" in confirmation Lou knocked on the door again, quite loudly, and Karen repressed a sigh.

"I don't really feel comfortable leaving these flowers on her doorstep. I can't imagine she's gone far, probably just to the grocery store or the bank or something, but I'd hate to have someone come along and take these."

"Well look, let's go round to the back. There's a fence so you can safely leave the flowers since no one will be able to see them sitting there. I'll just write Ms Posani a little note, I came by to drop off her resident's parking sticker – the Tenants' Association came up with these since they've been having parking problems – which I forgot to bring yesterday when I handed over the keys to her."

As he spoke he followed the bricked walk round the side of the building and led the way into the backyard from a gate leading off the common walk-way. More brick created a path across the lawn to the back door of the town-house. Karen put down her plant and was fishing in her purse for pen and business card on which to scribble a note when Lou, out of habit or curiosity, turned the handle and opened the door.

"Oh, great!" he said, walking in, "We can leave this stuff in here and.." That's when he noticed the blood. There were smears on the counter around the sink and splashes on the wall. It looked like Angelica Posani had run into the kitchen - hoping to grab a knife?- and her assailant had pursued with extreme violence. The evidence was all around them.

Karen, pale and shaking at the sight, abruptly squatted and hung her head down between her knees taking fast, gasping breaths. Completely forgetting all about his children, their day-care, the baby-sitter, and the dinner-date in Streetsville Lou stepped further into the town-house, thought better of it, and went back to his Lincoln to use the car-phone to call the police.

It was just as well he had the car-phone since the phone company, unable to get any answer to their knocking, hadn't been able to install Ms Posani's phones, as scheduled, that morning. Angelica Posani's death had inconvenienced many people.

Chapter Twenty-Five

Tuesday February 26 – Thursday February 28, 1980

When their daughter was sent to the Ministry of Correctional Services for her three-week college practicum Tanya's parents hoped she would do well and be offered a permanent placing once she'd completed her Medical Secretary course.

A position with the Ontario government meant job security, benefits, and a good pension, and when required, extended maternity leave would be available. The Beckett's had it all mapped out, a win-win situation for sure.

Tanya first discovered that her parents were nosy people when she was in elementary school. She'd had to take a school-bus so not all of her classmates were from the neighbourhood and when she came home with a tale about new friends she was immediately quizzed: 'What's Karen's last name?' and 'What does her father do?' and 'Oh, well why don't you find out?'

Now each night the dinner table hosted discussions about the work she'd done that day and what her bosses and co-workers were like: 'His name is Gold? hmm, he's Jewish then.' 'No, he's English from England.' 'He can be any nationality and still be a Jew.' 'Why does it matter?' 'It doesn't, it's just something to know.'

But tonight she would have to plead confidentiality or else lie because there was no way she could tell her parents the truth about today's work day.

The administration was currently short-staffed due to a stomach bug making the rounds and a number of employees enjoying an all-inclusive package vacation in the sunny Caribbean for a winter break. This added variety to Tanya's placement since she got sent to several different departments and she enjoyed learning about each section. Today it was the Office of the Chief Coroner – but that shouldn't have happened.

The typing of death investigation reports – which include transcribing autopsy audio and matching photographs to the exhibit list – is only given to mature secretarial staff. Material of this nature is never given to an 18-year-old temp, but unfortunately that's exactly what happened today.

Tanya arrived at her assigned desk interested and eager to begin but was soon horrified by what she saw in the file. She didn't realize this was far beyond the scope of her assignment and instead mustered her reserves to complete the task at hand. The Beckett parents would be furiously angry if they ever found out.

Tanya was determined to be do well in this placement so she tried to be detached and professional and the medical jargon shielded her to an extent.

Nevertheless, it was awful stuff.

She transcribed how many of the welts were bloodless because those strokes were applied postmortem, the victim's cheekbone was shattered, she was missing teeth, one eye was swollen shut, clumps of hair had been torn from her head leaving her scalp bloody, the four fingers of her right hand were pushed back to an unnatural angle – probably while she'd tried to defend herself – her left instep was crushed, she had splintered ribs, and a dislocated shoulder.

Blood had gushed out of her mouth when she bit through her tongue and run down her face when her nose was broken but there was little blood elsewhere. The body was marked with deep bruises and it was the internal injuries that actually caused death. Ruptured, displaced, and distended organs caused massive internal bleeding.

Tanya did very well up to that point but she found the description of blood-filled cavities sickening. Luckily at that moment an ambulance driver spotted her shocked white face – Tanya had the kind of looks men did notice even when she felt nauseous – so he hurried over and pushed her head down between her knees and rubbed her back until the faint feeling passed.

Catching sight of a photo showing the victim's damaged face he angrily demanded to know "why the hell this child is doing this type of work?"

The unit manager, a man with little compassion and zero social skills, came out of his office and loudly challenged the EMT saying: "What business is it of yours? and stop interfering with the female staff."

His P.A. followed him and took charge of the girl who was embarrassed, close to tears, and apologizing.

"No, no we're the ones who are sorry. You should never have been sent to this office, I don't know who's responsible for this mix-up but this definitely isn't the type of work we would ever expect a temp or a new employee to deal with. This just shouldn't have happened and I'm terribly sorry that it did."

As the older woman bundled the papers into the file she complimented Tanya saying: "I'm really impressed with how much work you got done, it couldn't have been easy and you did really well. I'll certainly pass that on for your evaluation. Meanwhile, I'm going to bring you back to HR and they'll get you set up with something more suitable after a little break."

Her boss and the ambulance man eyeballed each other then, leaving the insults unsaid, turned back to their own business in the wake of all this female efficiency.

The completion of the report on Angelica Posani's brutal murder would have to wait until a recovered – or suntanned – senior typist returned to work.

Chapter Twenty-Six

Tuesday February 26 – Thursday February 28, 1980

Dale walked into the Husky Truck Stop and was loudly welcomed by the group sitting at the centre table with shouts of 'Good to see you again' and 'About time you got back to work'. Gerry brought over another chair and the men shuffled to make room.

"I got the go-ahead to start driving again a few weeks ago and I'm already on my return trip." said Dale.

"You sure were a long time in hospital, eh? Must have had hot and cold running nurses there."

"And he'd be too shy to take advantage of them!" said Gerry, laughing kindly at his friend. "Of course that was some crash he was in so he probably couldn't have done much no matter how cute the Candy-Stripers were."

"I'm well enough to kick your butt so watch it."

"Truce! I've been warned by our dispatcher not to get into any more fights and she'd kill me if I put you out of action."

"Oh as if..." Dale smiled at the banter, feeling relaxed for the first time in a long time. It was really good to be back shooting the shit with the guys. The conversation his arrival interrupted got going again:

"I can't believe we're back to the Liberals already. Four years of being ripped off yet again." said Kenny. He drove for a different van line but all the household movers were friendly with each other, always ready to lend a hand, not like the freight haulers.

"Joe Clark should never have been Prime Minister. He's weak. He can't even control his own wife. You know she goes by her own name, right?"

The waitress overheard that remark as she came by with the coffee pot and responded saying: "Helloooo it is 1980 not 1918 and women do keep their own names – especially if they're well-known in their field."

"C'mon, Michelle she doesn't need a career, being the Prime Minister's wife should be career enough."

"I have to admit it doesn't seem like she's being very supportive of him." replied Michelle, always ready to take the traditional line that she found most of the truckers favoured. It was easy to agree with the customers who tipped so well.

"Awww he's a dick, you can tell just by looking at him, why would anyone vote for him anyhow?"

"Well I did because he was going to make mortgage interest payments tax deductible. Just like in the States. That really adds up, especially with interest rates always on the rise. Got to have a home for the wife and kids but it isn't easy paying two sets of living expenses."

"Try being divorced, it's even worse then!"

"So a bunch of homeowners liked him, big deal. What about everybody else? What was he going to do for them?"

"It wouldn't just benefit homeowners – or I should say mortgagees – because it would mean more people would buy homes and that's more business for home builders, tradespeople, appliance and furniture sales, and more jobs overall. It's a good way to boost the economy."

"Huh, more like boost bank profits."

"They don't need any help to boost profits they do just fine as is."

"Speaking of which is it true Murray Ames might be selling his truck? I heard he's behind on all of his bills trying to make his truck payments because the 14% interest rate is just killing him."

"I know he's missed out on rent payment to Jim Grubowski's ex, what's her name?" asked Eric, Kenny's brother, turning to Gerry since Gerry was everybody's who's who source. He didn't disappoint.

"Marie and yes, she is a 'Sweet Marie.'"

"Oh yeah I don't think you'd better let Jim hear you say that, even if he is her ex. Anyhow, Murray rents her basement suite, and I know she can't afford to carry him because Jim isn't giving her any money. He's pissed she got the house which she did because now she's a single parent."

"Don't get me started on poor single Moms."

"Hey, we're back to a Liberal government – the single Moms won't be poor anymore, just the Dads – whether they asked to be single or not!"

"Oh please, as if the lying Libs take care of anybody – oh wait a minute, they take care of their friends."

"Real well, too."

"Clark just didn't have what it takes. Last year Trudeau resigned and this year he's Prime Minister again – go figure."

"Hey you talk about why would anyone vote for Joe Clark but who the hell voted for Trudeau?"

"The immigrants. When they come to Canada they're told they were brought in by the Liberal Party of Canada and that they'll be sent back if they vote Conservative."

"It's old news anyhow, the election was in February."

"Yeah, a real Happy Valentine for Canada."

"Old news to you guys," said Dale, "but I'm still catching up."

"You look good, and you're moving OK."

"Yeah the doctors did all their tests before passing me fit for Class 1 and I feel good except for a headache now and then but sometimes those headaches are a real bitch."

"Well," said Gerry "Life's a bitch." and waited for the chorus from the rest: "...and then you marry one."

Dale hadn't joined in and Gerry noticed that his friend's forehead was creased in a frown and his lips were stretched tight, it looked like he was suffering the onset of one of his bad headaches.

Gerry knew what that was all about since he was still suffering his own. Dale stood up and headed for the washroom, stumbling a bit but before anyone else noticed Gerry loudly broke into song: "♫You picked a fine time to leave me, 'Loose Wheel'...♫" which always got a laugh and was a good distraction.

Chapter Twenty-Seven

Tuesday February 26 – Thursday February 28, 1980

It had all gone to plan except for that moving pad. He'd suddenly remembered about it and now he couldn't forget it. But it wasn't such a big deal... was it?

One moving pad wouldn't be a problem at all except he wasn't sure if the company name was stencilled on it like most, although not all, of his equipment. But anyone who had ever been in the warehouse had access to the equipment, and stuff often got left behind by anyone – helpers and drivers.

They had been moving out the living-room furniture when he heard the customer saying 'oh no!' so he left the crew to continue on while he followed the sound of her voice into the dining-room.

"I forgot to take down my light so it could get packed up and now the packers are gone." said Angie Posani.

"Fixtures are usually sold with the house." he began but she interrupted saying:

"When I sold the house I showed the new owners the original light fixture and explained I'd be putting it back on because this would be coming with me and it's noted on the Agreement to Purchase. But I should have taken it down so it could be packed. You will take it, won't you?"

The light was a modern sculpture in thick, heavy glass. It looked expensive.

"I'll take it but I don't have anything to pack it in. Wait, we can put it in the bottom of one of your wardrobe boxes, I'll wrap it in a pad for protection but it's not the same as proper packing in a china carton."

"No that's fine, I really appreciate it. This fixture has special meaning. I'll just disconnect it – it's really easy – and thanks so much for taking care of this for me."

And so he'd wrapped the light fixture and tucked it securely into a wardrobe which was still sitting unpacked in her home with his moving pad inside. Angie thought he was such a nice, helpful man, and so good looking too!

Now the killer was obsessing over that moving pad. It wasn't proof but it was a connection and that worried him.

Chapter Twenty-Eight

Tuesday February 26 – Thursday February 28, 1980

"Suzi what on earth..? you look like something the cat dragged in."

"And late, too." added Arnie, enjoying a coffee break before continuing his day's work in the warehouse.

"I'm either having a flashback or I'm still high, God only knows. I feel like shit."

"And sorry you're late too, right?" Arnie wasn't going to let it go.

"Yeah, alright I'm sorry I'm late – OK, Arnie? Not that it's any of your business – OK Pam?"

"Suzi, I give you work to do but I can't fire you so that makes me a co-worker, not your boss." replied Pamela mildly. "But I can give you a hard time if you're showing up to work stoned so what's up with that?"

"We did some Purple Microdot on the weekend and I think it's still in my system."

"Omigod do people still drop acid? I thought that went out of fashion ten years ago."

"It's back, so's heroin but I never mess with shit like that and not just because it's illegal."

"It's all illegal, Suzi."

"I know, eh? I can't believe weed is illegal."

"Well, regardless of what your opinion is we have a very strict no drugs policy here so don't ever bring anything to work."

Arnie jumped back into the conversation saying "If it was up to me I'd legalize everything."

"Even heroin?" asked Suzi as if seeing Arnie in a whole new light.

"Sure, it would break organized crime since it was Prohibition that got that started, and why not let the idiots kill themselves if they want to? There's too much money wasted on those losers."

"Wow, much sympathy or what?" interjected Suzi indignantly.

"Why would I waste my sympathy on people who are too stupid to take advantage of the great life they have here? Why should I pay for their needles when diabetics have to pay for their own?"

"Why should anybody pay for needles when we supposedly have this great free health care system?"

Pamela interrupted saying: "Um, can we continue the debate later? We've all got work to do, Arnie I think your break is over, hmm? And Suzi are you fit to work or what?"

"Work, eh? Oh sure. You guys just want to have some girl talk."

"Yeah us guys with the girl talk right, it's just a giggle-fest all day long."

When he left Suzi said to Pamela: "I really am sorry I'm late. The alarm when off and I thought I had hit the snooze button but suddenly I open my eyes and I'm like oh shit. I didn't bother with make-up or curling my hair I just figured I better get in as soon as I could so that's why I look like this."

"Well I've never known you to be late before so it's not a big deal this time but come summer it's going to be extremely busy here and I have to be able to count on you then."

"Totally. It won't happen again. Actually, Derek has got a job in construction for the summer so we won't be partying as much on weekends and he'll be so beat after a day's work that I probably won't even see him during the week."

"Oh yes Derek, the guy with the shiny Corvette. Won't he be chauffeuring you around anymore?

"Of course he will. We start early here so he'll be able to drop me off as usual and as for going home, well if he's got to work late he'll let me know and I'll call my Dad or something. No, what I meant was that we probably won't be hanging out or going anywhere on weeknights."

"So, is it serious with you two? Will wedding bells be chiming?"

"Piss off," laughed Suzi, "I'm way too young to be tied down. Besides, Derek is really smart. He's been accepted into Law at the University of Toronto so he'll be living there come September."

"We don't have a Law faculty at the U of A?"

"Oh, this is some specialized course that's only available there, I don't know exactly. He goes on and on about it so much that I've forgotten half of what he said."

"But you guys don't have to split up just because he'll be in Ontario."

"Yeah, we do. He doesn't think so, I mean he thinks we'll still be an item but let's not kid ourselves, he'll be there meeting new people and wanting to go out and everything and I'll be here and wanting to go out, too.

He's a super-smart guy who's got a lot of schooling ahead and then years building up a career which will be brilliant, I'm sure, and I'm not going to be sitting at home twiddling my thumbs while he's having a life. Of course if he wants to come and find me once he's a rich, successful lawyer that'll be great."

"I don't know if you're mature beyond your years or hopelessly shallow but you do make sense."

"I'm not a brain like Derek but I'm not stupid and I can figure out what the score is. Talking of scoring, how come you know what Microdot is? I thought you were just a small-town country gal?"

"No matter how small the town is drugs are going to be available at the high-school. Our sport teams travelled throughout the province, I played basketball and was on the track team too, and we discovered all kinds of stuff. But once I graduated that was the end of doing shit. As my best friend used to say 'someday we're going to have babies and we don't want them to be spazzy' so that was that for drugs."

"You don't get high at all?" Suzi was incredulous.

"I drink, but the goal isn't to get drunk but to enjoy the taste, enjoy the atmosphere and ambiance and the glow."

"Yeah, but what do you do for fun?"

"Suzi, we're already running behind since you came in late so let's try and get some work done before you leave for lunch, OK?" Pamela was suddenly feeling there was way more than a six-year gap in their ages.

"OK, but just answer, what do you like to do? What kind of movies do you like?"

"I like comedies that are silly. Pink Panther, anything by Mel Brooks, and especially Monty Python movies. I thought the "Holy Grail" was the funniest thing ever but I just saw "Life of Brian" and started laughing from the moment it started. The guy I went with was embarrassed so that was a first and last date.

Now, you can tell me what movies you like as soon as you finish typing all these bills of lading and don't say you can type and talk at the same time because Arnie checks everything over and loves it when he finds typos like Petewawa and Van Liens."

"Arnie is definitely not my boss."

"Luckily for you..."

Chapter Twenty-Nine

Tuesday February 26 – Thursday February 28, 1980

Dale came out of the bathroom with his collar wet from splashing cold water on his face. Michelle was waiting and taking his arm pulled him to sit at a high-top table.

"I wanted to let you know that everyone is so glad you're OK but also so sorry for what you've been through."

Dale shook his head saying: "Yeah, that's over now. I don't.." but Michelle interrupted: "Hey, I can see that you're having trouble coping with what happened and I want to make sure you know that it wasn't your fault. Nobody thinks it was. Except, from the look of you, maybe you?"

"Two little kids are dead, Michelle."

"Because of what their mother did. Not you."

"Right except that I was driving the truck that was pulling the trailer that wiped out the car they were in."

"And she's the one who put them there. NOT you. Listen, right now I'm a single mother because Pete's living in a work camp way up in northern Alberta. It's really hard to be raising kids on your own and this is by choice, Pete and I agreed to do this. So I feel for the woman - she's lost everything - but that's down to her. Everybody who was coming in here at the time was talking about it and not a single soul even hinted you were at fault. Maybe there would have been talk if that cop hadn't been following you and witnessed the whole thing, I don't know, but thank God he was there. And thank God you're here now. Bad as it was it could have been worse."

"Worse?"

"Dale you could have died too or ended up in a wheelchair for the rest of your life. The mother could have been killed as well."

"Her? Huh, she should have killed herself."

"You know what? I agree. I know I couldn't live with myself if I'd done something like that. And sure, I'd be angry at whoever was nearby, namely you, but that wouldn't change the fact that I'd know, deep down, it was my fault. All her fault."

"OK Michelle, I appreciate what you're saying and I think it does help a bit."

"It's what everybody is saying."

"Yeah, well 'everybody' wasn't there. But hey, thanks for this, you've got a big heart."

"I'm glad I got a chance to talk to you. You're one of the good guys, not like so many of the assholes out there. Speaking of which, why is Gerry Tanner making that stupid face at us? Oh I'm gonna sort him out right quick."

Chapter Thirty

Summer 2015

"You've heard me complaining about the Liberal Government before, right?"

Jake nodded his agreement.

"Seems most of the folk down here love the Liberals because they love their unemployment cheques – it's become a way of life – so they keep voting the Liberals into power. From Toronto east it's all Liberals.

Well it was Prime Minister Pierre Trudeau, the biggest Liberal of them all, who brought in the awful Metric System. Canada's main trading partner is the United States and it isn't using metric but that Trudeau he hated Americans, hated the British, and I sometimes think he hated Canadian too. He didn't care, he just made everybody change from Imperial, that's what I learned in school, to Metric.

It started off gradually but by 1975 the weather forecast was given in Celsius, the following year the grocery stores sold meat only by the kilogram, and the year after that, 1977, road-side speed limits were all posted in kilometres. It was tricky, let me tell ya. It was real easy to get a speeding ticket 'cause when you're going up and down the road all day you see signs but your brain doesn't really register so if the sign says 80 well... And we were driving 80 miles an hour so it was easy enough to make a mistake if your mind was drifting to other thoughts.

So everybody had to learn how to calculate and convert using the new numbers although people still used both numbers when talking like: 'thermometer says it's 30 today, that's about 90 degrees.'

Kids your age have only ever been taught in metric values, right?"

"Yeah, but we did learn that the American gallon is smaller than the Canadian gallon even though we don't have Canadian gallons any more."

"Well, we still have them, they're just made up of roughly four-and-a-half litres, and we sell gas and diesel by the litre so we don't use the word gallon. Except when the price goes up and then we say things like: 'I remember when it was 40 cents a gallon and now it's $1.40 a litre? Highway robbery, that's well over six bucks a gallon!'"

"Teacher said we use the metric system because that's how they do it in Europe and we're more European than American."

"Your teacher is an idiot and probably a Liberal or maybe even an NDPer. Canada is part of North America, along with the US and Mexico, we aren't European. Lots of people originally came here from Europe because they were offered free land but that was a few generations ago.

Anyhow, I was telling you about how Canada started using the metric system in the seventies but by 1980 we were still getting paid by a shipment's weight in pounds and the miles travelled from origin to destination. Our tariffs, which we got from the Government, spelled it all out in charts and they still weren't in metric. But that kind of half-assed job was just typical of the Liberals.

Hmm, I'm getting a bit off track here. But that's the thing – at that time most of the talk was about metric this and that and nobody really talked about the killings until it was all over."

Chapter Thirty-One

Friday February 29 - Monday March 3, 1980

In 1978 the moving company sent Pamela on a training course put on by the Household Goods Carriers Bureau to introduce the metric system to staff in the industry. The van lines declared these courses to be mandatory for all the sales and operations personnel in their agencies. Today she was scheduled to attend a refresher.

"I don't see why I have to go" said Arnie for the third time. He and Pamela were waiting for Fiona even though they were taking separate vehicles. Pamela needed to get straight back while Fiona would want to stay to schmooze and gossip with the other sales associates. She would follow in her own car. Pamela drove Arnie in her car since he didn't let anyone smoke in his.

"I shouldn't have to go either," answered Pamela, "because I went through it all two years ago and the tariffs are still published in pounds and miles. I've gotten used to the fuel conversions for my fuel reports but the tariffs haven't changed so this is just a waste of my time."

"This whole metric nonsense is bullshit and a waste of time." They looked at the big colourful poster hanging on the wall that showed the equivalent miles per hour to kilometres per hour for the most commonly posted speed limit signs. It was made by one of their saleswomen who was artistic and whenever American drivers came into the dispatch office they'd write down the numbers.

Those drivers had been driving 55 miles per hour on US highways since '74 so maintaining the legal highway speed of 100 kilometres (60 mph) should have been easy but instead they got tickets because they kept speeding up whenever they saw the number 100 on a sign.

It was widely believed that American tourists wouldn't get speeding tickets but commercial truckers sure would.

"I'm the warehouseman, I don't need to know about tariffs, you do all that calculation and billing stuff."

"Well maybe there's going to be something new about warehouse inspections for DND, like maybe space being calculated in metres instead of feet, something like that."

"That would be just typical – I swear to God someone high up in the Government has got a brother with a paper company and he's sure being kept busy printing out all this new stuff."

"You're probably right, so how come we weren't smart enough to apply for Government jobs way back when?"

"Because we don't parlez vous Francais."

"Oh yeah, I forgot that part."

Fiona joined them asking "What are we talking about kids?"

"Why we don't have Government jobs."

"Because we're all too smart, that's why. There's no money in Government jobs."

"No, just benefits, sick leave, and a pension."

"Earn big and buy RRSPs to fund your own pension. Come on, let's get going. I don't care if I sit in the front row but I know you two will."

Chapter Thirty-Two

Friday February 29 - Monday March 3, 1980

Cam Stillwell, a civilian analyst with the Royal Canadian Mounted Police, hadn't yet come to terms with a personal shake-up she'd had a couple of months ago. She couldn't get it out of her head, it filled her thoughts, and yet she was sure her situation couldn't be unique.

She'd come to realize that some time ago she'd fallen out of love with her husband. She was pretty sure she had loved him at one time but maybe those feelings then, like these feelings now, might simply be a phase in the course of a person's lifetime development?

She would never tell him, of course, but the real shock came in suspecting that Mark felt exactly the same way about her.

Mark was ten years older than her and he'd opted for an early retirement package. Not too early, he had his numbers in since he'd joined the Force young and his pensionable years with the Police transferred to the RCMP but early in actual years. She thought he'd left way too early.

Then he tried to nag her into retiring as well, telling her about his great travel plans for the two of them. That's when she realized that they'd grown so far apart they were strangers to one another. It started with brochures for a package tour to Russia but she squashed that idea.

"But whenever we watch movies set in Moscow you always talk about the architecture and how you'd like to see those buildings for yourself."

"Well yes, I've said that, but it's just something to say. I mean, the shapes and colours of the onion domes look so exotic that anyone would want to see them but to actually go to Russia? No way! Awful food and even worse prisons and probably the slightest thing could get a tourist landed in one of them."

"We'd be okay, I was a cop and you've worked for the RCMP for decades."

"That's worse – they'd probably accuse us of spying!"

At the time she couldn't think of anything she'd like less until Mark put forth the idea of training up and tackling Everest or at least making it to one of the base camps. That idea got a flat no, no argument.

Cam wasn't ready to retire. She enjoyed her job with the RCMP and although she wasn't actually a member of the Force – women had only been allowed to apply in the last five years – she'd achieved an interesting position through her hard work and intelligence.

So Mark announced that since she wasn't interested in travelling he didn't need to wait until she retired in order to set out himself. He'd joined a travel club of retirees, widows and never-married professionals, who wanted to visit foreign lands in congenial company and with shared costs.

Cam wondered where the money for this would come from then realized they had plenty of money in the bank and there was no reason why one or the other of them couldn't spend it however they wished. But it felt... odd.

Mark was currently on a train trip through the interior of China and Cam was so thankful that she wasn't on it with him. It was only in the last year or so that China had opened the doors to tourists from

Canada and Cam was certain there would be heavy restrictions on what could be seen and done, and that the accommodation, food, and entertainment would be primitive at best. To Cam her husband's enthusiasm for exotic foreign travel – inconveniences and all – was incomprehensible.

When she took him to the airport and met up with his travel companions it seemed to Cam that they were all women – very excited women – about to embark on adventure. She found she was feeling a bit sorry for herself since Mark was so keen to get away without her. And yet, she couldn't pretend to be jealous.

She had since discovered how much she enjoyed having the house to herself. She could pour a drink without needing a reason, stay up watching TV past their usual bedtime, and not have to bother cooking meals if she wasn't hungry.

Although she'd already reached her fifties she'd never actually lived by herself. She thought of young women nowadays who shared apartments with a best friend – or even rented a bachelor suite on their own – and had unimaginable freedom.

Cam had gone from her parent's home to her married home and although she'd gone away for training sessions at different times during her career in administrative law enforcement she'd never been on her own. Mark, content to have no further ambition, was the one who stayed at home. Now he was the wannabe world traveller, who would have guessed?

Cam had already run all of these thoughts through her mind at least twice and was only thinking about it again because she was letting some other thoughts ferment in her subconscious by engaging her consciousness with something familiar and repetitive and non-distracting.

She'd recently encountered a few things in her work that had stayed with her and the best solution was to think of something completely different and wait for the ideas to coalesce and surface. Cam always believed that it was her ability to see something more, to sense a connection that others missed, that had made her successful in a male-dominated profession. Even the Behavioural Science unit at the FBI had yet to shed gender-bias.

She'd learned long ago to only voice thoughts derived from the facts and experienced-based theories yet she was certain her detractors claimed any breakthroughs were simply "women's intuition" – as if that gave her some unfair advantage – yet she'd have been scorned and dismissed if she claimed the same. Although somehow when a male coworker relied on his "gut instinct" that was good enough for most of the other men.

Cam didn't get bogged down thinking it was unfair. Life wasn't fair and she had learned that lesson long ago: there had been no trauma and no drama, just factual observation and she was comfortable with that. She was a great example of someone experiencing "job satisfaction", a newly popular phrase. Her success was well-compensated, and her contributions appreciated by her boss and his team.

Cam worked in the Integrated Homicide Investigation Unit. It was her job to liaise with the different forces in each of the jurisdictions where such criminal activity took place and was believed to be connected. In other words, tracking multiple and/or serial killers.

There were Metropolitan police departments in major cities, there were Sheriff's departments in some counties, some provinces had their own Provincial police departments, and then there were the RCMP detachments covering the rest of the country. Plenty of forces to liaise with and bring together as and when needed.

Cam didn't go into the field. The face of the investigating RCMP officer was always male but she was the one figuring out the questions he should ask. Once she'd had to call the Royal Newfoundland Constabulary – a provincial police force – and the fellow she spoke to why "the Mountain Police were involved?". It took her a moment to realize that's what the man thought the M in RCMP stood for, Mountain instead of Mounted. Cam wondered if the man thought all of Canada west of Ontario was part of the Rocky Mountain chain? When she shared the story with her boss he told her he'd never ridden a horse in his life. The RNC had a Mounted Unit with a lengthy history of its own which made the question even more surprising.

Information about capital crimes committed anywhere in the country was reviewed daily and this is where connections were made. It was unfortunate that the links could only be found after the crimes had been committed but it wasn't her job to prevent murders. Cam drew conclusions based on the facts the data presented and then passed the information to the relevant law enforcement. She had no authority to make them act on her assumptions and her theories were often ignored.

Cam had read the reports of the murders in Halifax and Montreal and now her brain was tentatively linking them. There was a common thread: each victim had just moved house.

When people are moving they find themselves allowing all kinds of strangers into their home – everybody from insurance agents to realtors and prospective purchasers, the cable company to carpet cleaners. Access is granted without question which means lots of potential suspects because the criminally-minded can create opportunities out of this circumstance.

There was also a victim in Kingston. They had her identity but no idea why she was in Kingston when she lived in Edmonton. Had she hitchhiked her way there? Or had she recently moved as well?

When details of the Toronto victim came through Cam was convinced she had a killer travelling through three provinces and returning again, and from that idea she concluded that the most likely service person was a truck driver. He might be a trucker's helper but she knew that the majority of drivers travelled alone when making long-distance trips.

As a veteran member of the RCMP Mark had been relocated across the country many times so she had become quite familiar with the business. She knew, for instance, that once school let out in June the moving season was well underway so if her quarry was a household moving trucker Cam was lucky to be pursuing him ahead of the summer rush.

The Montreal killing wasn't necessarily part of the series because it was only a local move which would be handled by a local moving company rather than a long-distance trucker. But the timing fit, the MO fit, and it was still a moving scenario, so Cam wasn't ready to discard it yet.

She needed to order her thoughts so she could write out a step-by-step plan to be followed by the police in the local jurisdictions. How best to approach the moving companies to gain access to their information? and without causing a panic? How to get the different levels of investigators on-board with her still-developing theory? And most importantly – could she possibly foresee where the killer would be next in the hopes of preventing another murder?

It was just as well that Mark Stillwell was on a vacation halfway across the world, he'd have had little of his wife's attention if he'd stayed at home.

Chapter Thirty-Three

Friday February 29 - Monday March 3, 1980

From the moment Jacques Hirondelle awoke to the white light of an overcast wintry sky he knew he had a bad day ahead of him. He wanted, more than anything else, to roll back onto the warm spot in his bed and close his eyes to the world. Unfortunately for him there was pressing business to attend to.

First, his bladder. Too much celebrating last night although he had no idea what the celebration was all about. But he had to get up early today to check his trap-lines because he'd put it off and if he waited any longer he's be in violation. Stupid regulations, in his opinion, but the assholes who made the rules also had the rights and Jacques couldn't afford to lose his licence.

He stumbled out of bed and added a few more clothes to the ones he'd passed out in the night before. Such considerations as washing, shaving, changing his clothes, eating breakfast, didn't enter his mind.

The day was windy, a chill damp breeze, that did nothing to clear the befuddledness from his head or improve his temper. The sun was rising but it was pale and weak, providing no warmth and little light to the early morning darkness.

His old beater of a pick-up truck started although, perversely, he'd expected trouble and was half-disappointed not to find it. He drove as far into the woods as he could go then left the truck at the end of the path and continued on foot.

He hadn't even gotten to the first trap when the smell hit him. He hadn't noticed nor appreciated the freshness of the crisp, cold air but the stench was unavoidable. He was moving downwind and caught the odour long before he spotted anything. Didn't make sense, his kills were still fresh or at least fresh enough according to the laws of the land, but he felt more annoyed (after all this was just another aggravation to add to the troubles of his day) then wary or curious.

His trap was empty and there were no signs to indicate what was causing the stink so he progressed a little further until he spotted something yellow-coloured off to the left. He pushed through the bushes, wetting his feet and pant-legs amid much cursing, and so came upon the body.

He realized it was a girl but he couldn't say much about how she'd looked when she was alive because her face was a swollen mass of bruises and dried blood. She wore a shiny plastic raincoat and not much else from what he could see.

Something about the body, it's state of dress/undress and the mess that had once been a woman's face made the whole scenario bizarre and unreal. Like it was a stage-setting in a play. Jacques didn't use words like surreal even in his thoughts. He saw this as an added attraction to further fuck-up his day and, underneath the anger, was a little scared, a little queasy, and a lot repulsed.

Later on, while seated in the Police cruiser alongside Constable Renaud, he didn't mention those feelings. He'd already vented the acceptable reaction and had now moved on to complaining about the delay in getting on with his work.

He'd been half-tempted to pretend he'd seen nothing – and he didn't mention that, either – but in the end had trudged back to his truck and driven into the city to the Police Station.

With ill-grace he'd gotten into the cruiser and brought the Constable back to the spot. Now he was stuck here answering stupid questions: "No, I didn't touch nothing" and "I knew she was dead because I'm not fucking blind" while the machinery of a police investigation into sudden death (fucking murder, as Jacques put it) was put into motion.

Gerard Renaud had been able to identify the deceased as Denise Drake stripper and hooker and druggie a.k.a 'exotic dancer' in her lingo.

He'd busted Denise two or three times and knew her as an abrasive, argumentative, aimless, and none-too-clean woman in her early twenties. In her routine she played a sleeping woman screwing a cardboard cut-out of 'Casper, the Friendly Ghost'. Her props consisted of a floor-mat on which she stripped, lay down, spread her legs and thrust her pelvis in the air to an ear-splitting noise level of Donna Summer moaning 'I Love to Love You, Baby'.

She performed this act on the stage of a truck-stop bar-lounge, her more lucrative acts in the hotel's bedrooms, and then took her cash out to the parking-lot in a never-ending quest for drugs. Of course Denise would be hoping to pay for her highs with something other than cash. It was a well-known fact in her world that plenty of truckers have dope and so Denise would haunt the parking-lot searching for a stash and a party.

Constable Renaud wasn't looking forward to trying to track down Denise's movements in the hours prior to her death. No doubt half the truckers she'd hustled were already miles down the Trans-Canada Highway, always assuming they could figure out who was there at the crucial time, and then there would be the business of checking their current whereabouts – it looked like being a real headache.

Unfairly, he blamed Jacques Hirondelle for bringing all this trouble.

Thinking about the tedious tracking that would soon fill his days Renaud was in no mood to listen to Hirondelle's complaints. He was also fed up smelling the man's unwashed clothes and sweated-out booze. He kicked him out of the car and warned him to be available for further questioning.

Jacques's parting comment was "Oh and fuck you very much for being such a good citizen, eh? I guess you forgot to tell me that" while spitting a copious amount of mucus in contempt.

Constable Renaud rolled down the window to check that none of it had actually hit the cruiser thinking he was just in the mood to charge Hirondelle with assaulting a police officer if it had.

Chapter Thirty-Four

Friday February 29 - Monday March 3, 1980

The killer had no interest in the discovery of the murder. That business was over and done with. Finished.

It seemed impossible to believe that Denise-the-Piece had once given birth, was somebody's mother, and had actually been responsible for another human being's well-being.

She was still a young woman yet she'd become a useless, worthless piece of trash and that's how he left her: discarded like rubbish.

She wasn't even pretty, at least not to him. She was twenty-something with big breasts and narrow hips and bleached blonde hair. That's all she was: a body. A body with a foul mouth. She'd made a lot of noise and he'd enjoyed quieting her.

First of all he'd had to play along with her nicey-nice behaviour even though it turned his stomach. When she touched him he'd wanted to rub at his skin. Each caress, each suggestive remark, each one of her high-pitched giggles had earned her one more punch. He'd concentrated on counting up the hits he'd deliver while she prattled and postured.

She'd come to him. It had been easy. After her show, when she was cruising the bar for some stuff, he'd given her the nod. He wasn't a seller, as she knew, but figured he'd buy some of her time so she'd be able to score with his money. Once she'd gotten her hands on some cash she'd be aiming for the low-life dealers and one of them could take the blame for her death.

If she'd already had money she might not have bothered but Denise had come on to him before – or at least she'd tried – so she might have come out anyhow, and not just from a junkie's craving. When she was high she'd tell the world to go fuck itself but when she wasn't she tried too hard to be sexy and hated to be turned down.

Anyhow, it wasn't a problem. He hadn't been in the truck long before she came pounding on his door. He let her in and she'd made a big production of climbing over him to get into the passenger seat. She'd looked at the ceiling of the cab but he didn't have any centrefolds taped up there. From the scowl on her face that had ruined her usual opening line.

She acted like she'd made a conquest and fished for compliments before climbing into the bunk. He cranked up the volume on the stereo then followed her, bringing along his tire iron.

After he was finished he simply drove away. He'd passed the wooded area on his way into the city many times and that's where he headed for. He pulled into a lay-by, there were no other vehicles in sight, and got her body ready by tearing down the plastic garbage bags he'd sheeted the interior walls with and wrapped her up. There was no traffic on the Trans-Canada when he pushed her out of the cab.

He thought that for a skinny girl she was heavy as an inert weight but he was still pumped up and carrying her presented no difficulty. He went quite a way into the woods then dumped her. He pulled the plastic garbage bags away from the body and, shaking open a folded bag from his pocket, put them inside and brought the sack back to the truck. He knew he couldn't burn it and risk attracting attention to a fire even if it was winter and not forest-fire time. He also knew that the Queen's Hotel had several dumpsters in behind the kitchen he could use.

When he got back to the hotel he went to Jeannie, the girl at the front-desk, to check-out and made a point on mentioning that he'd already gone and fuelled up so he could head straight out early next morning. It was good to have a cover story in case someone noticed that he'd unhooked the tractor and gone for a ride.

It was never his plan to leave next morning but that didn't matter: truckers schedules were always changing so he had a plausible excuse. Next day he told Irene, the elderly woman who'd worked the front-desk morning shift for about as long as the hotel had been open, that the damn dispatchers had messed things up again and to book him back in. She'd remember that.

So he was still around when Denise's body was found and the police came around asking for information and checking who could be crossed off their list. He wasn't bothered by that because he'd already forgotten the actual killing and his part in it. Now he felt like he was just another spectator, part of the crowd watching and commenting from the sidelines.

Chapter Thirty-Five

Friday February 29 - Monday March 3, 1980

Police Inspector Warren Lund was nondescript in appearance and quiet, even mild, in manner. Unfortunately, unlike novels or the movies, his calm exterior didn't mask an ambitious, brilliant mind. He was shrewd, true, but he was bored. He was bored with his many years in the Police Force, he was bored with his many-year marriage, and, frankly, bored with his routine life.

Partly the boredom stemmed from a feeling of helpless hopelessness, a feeling which had only grown stronger over the years during his career. At no time, even in his youth, had he ever been going to "save the world" – he was too practical-minded for idealism such as that – but he had hoped to make some small contribution, a difference, and with luck, an improvement.

He'd been quick to feel disillusioned by the system and learned to adapt to the rules without letting them drive him crazy. But at some point he gave up caring. If forced to pin down his feelings he would blame them on the Young Offenders Act which seemed custom-designed to instill resigned misery in all the lives it touched: victims, juvenile perpetrators, and the families of both.

He'd dealt with vicious eleven-year-olds who committed crimes of assault, arson – even murder – and he couldn't stop seeing them as children. Even when they asked if his wife was a good fuck. He performed his job as well as the evaluation reports required but he'd lost any sense of purpose he'd had and he missed that. There had been a time when he was eager to come to work.

Waiting now in the Manager's office at the Queen's Hotel he reviewed the case in his mind and was struck by its inevitableness and discovering how little he actually cared about the victim or the fate her lifestyle had invited. Not deserved, no he wouldn't, please God, ever become that apathetic but the futility of her life and his involvement at the end of it.

The hotel manager, Joe Wysecki, could have doubled (and sometimes did) as one of his bouncers. He was in his fifties but the hard-muscled body had worn well and the lines in his face indicated his scowling, don't-mess-with-me expression was habitual. It wouldn't take much to provoke such a man. Had Denise Drake been provocative?

This was Inspector Lund's second interview with Wysecki, the first having been to accomplish victim identification. Denise Drake had no known family and, since she'd worked for Joe since before she was of an age to actually legally do so, he was asked to make the official identification.

He'd betrayed a softer side, or, more honestly, a more sober attitude, after viewing Denise's body but any sentiment he felt then was not apparent now. That was over and done with and now he wanted to get on with running his business.

"I need to know who was checked in here on Friday, Saturday, and Sunday. Denise was killed early Sunday morning and her killer could have hung around, or he could have checked-out before the murder, or the day after."

"Christ, I don't need this aggravation and neither do my customers but I should be thankful, I guess, that it's still winter and not summer. During the summer months we're so busy a lotta the time it happens that some truckers can't even get rooms."

"Well, it isn't summer now and it's darn cold at night so I imagine everyone did have a room."

"Maybe not." Wysecki said, determined to find obstacles. "They've got heaters in their cabs, some of them. We have a deal where a guy can sleep in his truck but plug in to our power and have use of the bathroom and shower facilities. Quite a lot save some money by doing that." He sounded like he begrudged offering this service to his clientele and then added resentfully "And half of them then scoop some blank bills from Jeannie at the front desk and submit for expenses! Not if I catch them, though."

"I see. So, tell me, do you think that's likely to be the case now?" asked Warren patiently.

"I don't know, do I? I can't keep tabs on everybody. And what's to say it was one of the truckers anyhow?"

"Nothing definite, but it's a place to start."

"Well, it's your time you're wasting so what do I care." So saying, Joe picked up his phone and dialled through to the front desk where Jeannie, an extremely well-endowed woman with the longest and fanciest fingernails Lund had ever seen, was told to provide the information the Inspector wanted.

"Well, then photocopy every fucking page. Yeah, yeah, whatever." Wysecki hung up the phone shaking his head but knowing Jeannie's attributes were a big ("really big", he thought) asset to him always decided that he could put up with a little stupidity. It was pretty definite that she put up with a lot more.

Warren Lund thanked him for his time and Joe Wysecki's acknowledgement was about as sincere as the Inspector's gratitude.

Coming down the hall from Wysecki's office Lund could hear the hum of the copy machine. He waited at the counter while Jeannie put the papers together for him. Her thumbnails were studded with diamonds, the nails of the baby fingers done in gold, and little decals, or hand-painted designs, were appliqued on the others. She manoeuvred quite well, he noticed.

"Jeannie do you ever have problems with the guys staying here?" She rolled her eyes at him and he added, "I mean has anyone struck you as creepy, frightened you even, something a little more than the usual, run-of-the-mill lines?"

"You mean like did anyone ever follow me home or something?"

"Could be that. Why, has it happened?"

"Sure, lots of times. But it's never really been a problem. I don't know, I don't think I can remember anyone ever scaring me. Mostly these guys are all just talk or like if they could get somewhere with me they would but just so's they could tell everybody else that they had, you know? It's not like anyone has ever made me feel he was really interested in me."

"So there's no particular incident, nothing that stands out that you can remember?"

"Nah, nothing special. Well, once we had a really goofy guy but he killed himself so it couldn't have been him. That was a couple of summers ago."

"Okay, keep it in mind and, if you could, ask around amongst the other women here, especially the dancers but also the housekeeping staff. See if anyone's encountered anything that maybe I ought to know about in light of what's happened to Denise."

"Sure. That was really a shame about Denise. She'd been talking lately of trying to straighten herself out and put some money together to go and see her kid. Who knows, maybe someday she'd have managed to get the kid back. Whenever she'd had a few beers too many she'd talk about that kid and how much she missed him. I figured, though, they don't take your kid away without a pretty good reason, or three, and maybe things were better left the way they were but who knows, I suppose she might have gotten her act together. You never know what could of happened."

"True." thought Lund, and felt a moment's fleeting pity for the what might have been. "But in Denise's case I think you and me could make a pretty good guess, Jeannie."

After thanking her with a reminder to talk to the other women Warren left but before he got far she called him back. "Inspector here come two more of the drivers who were here last night and might be able to help you."

She pointed to the front door where a few men were gathered and a couple more were coming in. "That's Dale Terry coming towards us and behind him, oh he's stopped to chat, well that's Gerry Tanner as well. "Dale hi, you've heard the terrible news about Denise, right?"

"I did, I can't believe it."

"I'm Inspector Lund of the Winnipeg police uh, Mr Terry is it?" asked Warren.

"Yeah, Dale Terry." said Dale. He didn't offer to shake hands and in fact took a step back and his face as he regarded the Inspector was closed and expressionless.

"Just a few questions right now, Mr Terry. Do you want to go into the restaurant? it looked like you were heading that way."

"No, I'd rather just get this done so go ahead and ask your questions."

"OK then, you're staying here in this hotel, correct?"

"Yes."

"And can you confirm that you were here in the hotel last night?"

"Yes."

"Do you, I mean did you, know the deceased Denise Drake?"

"Yes."

"OK good, did you know her well?"

"No."

"Could you tell me how you know her?"

"She worked here."

Jeannie fidgeted for some time before interrupting to say, "Inspector, Dale would just have seen Denise dancing when he was in the lounge. Dale is not like most of the guys around here – you know like what you and me were talking about before – he's a real gentleman, a real nice guy who always talks polite and friendly without coming on to anyone. He wouldn't have bothered with the likes of Denise Drake. Sorry, I know she's dead but we gotta be realistic here."

Dale smiled and thanked her.

"Well somebody had to speak up 'cause you're not saying much of anything!"

"I know, and Inspector I apologise but I'm beat. I arrived really late yesterday, I ran into bad weather coming in, and I had an early start this morning. Right now I just want to go to my room and lie down for an hour or so. If you're still around I can talk to you later on. I'll be hungry by then so you can find me in the restaurant."

"No problem, go and get some sleep Mr Terry and I'll catch up with you later if I need to."

Watching Dale as he walked to the elevators Jeannie told Warren Lund that some of the women who worked at the Queen's wouldn't have minded if Dale Terry did make a pass but so far as she knew that had never happened. She might have sighed, Warren couldn't be sure, but she sounded quite wistful.

Lund didn't completely accept Terry's excuse for not being more forthcoming. He could see there was Native blood there somewhere so maybe it was just a general antipathy towards the police. Winnipeg, Regina, Edmonton – all of the major cities experienced plenty of conflict between local law enforcement and the indigenous population so mistrust was common and commonly felt by both sides.

He'd heard it was even worse with the RCMP.

Chapter Thirty-Six

Friday February 29 - Monday March 3, 1980

Inspector Warren Lund felt an instinctive liking and a professional interest in Gerry Tanner.

He and Constable Renault had been interviewing hotel guests for a couple of hours now and Gerry was the only man who'd warranted more than a passing thought so far.

Gerry's open, plain face and engaging manner set off alarm bells in the Inspector's mind even as he felt himself warm to the trucker. There was something a little too "aw, shucks" about Gerry to ring true but that didn't take away from his charm.

He was in his late thirties to early forties, blond-haired with light blue eyes. He was neither thin nor fat and stood about five foot ten. He'd been at the Queen's Hotel for most of the week and would be picking up a load on the next day headed for Edmonton.

"How come you've been stuck here so long?" asked Lund.

"Actually I've been on a good assignment. Got an RCMP customer whose house wasn't ready until yesterday and he didn't want his stuff put into storage so I've been getting paid to hold it on my truck. This is the second customer in a row that's happened with and it's a really good deal for me."

"Well, Mr. Tanner, if you're as friendly and chatty with everybody else as you are with me I think you might make an ideal witness. Do you know many of the drivers who've been around this week?"

"Hey, call me Gerry and yeah, I guess I know just about everybody because you're right I'm a friendly kind of guy. Either that or I'm just nosy and always wanting to know who's doing what, where and when. And who, I guess" he chuckled.

"Did you know, or had you seen, the deceased? Denise Drake?"

"Denise-the-Piece, yeah I knew her. I really can't believe someone would murder her, though. If anything Denise went out of her way to be obliging, if you know what I mean. I mean, she's dead and everything and nobody should have to die that badly but it really doesn't make any sense because nobody would ever have to rape her. I don't like saying anything shitty about a girl who's been killed and all but that's the way she was. I can't pretend she was any different. No one would have had to rape her to have sex with her."

"What makes you think she was raped?"

"Because I heard she was naked and killed. You mean she wasn't?"

"I don't have that information and, frankly, I couldn't pass it on even if I did, but I can tell you Denise wasn't found naked. She was wearing her working clothes so, granted, wasn't exactly overdressed, but she had her coat on."

"That yellow thing?"

"You saw her that night?"

"Well, I know the coat. I mean nobody could miss it, but yeah I did see her that night. I was in the bar having a wobbly-pop and..."

"A what?"

"Huh, you mean you can't tell I'm a Newfie? A wobbly-pop is a beer."

"I did detect an accent but I've never heard that expression before."

"Stick around, I'm a home-grown Islander and I talk the talk all the time. Anyhow, I saw Denise's show. There was something wrong with her because she wasn't performing so good. I would have thought she was coked to the nines if I hadn't seen her afterwards really desperate to score something. She was like way off beat. Moving far too fast, way ahead of the music, and she was up and finished before the music was even over. So, something was up but I didn't really get a chance to talk to her. She came over to the table to see if anybody had anything, I was sitting with a couple other guys, but we didn't, of course, and she didn't stick around. She was pretty jumpy."

"Did you see her connect with anybody else in the lounge?"

"No, and I'm just about positive she didn't because she headed right outside, like to the parking-lot, I guess. I know that's what I thought at the time but I wasn't really aware of thinking it, if you know what I mean, like it doesn't really register but your mind spots something even though you're not really thinking about it? Anyhow, as I said I figured she'd gone out to the parking-lot because if she'd scored something in here I think she would have gone to the can for a hit and then come back and hung around for a few drinks or something. I didn't see her again."

"What about later that night?"

"No, but then I couldn't have, could I? She went outside and met up with her killer."

"It looks that way. It certainly takes her out of the hotel, or at least out of the bar, where you and your friends were until what time?"

"Oh, umm, there was one more dancer on after Denise, a real little cutie, and she was good. We watched her and had maybe two-three more drinks then went up to Rawley's room and played four-handed gin until two o'clock, or so. I made over eighty bucks so I was definitely there."

"I'm sure you wouldn't lie about something so easily checked, Mr. Tanner."

"Gerry, c'mon."

"Okay, Gerry, and how long will you be here if we need to talk to you again?"

"Let's see, I'm loading 6,000 pounds tomorrow but it's out of a townhouse so that's gonna take awhile but looks like I'll have lots of help so I should be ready to roll by two in the afternoon. I'll be here for the rest of today and all night."

"Okay, that sounds good. Once we wrap up these interviews we'll know who we need to have come back to the station to get signed statements. We'll probably find someone who talked to, or at least saw, Denise after you did but if you don't live here in Winnipeg then we'll definitely want a written statement from you with your home address and contact information."

"I'm living in Edmonton right now. Another driver, a guy named Dale, has been putting me up for about six months now. Yeah, that's right because it was October when my wife kicked me out. Then Dale got in a really bad accident so I looked after the place while he was in hospital. They kept him there for weeks and weeks and when he finally came back home he was glad to have somebody around so it's worked out really well for both of us. Sorry, but I can never remember the address 'coz it's not like I'm going to be staying permanently or anything. I know the building, it's a kinda crummy-looking apartment but really big inside, on Whyte just before it turns into 82nd Avenue. But here I've got a business card with the office address, that's where I get all my mail, and they always know where I am."

He handed over the card and Inspector Lund thanked him for his time.

"Hey, no problem. I liked Denise, you know. She wasn't the happiest person in the world but she could be fun when she was feeling right."

Warren Lund smiled and nodded. It seemed like a fitting epitaph for the girl she had become.

Chapter Thirty-Seven

Friday February 29 - Monday March 3, 1980

"Dale was asking me about you."

"What? What did he say? And when was this? I mean, when did he call?"

"About half-an-hour ago, he left a message saying he's in Winnipeg and has been held up because of a murder at the truck-stop. Well, they found the body a ways away but she worked there, she was a stripper."

"He's at the Queen's Hotel then."

"Yes, with Gerry too. The police are questioning everybody."

"But as a stripper she's probably run by the bikers and if they didn't kill her they've probably got a better chance than the police at finding out who did. And of taking care of it, too. They don't like anyone messing with their property."

"Jeez, you don't sound too sympathetic."

"Sorry, I don't know her but I do know of women like her and you're right I'm not sympathetic. They can cause a lot of trouble for the drivers: they steal, they do drugs, they ask for rides, and their boyfriend pimps have been known to beat up on drivers. These women are just really bad news for truckers."

Nothing was said for a few moments then Suzi asked: "Don't you want to know what Dale was asking about you?"

"Hmm? Oh yeah. What was it?"

Pamela figured she didn't sound as unconcerned as she was trying to be.

"He wanted to know if you were seeing anybody. He said after being away for so long he didn't know what was going on with everybody and so he wondered about you."

"Well I'm sure Gerry kept him up to date."

"How? You don't talk about your private life. And that's what I told Dale. I said Pamela doesn't talk about stuff like that in the office."

"Well that's true I don't."

"Not with words."

"What's that supposed to mean?"

"Well, it's pretty clear you're interested in Dale. And maybe Gerry, too. But I think it's Dale you really like and he's obviously interested in you."

"How could you know something like that?"

"Because he's wondering about you and wanting to know if you're available."

"What exactly did he say?"

"I already told you."

"You never mentioned asking if I'm available."

"OK he didn't spell it out but he didn't have to – I knew what he meant."

"Oh great, so this is your interpretation of what was probably just a friendly, casual remark, right?"

"Wrong. Yes, it's my interpretation but I know what I'm talking about and I know he's interested and was trying to sound me out to see if you're interested too."

"I feel like I'm back in high school."

"Did you like high school?"

"Yes, actually I did. I was on the track team, I pledged a sorority, and I was a cheerleader."

"Get out of here."

"Hey, I grew up in a small town."

"Oooh and I bet you were Prom Queen, right?"

"No, I didn't go to my Prom."

"Seriously? There's gotta be a story behind that!"

"Broken romance. End of happy time at high school and that's why I decided to move to the big city."

"Wow, what happened with you and the guy?"

"That's an old story and I've moved on."

"You don't want to talk about it?"

"Not ever."

"Oh. Well what's Dale's story? How come a good-looking guy like him hasn't gotten married yet?"

"He was married but his wife died of cancer, she was really young, and I guess he just adored her."

"That's so sad. I mean, everybody has an old relative who's got cancer but somebody young? Wow, that's awful."

"It is. When it was detected, it was in her ovaries or something, she had what they called aggressive treatment. I got all of this from our boss Eddie. He's known Dale for a long time and he'd met Dale's wife, too. Said she was just a living doll. Anyhow, the doctors said the operation was a success and maybe it was but the cancer came back. She was supposed to go for a six-month follow-up appointment but she skipped it. She said she felt fine and apparently the examinations were extremely painful, some doctors are real butchers, and with Dale on the road, well.. Afterwards he was angry with her, even though she was dead, because she didn't look after herself and he was feeling guilty because he hadn't looked after her either. I mean there really was nothing he could have done but people aren't rational when they're dealing with a loss like that."

"When did this happen?"

"About eight years ago. Like I said both Dale and his wife were young."

"Poor Dale. Do you think he's gotten over it by now?"

"I'm not sure that you ever really do get over something like that."

"Well from the sounds of it you had your heart broken but I think you've gotten over that now and are interested in trying again."

"A high-school romance is hardly the same thing."

"Hurting is always relative, no one can say what kind of loss is worse because no one knows how anybody else really feels. I mean one person might be absolutely and utterly devastated over losing their cat while someone else might be philosophical about having a kid die, you just never know with people. Everybody's got their own mysterious shit going on."

"It is true that not every parent loves their kids despite everyone acting like the exact opposite has to be true, it's just one of those accepted things that we're all supposed to believe."

"Sounds like you've experienced something that makes you think that way."

"Something I saw, actually. It was at Klondike Days – you know they have a Casino? Well outside the front doors somebody had put down a blanket and it was full of kids. The casino is adults-only so folks just dumped their children while they went inside and gambled. It wasn't anything official, I mean there was no babysitter or daycare attendant or anything. No one to take kids to the bathroom or get them food or cold drinks and it was really hot out. It shocked me.

Anyhow, Social Services showed up and one of the older kids opened the casino door and started hollering and there was a stampede of parents or maybe babysitters coming out yelling and that started the kids screaming. It was horrible to see but even worse was knowing that these parents had just left their children unattended. Kids can so easily get into mischief – and dangerous mischief like climbing heights or running in front of cars and stuff. In fact, there was nothing to prevent some pervert from coming along and grabbing a kid."

"Yeah that really sucks. Probably happens every day of every year at the exhibition and that's why Social Services was there. Did you go in and gamble?"

"No, I looked around though. It was really big, lots of table games surrounded by these Wheels of Fortune. I tried one of those on the

Midway and made a couple of dollars – literally just a couple of dollars – but I thought it was kind of boring."

"I can't picture you on the Midway and that's something I'd love to see. We should go this summer, we can eat mini doughnuts and go on the roller-coaster."

"I'm not a fan of the rides but I do love those mini-doughnuts."

Chapter Thirty-Eight

Friday February 29 - Monday March 3, 1980

Pamela felt like running but forced herself to walk to the bathroom at a normal pace. She was short of breath and knew her skin would be cold to the touch, moist with sweat. She was going to throw up.

Talking to Suzi had brought back the past with shocking vividness. Her heart had been broken but it was her gut that hurt. After all this time she couldn't believe that sorry mess still had the power to leave her disconnected and devastated.

Even at the time she hadn't understood the concept of betrayal. She thought she knew what the word meant but turned out she had no idea. She was operating in reflex mode and she thought she was handling things but in truth she was numb, cushioned from reality, and hadn't grasped the significance.

Driving to her part-time job one Saturday the truth hit hard and the depth of his betrayal left her paralysed. She burst into tears and had to pull over to the side of the road because she couldn't see to drive. She sat in a torrent of tears fiercely suppressing the urge to howl, utterly shattered.

Of course some good Samaritan type had to stop with an offer to help. Help? She couldn't stop crying long enough to answer and instead shook her head at him when he tapped on her window. Eventually he got huffy and left – thank God – because that forced her to control herself enough to start the car and drive back home.

She didn't go into work that day or the next or the following week or the week after that. In fact, she stopped functioning. Her parents worried on her behalf, her girlfriends got angry on her behalf, but nothing anyone said or did helped.

Pamela couldn't stop crying. She couldn't eat, she couldn't sleep, she couldn't talk about it. Finally her parents, full of loving concern, talked to her about entering a psychiatric facility as a voluntary committal to get the help they couldn't give. That suggestion finally penetrated the shell Pamela had been using to hide her thoughts.

Yes, she wanted to stop feeling the way she did, but no she didn't want a stay in such a place on her record. The thought of a stranger suggesting they 'talk it through' nauseated her.

So she'd pulled herself out of it or at least gave everyone the impression she had done so. Now she knew that in fooling everyone else she'd also fooled herself. But her tears dried up and after hiding indoors for so long she started taking long walks every day. The exercise enabled her to eat and sleep.

Beverley Wright wasn't convinced that her daughter had recovered but she couldn't fault Pamela's behaviour. She'd been self-contained as a little girl and was even more so as an adult. Because she was an adult the path she chose was her decision to make.

Pamela never told anyone, neither her parents nor her friends, the real reason that she and Rick had broken up. She told them the truth – that he had dumped her – but not all of it, not the why behind his actions.

Since Grade Six, when Rick's family moved onto Pamela's street, the two of them had been a couple. They were friends who believed they were soul-mates and, having found each other, knew they would happily spend the rest of their lives together. It wasn't puppy love or a summer romance or a teenage fling it was the real thing for both of them.

They remained a twosome throughout junior-high and high-school. Neither was keen on four or five years worth of University so they'd chosen two-year programmes at the Community College and were anticipating marriage within a year of graduating and finding jobs.

Rick played on their school's football team and Pamela was on the cheering squad. They were both fit and healthy except that she had very difficult, painful menstrual periods. She'd matured late so the problem didn't become a problem until Grade Twelve when Beverley insisted that their GP refer Pamela to a specialist.

It turned out that Pamela suffered from blocked Fallopian tubes, a congenital condition, resulting in infertility. Prior to that Pamela had never encountered any real problems, serious difficulties, or obstacles in her life so the news was a shock and a deep surprise. Her parents thought it was a tragedy.

She had never had clear thoughts or even daydreams about having children. Not like her friends did when they all swore off drugs. She figured it would happen when it happened. It never occurred to her think it wouldn't or couldn't happen. She didn't actually know how that made her feel – she wasn't bereft but believed she was being cheated out of something. She was curious to know if Rick felt the same.

When she told him the news and was explaining her feelings, trying to analyze the lack of a strong feeling one way or the other, he interrupted to say that he loved her and would never be able to love anyone else in the same way – not ever – but everything was different now. Because he knew that someday he wanted a family and since that wasn't going to happen with her well...

And after eight years of growing up together that was that.

Pamela was left feeling used and worthless but she fought her way out of the depression by deciding that if she wasn't going to have a family she could at least have a career. She had no intention of taking up her planned schooling but she didn't need a profession, she would be a receptionist who would work her way up to secretary then administrative assistant – maybe even a good job in personnel.

She figured her chance at success would be much greater in the city so she called up her married cousin in Edmonton and asked if she could live at her place until she got on her feet.

Pamela's parents kept their worries to themselves and helped their daughter move and get settled in. Beverley's niece was a cheerful, sensible woman who would look out for Pamela in a friendly and undemanding way.

Pamela got hired on at Big Sky Moving as a clerk-typist and as time went by and her job responsibilities grew so did her wage. She was able to move into her own place, a one-bedroom apartment in a co-op building for only $245 a month, and with the third-hand car her parents gave her she had transportation.

She'd locked away her secrets and her heartbreak, in fact she thought she'd gotten over that, until today.

As it turned out she wasn't sick to her stomach. Splashing cold water on her face killed that impulse for which she was thankful. She combed her hair with her fingers and studied her reflection. A little pale but not too noticeable. If Suzi probed she'd say she was on her period. No doubt that would invite all kinds of confidences about Suzi's own cycle which would be a good distraction.

Pamela decided that the young woman in the mirror was passable, even pretty, and figured that if someone like Dale, who she respected and admired, was possibly interested in her then, well, she felt she wasn't worthless after all.

Chapter Thirty-Nine

Friday February 29 - Monday March 3, 1980

"It's a serial killer." stated Ray. He and Jim had met up again with Dale and Gerry in the hotel bar. They'd just placed their order of two Labatt's 50, one Molson Golden, and a Pepsi, and were discussing Denise's killing.

"You just wait, there's gonna be more. It's a trucker and Denise-the-Piece was just the first."

"First? What about that woman in Halifax? and there was one in Toronto, too? I think you're right that it might be a trucker because both of them had just moved so there's a link there."

"And hey, remember when we all got stuck in Kingston because of closing the highway while the cops investigated some woman being murdered there?"

"That's not the same thing."

"It might have been, we don't know whether or not she'd recently moved."

"Or she could have been a hitch-hiker who got a ride with some psycho driver."

"Or it might just have been some pilled-up driver who flipped out."

"Remember Tony-24, the guy who was on bennies 24 hours a day? He told some story about getting busted for speeding in some little town in the States and he said to the cop 'you can't throw me in jail I'm too wired to be stuck in a cell' – what an idiot he was!"

"But funny, too. We were on a job one time and it was summer and you know what the summer's like in Toronto with the humidity so bad you sweat just reading the work order."

"Montreal's worse," interrupted Jim. "I once had a customer throw a hissy-fit because sweat from the helpers was dripping on her couch. Never mind that we're dying in the heat and our t-shirts are white with salt sweat while we bust ass for her.."

"As I was saying..." cut in Ray. "Here we are suffering in the heat and this bum is watching us work and while he's watching he's taking a pull out of the bottle he's got tucked in a paper bag. Watch, sip, watch, sip and so on until he finishes his drink and tosses the bag in the gutter. Tony-24 stops to light a smoke, he's been watching the bum watching us and when this guy says 'hey, can I have a cigarette?' Tony-24 says 'no way man, you didn't offer me a drink'".

Despite having heard that story before – and by someone else – everybody laughed.

"He was a nut but a good guy, lousy way that he died, though."

"Liver cancer is pretty quick. He was already dead by time I even heard he was sick."

Jim replied: "Yeah, but he'd been pissing blood for some time apparently. Still, cancer's a bitch." Then, remembering Dale was present he quickly changed the subject saying: "Ray, I think you're onto something with this serial killer idea. Even if there is no connection, and really that would be just too coincidental, the cops are going to start thinking the same way and they'll want to check it out – check us out – and that's going to mean a whole lot of shit for us between the cops and the RCMP and the newspapers."

"Yeah, but how are they going to figure out where everybody was and then track 'em down? We're always on the move."

"Well they could put a stop to that by making us hole up and wait while they investigate where we've been and when before they clear us. That'll cause a real shit-storm."

"Well, if it is a serial killer they better catch this guy quick because the summer season hasn't even started yet."

"Enough with the serial killer bullshit. Denise was into shit with the bikers. I don't even know which motorcycle club is in Winnipeg but they're all gonna be pretty much the same with these broads: toe the line and hand over your earnings. Denise must of screwed up or tried something on, I don't know but something like that, because it must have been a biker who killed her."

"I don't know about that. Nowadays these motorcycle clubs are run like businesses and killing your employee isn't good for business."

"Oh right, like they're all level-headed middle-management types and not psychos with tire irons, knives, guns.."

"They aren't psychos, well not most of them, but they are dangerous guys. If I see a bunch of bikes parked outside a bar I move on to the next location, I don't want to get mixed up with any of their stuff, but sometimes I'll see a biker in a bar by himself and we'll get talking..."

"Gerry you get talking with everybody!"

"Hey I'm a friendly guy and I'm interested in all kinds of people. I mean I wouldn't accept an invitation to their clubhouse, I'm not stupid, but people are crazy and funny and it's a great mix."

"Talk about mixing it up did you hear about the Rebels in Edmonton and their fight with some Air Force guys a few years back? They kicked ass and put about a dozen paratroopers in hospital."

"No, I never heard about that, well I'm from the East. So the Rebels are a biker gang, must be pretty tough, eh?"

"They are but I don't know how things would turn out if there was a war between them and the Reapers, the Grim Reapers from Calgary."

"Well none of those guys would have come here so they weren't killing Denise but some biker was, bet your ass."

"If she was ripping them off maybe they're sending a message to the other strippers."

"Oh c'mon, they're not the Mafia: 'sleep with the fishes' and all that."

"Great movie, eh?"

"I didn't really like Part II, did you guys?"

"I guess it was a good movie in it's own right but I was expecting it to be more like 'The Godfather' which was so good."

"Marlon Brando – what an actor. First way back when and still killing it, have you seen 'Apocalypse Now' yet?"

"I haven't even seen the first 'Rocky' yet" said Dale. "Who has time to go to the movies?"

"Yeah forget the movies, let's talk hockey. Specifically, let's talk about that new kid Wayne Gretzky."

Chapter Forty

Friday February 29 - Monday March 3, 1980

Sondra Cardinal sat in a Ford pick-up, parked behind the hotel, waiting for Gerry to come out. The temperature was bitterly cold and she had the heater on, trying to keep warm, but there wasn't a lot of gas so she kept switching the engine off and then back on again. When Sondra was in a bad mood a nasty, violent streak came out and she was a vicious fighter but now, since she wanted a favour, she waited patiently.

When Gerry arrived he said he was expecting to see Jack, his swamper from the RCMP delivery, not a woman. Jack was paying Gerry to take a small shipment of several boxes to Saskatoon. They'd agreed to meet in the parking-lot where Gerry would get the delivery information and payment up front.

"Jack's around somewhere, he'll come over now that you're here. I'm Sondra and I'm waiting because I want to get a lift with you to Saskatoon."

"Is it your shipment? are you moving there?"

"No, the boxes aren't mine. Actually I'm heading for PA, I need to visit someone in the Pen."

"But I'm not going north, from Saskatoon I'm straight through to Edmonton."

"That's OK, I'll hitch to Prince Albert. Listen, can we party? because I don't have any cash to pay for the ride."

Gerry wasn't surprised by her offer. Many long-distance truckers formed mutually beneficial relationships with hitchhikers, working girls, and working travellers. Life on the road was different. It suited Gerry who was easy-going and loved all kinds of women, but Sondra's dark skin, hair, and eyes didn't turn him on – he preferred fluffy, feminine blondes.

"Sondra, don't worry about it. I'm going there anyhow and I like company, especially the female variety, when I'm driving across the prairie, You can tell me your life story and even make it all up if you want to because how am I going to know?"

He went on to explain about being questioned by the cops, 'fuckers' interjected Sondra, and said he was sorry she'd had to wait in the cold. That earned him a funny look.

"OK, cool. And I'll hang out with you in Saskatoon until the guy shows up to get this shipment just so he knows he can't mess you around or anything."

If Gerry was amused by this comment he was careful not to let it show when he said thanks and offered a cigarette. They smoked in companionable silence for a few minutes before Jack showed up. Jack was big and scarred and, wondering what the guy at the other end would look like, Gerry thought there might be something to Sondra's suggestion after all.

Once they were en route he explained that if things went wrong he'd appreciate the help because he himself wouldn't be much use in a fight: "I just got out of the hospital about six weeks ago. Was banged up pretty good but I've always been told I've got a thick skull and seems like that's right. My ribs are still sore and my leg's gimpy but my arm's okay although I doubt if I pack much of a punch."

"You don't need to if you've got a knife. The thing with a knife is you just stab and stab and stab. It's not like the movies where they weave around like snake charmers or something, no what you want to do is get in a lot of punctures – doesn't matter where – to make the blood pressure drop down to nothing. Guy will be dead in minutes. So just go in for the side of the body fast-fast-fast and do as much damage as you can."

"Good to know, thanks."

"Well I'm Indian so I know about knives. Cops never bother much about knives, they only get excited when we get hold of guns."

"One of the drivers at our company is Native, from the Driftpile Band."

"Yeah, that's Cree, too."

"Donald just drives locally but is saving to buy a share in his truck and take longer trips. His wife travels with him. I asked him if it's true that if he lives on the reservation he doesn't have to pay income tax because he could really save a lot of money doing that and you know what he said? He said they couldn't live there because his wife would get killed for being white!"

"Yeah, probably. I guess Donald knows his business."

"But that's oh... huh, I guess I should mind mine, eh?"

Sondra rolled down the window far enough to flick her cigarette out then she settled herself against the door to sleep.

Chapter Forty-One

Friday February 29 - Monday March 3, 1980

Inspector Lund called for Constable Renault to come into his office saying: "Sit down, Gerard. I've got an idea I want to bounce off of you, see if it makes any sense. Plus, there's something in the interviews – someone I spoke to, or something someone said – that's nagging at me. I don't know what it is so don't bother asking but I know something inside me went 'click' and it'll come to me if I don't worry at it. So if I think out loud about my idea maybe that niggling fact will come back to me."

"Was it one of the truckers?"

"I tell you I don't know. I think it was. I also think it was a trucker who killed Denise."

"But why? That's the bit that doesn't make sense. Why would anyone kill her? Unless it was a senseless killing, unless he killed Denise simply because he could."

"Why not? If all he wanted was a victim then it wouldn't matter who she was. In fact, considering what we know about Denise it seems no one would want to kill her. It couldn't be jealousy, anyone who knew her knew what she was like, she had no money, and I can't imagine she had any knowledge that would harm anyone."

"Drugs?"

"Maybe, but I doubt it. She was using too heavily to ever be trusted with selling the stuff and if she'd ripped somebody off then she wouldn't have been hustling in the bar trying to get set up. No, I'm inclined to believe that she was available to kill and so was killed."

"And you think it was one of the truckers."

"Yeah, I do. Being on the premises meant he had a reason to have contact, he knew her and knew how to get hold of her. He has a vehicle so transporting the body wouldn't be a problem. That bit of woods where she was found is right on the Trans-Canada so every trucker who arrived at the Queen's from the East drove past it. He would definitely know of it."

Gerard digested these facts for a moment before saying: "But if it was a killing just for the sake of killing then what's to stop this guy from murdering again?"

"Absolutely nothing. Well, nothing except, perhaps, us. I realize we've got practically nothing to go on but we've got to try."

"So what do we do now?"

"I want to put all the actual facts together, the relevant parts of the statements, the path. report, times, etc. into a report, and then I'll take that along with my speculations to the boss and see if he'll let me contact the RCMP for assistance."

"Those assholes? We don't need a Musical Ride!"

"We don't have a choice. They're the ones with the linkage to all the other police forces. The fact that he managed to go unnoticed before the crime and after makes me wonder if he's done this before. I mean he hasn't left us a thing to work with. If this guy is a trucker there might be other murders en route to Winnipeg, or, since he's gotten a taste of success here, maybe there will be more murders to come. Almost all of these truckers came into Winnipeg out of Ontario and in Ontario you've got the O.P.P. and the metropolitan police forces as well as the RCMP jurisdictions and we can't be calling everybody. We have to pass on the information to that special liaising division of the RCMP and see what, if any, connections they can make. Or what possibilities, tie-ins, anything, they can give us."

"You really think this guy might be a mass murderer, something like that?"

"Something exactly like that. I think it's very, very likely we've got ourselves a serial killer."

"Holy shit, a Canadian Ted Bundy guy? That's creepy. Hey, did you remember the other thing?"

"Not yet, but it'll come to me."

Chapter Forty-Two

Summer 2015

"You know I was what's called a broker driver way-back-when, eh Jake?"

"Yeah, you said you were called that because you were always broke."

"The stuff you remember, boy oh boy. Anyhow, what it meant was that I owned my own truck that pulled the moving company's trailer."

"Big Sky Moving."

"That's right, I worked for them for over 30 years. I'd be assigned jobs by the van lines and both me and Big Sky would share the money since we both provided the equipment. Prices were based on tariffs put out by the government and based on the weight of the household goods. That meant that before loading at the home I'd have to go to the weigh-scale and get the truck weighed empty and then after I finished loading up at the house I'd have to go back to the same scale for a gross weight. The difference between the two amounts was the net weight of the shipment. You got that?"

Jake nodded: "Uh-huh."

"Now the truck is supposed to have full fuel tanks for both weighings, because otherwise there could be a big difference – hell it could be as much as an 1,800 pound difference – which would really jack up the price of the move. We drivers always tried to make friends with the operators at the scales because even if they didn't do you any favours they could sure hold you up if they were jerks and some were. It's always the way when you give somebody a bit of authority you see because some people are just natural-born a-holes and given the chance they'll prove it."

"A-holes!" giggled Jake.

"Never mind. Anyhow I always tried to form relationships of mutual benefit and this is a good lesson for you to take on with you for the rest of your life. Mutual benefit. Can you remember that as well as you're gonna remember me saying a-holes?"

"Yeah, mutual benefit. I'm pretty sure I know what that means."

"An example of what I did, back when the anti-smoking lobby which, as you know I totally support, now, but back then when I was a nicotine addict I just hated them, and that's because I was an addict and my anger was really fear – fear of not being able to feed my addiction because it's so damned hard to quit. Anyhow I lost track of... oh right.

Back when that lobby was first cutting its teeth a carton of name-brand cigarettes costs $23 in Ontario but only $8 in Alberta, all due to provincial taxes and anti-smoking lobbying. So I'd stock up in Alberta, and you know all about why I had to quit smoking don't you? So don't even think about starting because quitting is a bitch but when the choice is between smoking or dying there really isn't any choice. And it's still hard as Hell to quit even then! But we really didn't know about that then. I mean we did because it was in the news (I think it all started with a Reader's Digest article, there's good stuff in that magazine) but of course you never think it's going to happen to you, plus everybody knows some 95-year-old who is smoking two packs a day and has been doing so for over 80 years.

Thing is, when you're hooked you don't want to believe anything bad about the stuff you're addicted to. In fact you make jokes like 'at least I know what I'm going die from', or 'go ahead and charbroil that steak because I'm a smoker so who cares?' So I always carried a few extra cartons and gave away smokes as a thank-you gift at the scales and that kept things friendly.

Now the weigh stations along the highways are for inspections, not commercial use, and those agents have lots of authority. They can make a guy re-load his trailer to shift excess weight off the axles, or even keep a trucker off the road if his vehicle is deemed unsafe. The inspectors check the driver's logs and paperwork, that's the bills of lading, to make sure that the pay-load adds up to the registered weight. Of course it's completely against the rules for a driver to have blank bills of lading but smart drivers always carried a few in their briefcases. Friendly dispatchers have been known to produce a nicely typed but totally fake bill of lading as well."

"Especially if they were smokers?"

"Boy, you catch on fast! High five me. Thing is a lot of people couldn't afford the tariff rates of a long-distance move back then and I'm sure it's even worse now despite no longer having government tariffs. So we had a cash-under-the-table solution called a buckshee shipment. People would ask a moving company dispatcher, or driver, or a helper, warehouseman, or even a salesman, to see if they could fix up something cheaper and everyone involved would get a share. Sometimes it was just a favour, somebody's kid off to university and needing a few boxes shipped, and those were freebies or the price of a few drinks in the bar. There was a lot of give-and-take and that's something that probably hasn't changed with the household movers even today.

Of course a company could fire you over it since you're using their trailer and they aren't getting a piece of the action but, like I said, everybody did it and everybody knew it went on including the company owners. Most of them grew up in the business and had had their turn as drivers so of course they knew the score. But it wasn't always just helping someone out and making a quick buck at the same time, oh no, sometimes it could be dangerous."

"You mean people gave you like guns or explosives to carry?"

"Well, I guess that sort of thing could happen – boy, what an imagination you've got – but I was thinking more along the likes of drugs."

"Oh yeah, the criminals are always moving drugs and money by boats and planes so it makes sense they'd try it with trucks too. I mean you don't really notice trucks because there's so many of them."

"Well I notice them because I'm interested in the trucks and the trucking companies but you're right, when car drivers see a big unit all they can think of is getting past it. Unless it's like foggy or a dead dark place on the highway with no lights – then cars are quite happy to get behind and follow a truck. But trucks have been hijacked and sometimes the drivers were in on it and sometimes they weren't and got badly beat up or even killed. I never had my trailer stolen.

I used to carry a gun but quit that years before I stopped driving. After I had my bad accident the gun I had disappeared and I never thought about it again for the longest time. I figured one of the cops took it and he probably did me a favour by doing that. After that there was only the one time when I was sent way up to Northern Alberta for an RCMP move and at the detachment they gave me a rifle because of bears. Sheesh, I'd never shot a rifle in my life – still haven't – but I guess if I'd had to I could have. I suspected at the time that they were just messing with me and you know I still think that's true. I mean yes, of course there's bear activity in places like that, but in such a remote location big trucks sure wouldn't be common so the bears would probably stay away from something so noisy."

"Did you see any bears at all when you were up there?"

"Not on that trip as it happened, but sure I've seen plenty of bears. Usually just they're just eating berries along the side of the road but sometimes they're crossing the road and you've got to be careful because they're not scared and they don't run out of the way. Especially if there are little ones, they love to run and scramble all over the place until Mama Bear gives them a smack. You do know to never ever exit the vehicle if you see a bear on the road, right?"

"Huh, natch."

"I have been robbed you know, but I'm glad I wasn't carrying a gun, even though most of the drivers I knew kept one tucked away out of sight but still handy, just in case, but I always thought having a gun could easily make a bad situation worse."

"Bet the serial killer had a gun."

"No he didn't. Huh, I didn't realize how much of that I'm starting to remember now that you and me are talking about it so much."

"Does it bother you?" Jake looked quite concerned at his Granpa who smiled down at the boy saying: "'Course not. It was a long time ago."

Chapter Forty-Three

Tuesday March 04 – Wednesday March 05, 1980

Warren Lund was surprised, happily, when on coming into the station the Desk Sergeant told him he'd had a phone-call from RCMP headquarters in Ottawa. Lund hadn't expected such a quick reply to his call about linking up his murder case with any other possibilities. The Ottawa time zone was ahead of Winnipeg by one hour so it looked like the call to him had been made first thing.

When he returned the call to Cam Stillwell Warren was further surprised to discover that his RCMP liaison was female, and, from the sound of her voice an older woman – maybe about his age. Cam gave him a quick background on her department and explained her role in investigations. Sometimes there was bad feeling between the RCMP and the police departments but Warren immediately felt confident in the ability of this woman. That was his third surprise of the morning.

"First of all I appreciate your call. Although it's our business to provide the facilities to liaise between police forces across the country all of our fancy equipment can't be put to the use it was intended without the police departments first making the queries. Using your query about murder victims who had recently moved I came up with three 'likely' cases, one 'maybe' and at least half-a-dozen because some idiot thought 'recently-moved' meant two or more years had passed. If tying this together all sounds a bit sudden it's because I'd already flagged some possible connections and discussed it with my boss, Superintendent Petersen, before your call came in. That's why we're so pleased to hear from you."

"Well, I'm not sure..." began Warren but Cam interrupted him saying: "You don't need to be. We're all on this path together and some of what we learn will help guide us forward and some things will lead us astray but not for too long. I'm sure you can tell I've used that analogy before, it's a good way to describe our process. So, let's begin with any questions you have."

"OK, let's start with why the 'maybe' case you mentioned is only a maybe."

"Good point. I've included it because the woman was killed on the same day she moved but it's a maybe because she only moved locally and I thought your suspicion was of a long-distance truck-driver. Anyhow, the victim had moved in the city, Montreal by the way, and she moved into an area of town with lots of low-income housing so, of course, a high-risk area. She was divorced and didn't make enough money at her office clerking job to afford anything better.

The Montreal police think the killer might have been targeting the previous tenant. The name at the buzzers hadn't been changed yet, but they were never able to get a lead on the previous tenant other than his name. It wasn't a building where the residents socialized or looked out for each other although the elderly woman who called 9-1-1 certainly kept an eye out – the report of her interview is hilarious, I'm surprised the responding officer didn't arrest her out of sheer annoyance!

Theoretically the victim, Jasmine Brown, would have had to let her killer in but you know what goes on in these apartment buildings. People will buzz in anybody who rings. Now, the ex-husband (actually they were only separated but ex is easier) said Ms. Brown wouldn't do that. He said she was a nervous, worrying type and was over-cautious as a result. Used to drive him crazy, checking three or four times that the stove was turned off, that sort of thing. But it could be that she was coming into the building, maybe had gone out for some milk and stuff, and someone just followed her through the door.

She'd just moved in so she had no idea who was a stranger and who was her next-door neighbour. It might even have been a neighbour and not somebody from outside. The police in Montreal are satisfied the ex-husband's in the clear. He does have custody of the son but that was the kid's choice and apparently the mother was okay with that arrangement."

"It doesn't sound too hopeful because of it being a local move but maybe the move could have been handled by a company that also does cross-country work?"

"That's why it's a maybe. I checked with 'K' division, they handle our re-locations, but they weren't much help because they only do long-distance moves. I don't know anyone who works for a moving company so I'm not sure how the business is divided up and how the work is done."

"I do. I golfed at a CFB Winnipeg tournament in the summer and one of the guys in my foursome was a salesman for a moving company. I could try and get in touch with him for some more background."

"That would help but for a start I checked the Yellow Pages of the phone-book and there are fourteen pages of ads for moving companies and all the big van lines: North American, Allied, United, have full-page ads stating their agencies do 'local, long-distance, and international moves as well as packing services, storage, the whole bit. So I think it's possible, especially because of the COD: Ms. Brown died as a result of being battered to death. Two of the other three cases had victims battered to death and the third one, which incidentally was the first killing, had the victim severely beaten before being strangled.

Now, either the killer (if it is the same guy, of course) felt she was taking too long to die and strangled her to finish it or he's getting too violent with the subsequent women who are dying from his blows before he can strangle them. Escalated violence – it's a classic pattern."

Lund drew forward a pad of paper and taking up his pen said: "I do better if I can visualize so can you give me the dates and cities of the murders and I'll try to chart this."

Cam provided the information and the chart they devised read:

Murdered	City	Moved From	Victim's Name
Wed Feb 20	Halifax	Grande Prairie	Tammy Bluett
Mon Feb 25	Montreal	Montreal	Jasmine Brown
Tues Feb 26	Toronto	Fredericton	Angelica Posani
Sun Mar 02	Winnipeg	Winnipeg (Truckstop Dancer)	Denise Drake

"Well, right off we can see he's moving east to west."

"And that he can't seem to kill fast enough.. but whether that's a question of circumstance or his own rage building, I don't know."

"We need a few more columns and quite a few more details starting with "Who was the trucker who moved them?" and "What moving company was involved?""

"I think, at this point, we'd better get the local police departments to check out that information. I don't want to go to the head office of a nation-wide moving company yet. If there is a connection I don't want our boy tipped off by anyone."

"How could anybody do something like that? I mean, this guy's a killer, who would want to shield him?"

"Hey, who'd believe somebody wanted to marry Ted Bundy and did so in the middle of one of his torture/rape/murder trials?"

"Sometimes, with some of the things we come across I feel so alienated from the people and from the things people do in this world that I live in. Makes me feel too damn old! That and the fact that I seem to be losing my memory!"

"Well if you're trying to recall something that's just out of reach don't probe at it like a loose tooth, just let it swim to the surface on its own."

"You paint quite a picture I must say.."

"Yeah," Cam laughed, "I can mix up my metaphors with the best of them."

"Metaphors? That stuff's all Greek to me."

"Oh good one Warren, I can tell we're going to get along great."

Chapter Forty-Four

News of the Winnipeg murder reached the Big Sky Moving Edmonton office before the truckers did but Gerry Tanner told a story so well that when he arrived they all crowded round to question him and hear what he had to say. He told his tale, having to repeat himself every time the story got interrupted by a phone-call, then took a couple of swampers out to deliver his shipment.

Now it was the quiet time of the moving company's morning. All the trucks had been started, packing materials loaded, helpers matched up with drivers, petty cash issued, street maps photocopied, envelopes of paperwork: bills of lading, and inventory sheets, with rolls of tags, handed out.

The Dispatch room was empty except for Pamela. Suzi had gotten called over to the Sales Department to type up some quotes and letters for the staff who'd come in.

Dale arrived and sat down at an empty desk. Pamela saw his briefcase and said "I hope you've got fuel receipts for me. Just because you've been sick doesn't mean I'm cutting you any slack. I still have to keep up-to-date with the monthly reporting."

It was an ongoing joke between Pamela and the broker drivers. When she'd first started working at Big Sky Moving her job was secretary to the dispatcher who, at that time, was a fellow named Tony Moretti. He'd had the job for years and when he quit to take on a job at Schenkers the company had scrambled to find a replacement.

First it was a guy named Dave who got fired after a screaming match with Eddie Ferragamo, the boss, almost turned into a fist-fight.

Pamela covered until they hired another guy, John, this time the son of a friend of Eddie's so no conflict there. In fact he was well–liked, a nice personable guy who was always up for a friendly drink, but it turned out he was hopeless at the job. He was way too disorganized for work that was all about co-ordinating schedules, time-tables, and available staff. Everybody liked John so for a long time everybody covered for him, after all there's a lot of boozing in the moving business and always has been, but it soon became evident that John had a serious drinking problem. When the early morning coffee wagon came round he'd be buying pop – as a mix.

Once again Pamela stepped into the breach while Eddie looked for a real dispatcher.

It seemed like they'd struck lucky when he lured Peter away from another moving company. Peter knew the work and was good at it. He held his own in the standard introductory pissing match put on by the drivers and warehouse crews and everything went well for about a year when he got headhunted by the van line itself. Not a big step financially but great career potential.

The busiest season of the moving year, when the kids got out of school, was about to start soon. Pamela stepped into the job and this time the men in operations went to Eddie and demanded he keep her in the job. There was no time to find and train up someone new.

Eddie Ferragamo was old-school – he thought Pamela did a great job filling-in but would never have considered for the position permanently because he didn't think the men would accept a female dispatcher. It was a man's job to deal with these guys.

If he'd picked a woman as a new hire that might have been true but every time Pamela had temporarily filled the position she'd relied on the guys for their help and in turn had listened to their input and implemented some new policies that everyone appreciated. They were protective of her if visiting drivers got out of line, and besides she'd started her job under Tony, their old favourite, and his training had stuck.

She'd had the dispatcher job for two years now and was delighted to have doubled her weekly pay. Since that was still half of what Eddie had been paying the men everyone was happy with the arrangement.

Dale opened his briefcase and pulled out a couple of manila envelopes which he handed over to Pamela. She had a quick look at the contents then put them aside until after she'd started pencilling in her new orders. She was very much aware of Dale sitting a mere half-a-dozen feet away.

He studied her thinking Pamela was a nice girl and looked it. Pretty face but not a beauty, nice figure but not sexy. The kind of girl a man would take home to meet his folks, a date for a family wedding, that sort of thing. She was twenty-five years old and lived alone in a small apartment.

One day one of the crews came back from a move with a couple of kittens that the previous home-owner had left behind and the new home-owners couldn't keep because their kids had allergies. The driver figured Pamela could take them home but she flat-out refused. She worked at least 12-hour days during the spring and summer and enjoyed winding down with a cold beer in the warehouse or a meal out before heading home. It wouldn't be fair to leave a pet alone for so long. He approved that kind of consideration which was typical of her.

Instead the kittens found a home in the warehouse and a pretend job catching mice, pretend because the warehouse followed strict safety and cleanliness protocols with the cats always re-located to the office during the DND inspections.

When Dale got on the phone Pamela surreptitiously studied him. He was dressed in the trucker garb of plaid flannel shirt, jeans, cowboy boots, with the inevitable bunch of keys hooked to a belt with a Peterbilt buckle. And of course a padded vest, a garment that keeps the kidneys warm but leaves the arms free for easy movement.

Dale wasn't a conventionally handsome man but he had a quiet solitariness that looks like confidence and that targets certain women with particular appeal. Many women did find him attractive. Pamela found Dale very attractive indeed.

Pamela knew Dale had been married but not for long before his wife got cancer and died. She'd never heard any rumours about him and other women. Not like some of the long-distance drivers. Men who had women in every city, women who called looking for phone numbers, asking about schedules. Dale wasn't like that. He was quiet and friendly and, with Pamela, a bit flirtatious.

At least, that's what she thought. She couldn't be sure because she couldn't trust her own judgement, not once she learned how wrong she'd been about her long-term relationship with her high-school sweetheart. She'd shied away from dating after that but for some time now she suspected Dale was attracted to her, or at least admired her. But she wasn't sure and wasn't about to make a fool out of herself in case she was wrong. Wrong again.

He looked up at her then, of course he would just when she was staring at him, and gave her an interested smile. She wished she could blush on command, she'd always thought that was a pretty and feminine way to subtly indicate her feelings, but instead she smiled back and looked away. She was rescued from further embarrassment by the sound of high-heels purposefully marching down the hall towards her office.

The Sales and Dispatch departments often clashed as is probably the case in most businesses where someone has to fulfill the promises made by a person on commission.

Fiona Dawson-Smythe ("pretentious, isn't it? but I'll drop the hyphen once the youngest is out of school") was a woman in her early forties with bold good looks, a flair in her dress sense, and well made-up. Pamela liked her, but she didn't always like working with her. She suspected Eddie spent a fair bit of time pacifying both of them.

Right now Fiona's presence was welcome as she entered carrying a file folder in one hand and an unlit cigarette in the other. "God, I hate it now that they've made the sales room non-smoking." she complained, reaching across the desk to borrow Pamela's lighter. She lit up, inhaled dramatically, then opened the file folder expecting Pamela's undivided attention.

Fiona was the extremely successful marketing manager and head of sales. She was chameleon-like in her ability to blend in to whomever's company she found herself.

"But that was your idea! You're head of the Sales Department." exclaimed Pamela. A heavy smoker herself she'd shuddered at the thought of a smoke-free workplace. She even joked that she couldn't answer the phone unless she had a cigarette in her hand.

"Well I had to, I was smoking way too much and figured this would make me cut down."

"What about the other salespeople?"

"It's for their own good. But never mind that just now. I want to tell you that I've just finished speaking to Heather Morrison, this is the perfect time of day for her, and we're all set for tomorrow. I wanted to do the move today, in fact just told her we could squeeze things in (because, of course, I knew you'd find a way to help her out) but it's no go. She says that now the kids have left it finally gives her a chance to get things sorted out and finished up. She didn't dare do anything when they were around in case they said something... oh, I'll let you deal with these folks since they're probably on the clock."

She turned towards a couple who just walked in and the man, unmistakably a trucker, doffed his ballcap to Fiona saying: "Kind of you ma'am, we're not exactly in a rush but we do need somebody with know-how to help us out." His southern accent proclaimed him to be an American and it turned out he needed directions and instructions for clearing his shipment at Canada Customs before making his delivery in Edmonton.

Arnie came in at that point and asked where the couple were from and where they were going. Then Pamela, with some input from Dale, was able to help out.

"Well aren't you just the ticket!" exclaimed the driver. "We don't get many lady dispatchers on the other side of the border."

"Yeah, you must be a Women's Libber, I'm not that type." drawled his wife or girlfriend, or maybe she was just one of several girlfriends, you could never be sure on the road.

"And yet you dress like one." said Arnie.

"What are you talking about?" she asked.

"Obviously you burned your bra."

Like everyone else in the room Pamela's gaze settled on the woman's chest and yes, her braless state was obvious. She braced herself for the uproar but none came in fact the woman straightened her back to show off her assets and the man smiled proudly.

"He must have bought her a boob job." hissed Suzi. Pamela hadn't seen her come in and pretended not to hear.

"I say if you've got it flaunt it!" the woman happily proclaimed, enjoying the attention until Fiona burst her bubble by saying: "You say you're not a Women's Libber yet without the movement you could be arrested for dressing like that, and if you were raped it would be your fault because of what you're wearing – or rather not wearing."

Before anyone could reply Pamela added: "And if you have your own bank account, or got a car loan, or ever rented an apartment without a male co-signer then you certainly have benefited from the Women's Liberation Movement."

"Plus if your doctor was willing to prescribe the Pill before you were married, or if you never needed your husband's permission take birth control, or have an abortion, or wanted to get your tubes tied, then you certainly are a Women's Libber or at least you've taken advantage of all the stuff other women fought for on your behalf." Suzi chimed in.

"Yes, and that's without even mentioning schooling, working in any profession, voting, owning property, choosing your own husband or choosing to have no husband, having your own passport... this is a new decade and you really should be more supportive of your sisters." chided Fiona. She waved the file she'd been reading from at Pamela saying she'd be right back and gave the woman an appraising look before leaving the room.

"Wow, she must be a dyke or something" stated the woman with a weak laugh.

Pamela pretended not to understand saying "A what?" while Suzi snorted a suppressed laugh.

The trucker thanked everyone for their help and the Americans left. Fiona returned and immediately continued from where she'd left off saying: "Heather's parents flew in last night and they've picked up the kids for a day at the Waterpark. They booked into the West Edmonton Mall Hotel – I wonder if they got a theme room? and they'll be keeping the kids while Heather gets the move done. Any other time that poor excuse of a husband's refusal to allow her parents to come to the house would be a big deal but this time the asshole's played right into our hands. The parents will keep the kids out of the way and we can get in there quick, move the stuff out, and Heather will finally be free of that vicious bastard.

So, the arrangement is we send the truck over for 9:30 tomorrow morning but phone first, it's essential. If he answers just hang up, no wait that might make him suspicious, do a foreign accent or something asking if it's the Unemployment Office or, well, whatever. If she answers just say it's you and is the coast clear. This is starting to sound like a spy story or something, isn't it? But seriously, you know what a bad situation she's in and I'm so thankful she's finally going to get shut of that jerk. I'd just feel happier if we had her out of there today. That girl is really in danger. It's not like I'm not psychic or anything.. you know how many times my gut feelings have been spot on."

"Psychic and psychotic?" interjected Pamela with an innocent smile.

"Darling, does it have to be said? but seriously, I am really concerned about Heather. She's in a bad way but by tomorrow it will all be over, thank God. Who've you got on the move?"

"Dale, here, is going to do the pick up for us. He's already loaded for Vancouver but will have room and that means the furniture will be on the way tomorrow night. Well, afternoon, really. By the time hubby figures which moving company helped his punching-bag to escape the stuff will be delivered before he can get a court order or Sheriff's order or whatever it is to stop it."

Fiona turned to Dale and flashed him a winning smile. As a rule she never noticed the workers but charm was a big part of Fiona's success and she knew when to turn it on. "Dale Terry, thank God. Someone with sense and discretion. You understand the situation?" She hurried on before he could answer to explain about Heather Morrison and the abuse her violent husband subjected her to, and about how guilty Fiona felt when she learned the truth of what was happening in that household.

She'd met Heather through a mutual acquaintance and the two had connected deeply and immediately which only made it worse when she discovered what was going on. Was she so self-involved that she'd enjoyed the friendship without paying attention to her friend? After all there must have been indicators. Had she become so complacent in her own marriage that she'd somehow unconsciously refused to see the signs? As a result Fiona pushed hard to convince Heather that they could move her out safely.

Dale listened, nodded appropriately, and assured Fiona he'd make sure everything went smoothly. She crushed out her cigarette and gave a little scream as she glanced at the clock then hurried away as if they'd been keeping her.

Pamela gave Dale a lopsided smile and shrugged her shoulders. "Come here in the morning while I make the call just in case some snag comes up or something."

"Sure, just let me look over the papers first. Gerry said he'd help out if he finishes up at the garage early enough but he's going to meet me at the location so I need to give him the address tonight."

Pamela flipped through her standing file and found the one labelled "Morrison". She opened it up and glanced over the paperwork before handing Dale the Bill of Lading.

"Where is this place? I'm not too good on the named streets in this city."

"I know what you mean but frankly I prefer them. At least I do when they make sense. In my little home town every street had a name and when I first moved here and learned about the numbered streets and how streets run north-south and avenues east-west and even numbers on the north and west sides I thought 'what a super idea' but that was before I discovered that often streets don't join up where they should because there's this huge river running right through the city and a limited number of ways to cross it.

This address is here on the south-side. Actually just a few blocks from here. Say fifteen minutes drive. Just off 38th Avenue. Apparently all of the named streets go diagonally. There aren't a lot of houses just there. There's a strip-mall with a bank, a bakery that's now closed down, a dry-cleaners, Chinese restaurant and a day-care. I used to stop at that bakery sometimes but apparently the owner had a gambling problem and lost the business. At least that's what they told me at the restaurant. A real shame because the treats were excellent. On the other hand I don't need to add any more calories."

"You look alright to me just as you are."

Pam faltered for a moment, smiled, then continued saying: "Uh, thank you. Anyhow, Heather Morrison isn't supposed to be taking much stuff according to this estimate. Just the kids' beds, toys, clothes, (probably bicycles too although it doesn't say so), and some kitchenware and linens, stuff like that. I'm glad that Gerry's helping out, you two have been working together quite a bit this trip, eh?"

"Yeah, I think he's keeping an eye on me, making sure I'm OK to be back at work."

"Huh, he's the one who needs taking care of. Anyhow this little move shouldn't take you long."

Dale agreed it wouldn't take long. What neither of them knew then is that the move wouldn't take place at all.

Chapter Forty-Five

Tuesday March 04 – Wednesday March 05, 1980

Gerry considered himself to be Dale's best friend. They were of an age, same profession, both basically single since one was widowed and the other divorced. Well, almost.

Gerry wasn't sure if he thought of Dale as his best friend, though. Dale wasn't that much fun to hang around with. He was okay and everything but Gerry preferred to enjoy life with big bites, savouring every experience. Dale wasn't up for the 'two wild and crazy guys' antics. Of course the characters in the Saturday Night Live skit weren't too successful either.

After finishing his delivery, and after the crews had left the for the day, he met up with Dale at the office where he was with Pamela over coffee.

"I didn't think I'd see you till I got to the hotel. I got the address for tomorrow so here it is." said Dale handing Gerry a photocopy of the map, "You're going to meet me there about 10:30 or so, right?"

"No, sorry I've already been assigned. Shit sorry about that. Do you have a swamper lined up?"

"Hey, it's no problem. I'm taking Absolute Zero, hmm, maybe it is a problem..."

"He's not that bad," interjected Pamela.

"Right, it's just his IQ that's absolute zero – he's certainly strong enough."

"Yeah, we'll be fine. It sounds like there won't be too much stuff to move but there's the threat of a mean fucker, sorry Pamela, of a husband showing up so I wouldn't mind someone watching my back but you're right AZ is a strong guy."

"I hope this won't be a dangerous job. I don't know what Fiona was thinking getting us involved but you know how it is – once you hear about a bad situation you feel you've got to help out if you can. However, Dale do not get yourself hospitalized again because there's just too much work coming up. So tell us Gerry, what's going on with your schedule?"

"There's something going on all right, something at van line dispatch but, since I'm on the receiving end of a good thing, for once, I'm not bitching. One of the prima donnas from the A fleet must have screwed up somewhere because I got a real sweetheart of a load. 16,000 pounds off the Base. The only drawback is the customer's a Major and that means major-pain-in-the-arse but, Hell, I'll be coming into Vancouver right behind you, Dale. None of the usual hanging around waiting to fill out and end up leaving with way too much room anyhow because nothing's come up."

"Whose booking is it?" asked Pamela.

"Alberta All-Way, who else screws up a big move like this?"

"There is no way a Major's move was overlooked. I'll bet anything they were planning to put it on one of their own trucks and then something went wrong. Van Lines probably got the P.O. and caught on that way. I can't believe that outfit. What if they'd messed up (which is practically a given) and had to bring Van Lines into it then? They're really pushing their luck. I mean they know perfectly well that they can't be requesting self-hauls this early in the year. If we don't keep the A fleet going in the winter then we sure aren't

going to have it around in the summer when we're all desperate for
equipment.

That George Lancaster is such a greedy prick. I wonder how they
explained the last-minute booking? Probably blamed it on one of
the girls in the office or else said the salesman left the order in his
briefcase or something. What jerks."

"Well you really lucked out, Gerry. We can meet up and I'll help you
to unload in Van."

"I'm racing to the city and hoping to get it into storage. I probably
won't get it – I already got a break with the Halifax delivery and I
can't be that lucky, can I?"

"You shouldn't be but you probably will. A Major is going to take
his sweet time travelling in order to get the maximum allowance, and
you'd be smart to get it into warehouse if you can because you know
he's already writing out the damage report he's going to claim!"

"God, isn't that the truth – and he's a cop! I don't know how they
get away with it. Still, storage would be so sweet. What do you think,
Pammy? can I get lucky?" Gerry smirked but didn't bother waiting
for a reply. He overrode her saying "Don't call my Pammy!" by asking
Dale: "What have you got happening?"

"Just this small shipment to load tomorrow morning. It'll fill me
out nicely and then I'm gone. It's a fly-by-night split-up case, here."
Dale handed the bill of lading over to Gerry who read through the
particulars saying,

"Sort-of single, vulnerable, leaving a bad situation – sounds like a
woman who could use a little T.L.C. of the Gerry variety, what do
you think Pamela? would I stand a chance?"

"You're a such a pig. Thank God Dale's got the load and not you." she laughed.

"Anyhow, I probably won't be seeing you again, sweetheart. I've got to get my labour from Alta-All, Van Line directive, so I'll be heading straight out once I finish tomorrow. I don't know how long I'll be twiddling my thumbs in Vancouver but of course I'll spend all my time missing you."

"Gerry, you are so full of it. Anyhow, it's been fun but my working day is now over. I've got a ton of stuff to do at home so I'm getting out of here now. Dale, I'll see you in the morning and Gerry I'll see you whenever."

Chapter Forty-Six

Much later he found himself reliving the killing of Heather Morrison. This one had been different, her reactions were different, and he found that he didn't want to think about it. Conveniently for him it would be attributed to her husband.

Thinking about husbands and wives led to thoughts of his own marriage but that wasn't a good place so instead he thought of stories he'd heard from acquaintances on the road.

He'd heard stories about wives who were tired of raising the kids on their own and tired of having part-time husbands and all that sounded reasonable but it wasn't the truth. That's what they said but the truth was they'd met somebody else. That's what it always boiled down to. Women didn't end a relationship until they had another one to go to. Even if they hid it well.

Heather Morrison definitely had a guy in the background. They always did. No doubt her husband was an asshole who beat the hell out of her but she'd put up with it for so many years why would she change her mind about him now? Hardly for the sake of the kids because they weren't babies, they'd already know what was going on.

No, she'd met somebody. Maybe the husband knew about this guy and maybe not. Who could tell? If he did know then the police would have a motive to go along with his track-record of spousal abuse.

The killer felt pretty safe.

Of course he'd been careful anyhow. It was a bit soon after the murder of that Winnipeg slut but the opportunity arose and things had fallen into place.

He'd left the truck stop and walked to the local mall. There were always taxis waiting outside the Safeway and he'd got one to take him to the strip mall. He told the driver, a man this time and not in the least bit curious, that he was going to a Chinese Restaurant on 34th, he couldn't remember the name of the restaurant but knew where it was. The cabbie simply headed in the right direction without comment.

The killer was obliged to actually enter the restaurant while the cab remained outside; the driver communicating with his office. The restaurant was, fortunately, crowded, and he was able to make a show of looking around as if seeking someone. Keeping watch on the cab he was able to leave as soon as the car left the parking-lot, neatly escaping the hostess who came to seat him.

He walked round the back of the building and, sure enough, found the path that led across the yard to the housing subdivision. Not an established path but a short-cut marked by many passing feet. Finding the Morrison home presented no difficulty.

Heather Morrison wasn't at all pleased to see him, in fact was terrified, but he was able to calm her fears and explained this quick trip now would save valuable time next day. She let him in, explaining her husband would have stopped for a beer or two after work but she was never certain what time he'd actually arrive home so this would have to be quick. It was.

He let her keep talking until she'd closed the door then he took it upon himself to give her marital problems a permanent solution.

Perhaps it was because of her previous experience with a fist-swinging enraged man but Heather Morrison made very little noise and that surprised her murderer.

She'd grunt or gasp with the pain but no screams and no terrified, hoarse yells. She submitted to the blows, turned into this or that protective position, and, eventually, died having said nothing more than 'No more, no more'.

Chapter Forty-Seven

Tuesday March 04 – Wednesday March 05, 1980

As usual on a chilly morning there was a long line of cars waiting at the McDonald's drive-thru. Plenty of cars in the parking lot too which meant service would be slow. Fiona drove past without stopping and decided to head for the Country Style Doughnuts instead.

She knew she was using the crowdedness as an excuse and the extra drive to pick up coffee was wasting time. She didn't want to go to Heather's place but felt obligated to do so. She hoped that arriving with a treat would cover some of her embarrassment.

Fiona had been happily married for almost thirty years. Edward Smythe was an easy-going, affable husband and father, successful in his legal career, and an active volunteer in youth sports. Fiona knew she was being silly but somehow felt that her good fortune seemed to emphasize Heather's troubles. No, troubles was a ridiculous word to use for the hellish life of fear and brutality her marriage had become.

Heather wouldn't say how long the abuse had been going on. At first Fiona accepted the explanations when she noticed bruises – why not? Spousal abuse didn't happen to people like them. But eventually she had to accept that her friend was lying to cover up, and that Heather became very angry and defensive when her excuses were challenged.

It was a long time before Fiona realized the poor woman was ashamed. Once that sunk in Fiona stopped criticizing and stopped making demands and instead she listened and hugged and cried.

Of course the abuse continued and that put a real strain on their friendship because it was hard for Fiona to keep her nose out but she managed by avoiding any contact with Hugh. She'd told Edward and was thankful it was just the women who were friends, not the couples, because he was so angry on Heather's behalf.

Edward was able to pass on some shocking stats, like how women would leave up to fourteen times before making the break for good, but also helpful legal information which he cautioned Fiona to present without expectations.

Eventually, after much talking and listening, Heather started to view her life from a different angle and at last it looked like she was ready to take the next necessary step.

Now that the children were older Heather feared that someday Hugh would turn vent his violent anger on them. She also worried about what they were witnessing at home and what lessons they were learning about relationships.

Fiona was happy to encourage Heather but the last thing she wanted was gratitude. Instead, she wanted the best possible outcome for her friend even though it meant they'd have to continue their friendship from a distance. Heather needed to move away from Hugh's influence – and his fists.

The coffee shop wasn't too busy so Fiona soon had a cardboard carry-tray filled with coffees, a small bag full of milk containers and sugar packets, and a family-size box of doughnuts. All chocolate-dipped so there would be no arguing over who got what and because chocolate was Fiona's favourite.

She got to Heather's home before the moving truck but thankfully Hugh's car was already gone for the day. Loaded up with treats she followed the gravelled path round the house to the kitchen door.

It wasn't locked so she dumped the food on the counter and called hello. No answer so Fiona went looking for Heather. Unfortunately she found her.

Chapter Forty-Eight

Tuesday March 04 – Wednesday March 05, 1980

"Gerry! I thought you'd be halfway to Vancouver by now?" exclaimed Pamela when the amiable trucker came into her office.

"No need. You were right about the Major taking his time – the shipment's definitely going into storage. This trip has worked out great and I can't believe me luck me darlin'. So now that I don't have to rush to get there, and since I've got a little bit of room, I thought I'd scout around the hotels to see if anybody's got a cash deal going."

"If it's a buckshee shipment I don't want to hear about it. You know that's a big no-no and if you get caught I'm not getting involved."

"Well, you're one of the few dispatchers who doesn't. Most of them set it up for a good-size cut of the cash."

"It's not worth it to me. Besides, I can see the owners' point of view and I don't blame them for resenting their trucks being used."

"The only thing the owners and the Van Lines don't like is the fact that they don't get a piece of the action."

"Exactly, after all they own the trailer."

"Anyhow, Dale, what are you still doing here. I thought you said you'd be gone by now?"

"Huh, I should have been, but we've had a lot of trouble here; another murder, like in Winnipeg, and I'm waiting for an okay from the police before I go anywhere." answered Dale.

"What do you mean?"

Pamela replied, saying: "One of our customers was murdered. The one Dale was supposed to be moving so the police have been questioning him but the whole thing is stupid because, obviously, her husband's the killer."

"In fact, it was the one you were going to help me with, remember Pam got a map for you? but then you got that sweet new assignment. This was a runaway from a wife-beater, a moonlight flit at ten in the morning, and I guess her old man found out about it and killed her. The two of them were home alone the night before she was leaving because her kids were away with her parents and next day she was found dead."

"By Fiona." added Pam.

"Oh Hell, that sucks. Poor Fiona and poor lady."

"Yeah, it was one of those 'phone first' moves but the phone was disconnected. Too early, but you know what the phone company's like. I'm guessing it was in the wife's name and she figured if she wasn't going to be around she wasn't going to pay the bills so Dale headed out to the house anyhow. When he got there he found Fiona in the driveway crying and shaking."

"She couldn't tell us what had happened, she tried but she just couldn't get the words out and wasn't clear. The front door was locked so I walked round the house and the back-door was standing open. AZ was swamping for me so we went in, the door opened into the kitchen, and hollered, got no answer, and then we saw the blood. AZ spotted it first. We went right into the house and found her in the bedroom. Then we got the hell out of there. It was an awful sight, poor woman, and I feel bad that Fiona had to see that. I called the cops, and the office, from her car-phone. I had to hang around most of yesterday and I'm just waiting to be interviewed again today."

"They don't think you had anything to do with it, do they?"

"No, they don't but we were in the house. I told them we hadn't touched anything but they want to fingerprint us anyway to make sure. The cop said the whole thing really is routine because they've got the husband. They had him last night actually 'cause he got arrested in a bar and spent what was left of the night in the drunk tank!"

"Holy shit, we've been on the road how many years with no real cop trouble and now two murders happen just like that and we're connected. It's a weird coincidence."

"Actually I've had several deaths with my customers." said Pamela, " There was that woman who died of toxic shock – you know the well, um, tampon thing – and then a really bad one, a special constable with the RCMP: she was in a plane that crashed and we had to ship her belongings to her family, I think she was only twenty-one or two.

And there was that guy from the explosives company who died out in the oil-patch and the company was relocating his family back to Peace River, also another oil-patch guy who lost control of his motorcycle or something, nobody knew for sure because it was one of those single-vehicle fatalities. Yeah, there have been quite a few deaths. But not murders."

"This one here sounds straight-forward enough all right – for a killing, that is – but I still can't get over Denise's murder."

"But a lot of these stripper-dancers are run by biker gangs, right? so they're in a risky job with scary bosses." Pamela said.

"Actually not at the Queen's and I don't really think any of the trucker bars have the biker girls. I guess bikers and truckers just don't mix."

"So you both knew this dancer?"

"Oh yeah, she'd been working at the Queen's for a few years. Everybody knew Denise."

Further conversation was interrupted by a phone-call from the police for Dale. He left to pick-up Davey the helper, aka Absolute Zero, to go to the station for fingerprinting and signed statements.

Left alone Gerry became more personal with Pamela. "You know he's never going to say anything to you and I know you're never going to say anything to him but it's really obvious that you two have the hots for each other so how are you ever going to get together?"

"Gerry, you don't know what you're talking about."

"Hey, I know I'm right about Dale. I know the guy, after all we've been rooming together for about half-a-year now. Whenever he talks about you which, come to think about it is quite a lot, everything he says is complimentary so I know how he feels. And if you don't feel the same then how about you and me going out? You know I can make really cute-looking kids."

Pamela smiled and shook her head at him.

"You are such a flirt but I know you well enough to know that your argument is charm and not logic so no, I think you and I will just stay friends. Besides, I know about all the other women. I'm the one who gets the phone-calls from them, remember? Which reminds me I have a letter for you. I didn't put it in your slot because some nosey jerk would be sure to pry, it's here in my desk and it smells lovely."

She opened her desk drawer and pulled out a violet envelope addressed to Gerry. He read the return address and gave her a wry grin.

"Probably her car payment's overdue."

"Let's hope nothing else is!" Pamela retorted.

Chapter Forty-Nine

Tuesday March 04 – Wednesday March 05, 1980

Dr William Taylor, the Medical Examiner for Edmonton, prepared to do the autopsy on Heather Morrison.

He had decided against an inquiry, as was his right, because the police were already investigating the death. In fact, they'd arrested the husband and when he was brought to trial the results of this autopsy would spell out in sickening detail all of the pain and damage he'd inflicted on his poor wife.

Although William Taylor had lived in Canada since the age of twelve a Scottish burr never fades entirely and his slight accent was even more pronounced as he recorded aloud the facts of this woman's horrible death.

As a young, single man who lived alone the doctor had never experienced first-hand how a couple can rub up against each other in both good and bad ways but he was quite certain in his own mind that he would never, ever strike a woman never mind batter one to death.

Mrs. Heather Morrison had been punched, kicked, hit with a heavy blunt object, and stabbed with a sharp-edged object. Her face was smashed while her arms, hands, and feet were crushed.

Last night's beating was yet another attack on a body that showed past abuses like a road map to Hell. Multiple breaks, only some of which were treated professionally, layers of damaged tissue, organs bruised beyond healing, missing teeth...

He felt badly enough when he had to work with the bodies of crash victims mutilated in a variety of horrific ways by twisted metal and gasoline fire but this deliberate rage-fuelled action by another human being – especially the person who had sworn an oath to love and protect – was beyond his ken.

Chapter Fifty

Tuesday March 04 – Wednesday March 05, 1980

Normally Pamela welcomed the comfort and solitude of her apartment – she worked long hours and was always glad to get home and relax – but not tonight. The apartment had finally acquired a comfortable lived-in look now that she'd finished furnishing and no longer used moving boxes for drawers.

The place needed dusting but it was tidy. Pamela spent too little time at home to make much of a mess.

When she got home from work it would be to eat, maybe watch a sitcom like 'Taxi' or 'Mork and Mindy', do laundry, sleep. It seemed most of her free time was taken up with running-around chores outside of the apartment. As of yet, she hadn't done any socializing at home.

Sometimes, when making her bed in the morning or climbing into it at night, she'd fantasize about who the man would be who'd christen her new double. She wondered if it was someone she already knew or someone she hadn't yet met.

Gerry was forever volunteering his services but Pamela found herself thinking (hoping!) that Dale would be the one. He had such a deep voice and she loved listening to him talk although he wasn't a big conversationalist – it was Gerry who had all the jokes, anecdotes, and wisecracks. Gerry was a funny, entertaining man while Dale was a more serious prospect.

Now she couldn't settle down to anything because she was too worried about both of them. The visit from the police this afternoon had shocked her beyond rational thought. She couldn't keep her mind from jumping about, couldn't concentrate on anything except that the police must be wrong. Must be. To think anything else was inconceivable. It was disloyal, it was stupid. She knew these guys, had known them for a couple of years. There's no way she could be fooled like that.

True, the evidence showed one of them could be responsible, even in her thoughts she shied away from the word "guilty", but there was no way Dale or Gerry could have committed those crimes. To batter women to death? It wasn't possible. They couldn't be involved.

The police had come into the office and requested an interview with her. Not her, specifically, but her because of the position she held in the company. The dispatcher with the records of all the trips the drivers made.

They hadn't said much by way of explanation but she'd persisted and knew, at least, what they were looking for. The schedules of Dale and Gerry, looking to place one or both of them in the vicinity of the crimes.

For the Edmonton murder, the killing of Heather Morrison, both men were in town and knew of the Morrison move, even knew her name and her address, but that meant nothing, it was part of their regular working day. There was nothing else in it. Unfortunately Dale discovered the body and there seemed to be some police maxim about the discoverer being the murderer. Or likely to be, or something.

Pamela's knowledge of police procedures came from Agatha Christie novels, obviously not the most accurate of sources.

Both men were at the Queen's Hotel in Winnipeg when the stripper, Denise something-or-other, was murdered. But about forty or more other truckers were there as well. It was a coincidence and coincidences do occur in real life.

Pamela had tried to convince the police of this, tried to persuade them they were following the wrong leads, but they hid behind police platitudes about "routine" and she got nowhere. She could feel the futility as strongly as the need to, somehow, show them they were wrong.

One of the police, a female officer, was looking at the Dispatch book, a huge leather-bound ledger, that was spread open on Pamela's desk. Apparently she read that the brokers daily calls were logged in with times and locations. The officer asked: "What was the Toronto date?" and when told flipped back through the pages and noted that both men were there at the same time a woman, recently moved from Fredericton, was murdered.

Pamela had asked "Who? what woman?" but the police had stopped explaining anything then – instead requesting permission to take the records.

The police never mentioned it but Pamela knew from Gerry that both of her drivers had been near or passing through Kingston when a woman's body was discovered on the highway. She didn't mention it either.

At that point Suzi joined the conversation to tell the police they couldn't be allowed to take the Dispatch book, it was essential to operations. When told she could photocopy the pages she needed she said: "No, you can tell us what dates you're interested in and we'll give you photocopies of those pages, you can't rummage through the whole book on a fishing expedition, our staff and our customers are entitled to their privacy."

Pamela was impressed, despite the mixed metaphors, at the way Suzi stood up to authority. She had no idea if any of it made sense but it sure sounded good.

She had no idea whether or not she could refuse, she thought she could but was unable to make that decision. By that point she was incapable of any decision so she'd called through to the owner who came upstairs.

Eddie dealt with the police; listening to their request and agreeing to provide the information. He instructed Suzi to photocopy the whole year's entries which, after much sighing and huffing, she did. Luckily it was only the beginning of March so it didn't take long.

Once the big ledger was returned Pamela leaned over it protectively. There were still jobs in the book which she hadn't invoiced and for which her drivers hadn't yet been paid and she needed the records for reference.

After the police had gone the two women and their boss had talked things over and what he'd said made sense. He knew there was no harm in handing over the records because he was sure neither Dale nor Gerry had any involvement in any crime.

"Especially Dale. He does everything by the letter and there's nothing psycho about him. And Gerry would never harm anyone, particularly a woman. He loves women far too much and besides he's too irresponsible to ever be in a position where commitment or finer feelings for any woman would ever interfere with his enjoyment of life. He'll never have any reason to do any woman any harm. There's nothing wrong in helping out the police, Pamela and you too, Suzi. In fact, it'll help both the drivers because now the police can clear them of any suspicion. We know they're both innocent but we can't expect the police to take our word for it, right?"

Suzi grumbled a bit about police abusing their authority but Pamela agreed with Eddie's assessment. He was right: Gerry didn't care deeply enough about women to feel anything as strong as the rage that caused their brutal deaths, and Dale? He was very respectful.

On an especially hot day last summer she'd walked into the warehouse where a few of the men were working shirtless and Dale had his shirt undone but he immediately buttoned up when he saw her. Dale was a meticulous, fastidious man. Very much the type to dot every "i" and cross every "t". Why his daily logs were... and the thought stopped there.

By law all truckers had to carry log-books showing each day's working hours, specifying how much time was spent actually driving, how much was spent on other work like loading, on rest periods, what cities they were in, how many miles they'd driven, how much fuel they'd bought and in what province the purchase was made. What work they actually did, who it was for, how much work was involved... in fact, everything. The dispatch book was nothing to what the log-books were, at least not in Dale's case.

Most of the drivers caught up on their record-keeping on a weekly (or more) basis but Dale filled out his logs daily. Gerry filled out his when Pamela had nagged long enough that she couldn't complete the monthly fuel tax reports without them, or when word had gone along the highway that the inspection stations were actually checking logs and everybody better be up-to-date or get fined.

Gerry enjoyed inserting cryptic notes, like "SFP", so that when Pamela questioned something he could enjoy himself by teasing her with the answer: "Stop for Pee, Pammy, everyone knows that."

"Very funny, and don't call me Pammy. Everyone else writes 'check the tires', no, actually Gerry no one else writes that down, or anything like it, at all. Nobody else figures I'm interested and you know why? because I'm not. Now stop playing the 'goofy Newfie', OK?" she'd sounded annoyed but was actually amused. Gerry could always be counted on to provide a little, sometimes much-needed, comic relief. Being caught out falling for one of his silly stories often exasperated her but his phone-calls were always fun, he was never bad-tempered or sulky.

She smiled at the recollection and relaxed enough to finish off her work day but, once home, the reassurance her boss had given her evaporated. She fretted over the crazy suspicions the police had and worried about the repercussions of their investigation into her guys. Too often innocent people suffered when false, or misleading, evidence pointed in the wrong direction.

One of their clients – a man she'd never met but had had a years-long phone relationship with – was accused of rape and although the charge was soon dropped and he was able to prove he'd been somewhere else at the time, the suspicion was devastating for his family.

Of course she could see the police viewpoint: if the murderer was a truck driver then they needed to track down which truckers were in each of the areas. It made sense. But there were about five times as many freight trucks as there were moving trucks on the road – except in July and August – so why did it have to be a mover?

"There must be more to it, the police must know more" she thought, and then wondered, "Exactly how many murders have their been? And since Heather Morrison in Edmonton can't have anything to do with some woman in Halifax or another in Toronto then the connection must be... moving. And something all three women have in common like the same driver? No, that can't be right but..."

With such thoughts going round and round in her head Pamela couldn't relax until she talked to her guys. She had to let them know what was happening with the police and their suspicions and everything that was going on.

It wasn't just the police who were asking questions either. She'd seen the sales women clustered into a gossip and overheard some of what the guys hanging out in the warehouse were saying. None of them believed the police were investigating without a good reason. A 'no smoke without fire' kind of thing. It was vital to get this cleared up.

Dragging her bedroom phone with its extra-long cord into the bathroom she filled the tub, climbed into a hot bubble-bath, and set about tracking down Gerry and Dale.

Chapter Fifty-One

Tuesday March 04 – Wednesday March 05, 1980

Warren Lund had a cup of coffee on the table in front of him and the ashtray was already half-full with butts when Cam Stillwell called. His response to her greeting skipped the niceties and went directly to what was foremost in his mind: "Can I go to Edmonton and look at the moving company's records?"

"The locals couriered a copy of the dispatch book but you feel you need more detail? Do we have enough to get a warrant for access?"

"Is a warrant necessary? Don't you think the staff will co-operate with the police?"

"They might but that's not the point." Cam heard Warren's huff of annoyance. She was pleased to hear the reaction and, after pausing to get her thoughts together, continued: "It seems to me that you think you've found the killer of all these women. I don't know if it's brilliant deduction or gut instinct or just cop sense, whatever you want to call it, but I think you've targeted a man. And it's because I sense you're right that I want everything done to a tee with no leeway for argument or reasonable doubt. We don't want any screw-ups on this one. I know you're impatient to get moving on it. Makes sense, it's the reason you became a cop in the first place, and also because we're running out of time, or rather the next victims are. But we've got to do everything by the book, you know that, we can't jeopardize our case."

"And, as you just said, while we pussyfoot around some other lady gets beaten to death?"

"You know I don't want that to happen, Hell, I don't even have to say that. But you also know that if we can't hold him, if he walks away from this on a technicality, then there will be even more women down the road."

"Down the road, very appropriate."

"So we've been working on the premise that the killer's a trucker but you have a particular trucker in mind, don't you?"

"Yes, I do. This is definitely gut feeling, instinct, or what did you call it? cop sense? that works just as well." Warren lit another cigarette and leaned back, squinting against the smoke. Although Cam couldn't see him he gave a lips-only smile saying: "I think the killer is Gerry Tanner."

"You interviewed him here in Winnipeg, at the hotel, didn't you?"

"He was here when Denise was killed. He'd come into Winnipeg from Toronto. He was in Edmonton when that woman married to the wife-beater was murdered, and he left Edmonton for Vancouver."

"That's not an uncommon routing for these drivers, especially since his company office is in Edmonton. You talked to him, what's he like?"

"He talked to me very openly, very friendly. Definitely the kind of guy whose table you'd choose to sit at even if there's a whole crowd in the room. A life-of-the-party kind of guy. You'd be sure of having a few laughs with him. He looks you right in the eye when he talks to you. He makes jokes about himself and he's always in motion. Talks with his hands and his face expresses every thought and the whole thing just sent warning bells off in my head. I felt like I was being conned, very pleasantly, but I felt the man's whole personality was bullshit. The type who lies even when it doesn't matter – like he's keeping practise, honing his skills, laughing at you.

He's separated, said his wife threw him out last fall, so maybe there's a lot of resentment there that could have built up into anger against all women. He shares the home of another trucker, same company too."

"Any chance that man.. what's his name?"

"Terry."

"No, not Gerry. I meant the other trucker."

"Yeah, Terry. Dale Terry is his name. I interviewed him in Winnipeg too."

"Similar names, strange. Anyhow, could he give you insights or information about Gerry Tanner, do you think?"

"Not likely. I could barely get more than a 'yes' or a 'no' answer when I questioned him about Denise Drake. The guy's not exactly forthcoming.

No, what I need are the driver records in order to be absolutely sure but I think I can place him on site for the murders. And I think there's something wrong about him."

"You know he's a hero, right?"

"What do you mean?"

"Back in January there was a big brawl at a stripper bar in Montreal. Police thought it was just truckers and bikers fighting – there was a story about some guy roughing up a girl with the action moving outside – but turns out it was a hijacking, a Sanyo truck loaded with high-end electronics, and your Gerry Tanner stepped in which probably saved the driver's life but before rescue came he got a real kicking badly injuring him along one side - arm and ribs – and nerve damage to his leg, finishing with a severe blow to the head which had him hospitalized for quite awhile. Apparently it was the fourth hit, or attempted hit, on a Sanyo truck so the company made a big deal about Gerry Tanner the good citizen stepping in."

"I didn't know that but it fits the kind of guy he is, personable and ready to help out. That doesn't jive with being a serial killer but maybe his injury resulted in brain damage or something."

"I can't get a warrant with what we've got but I think I can if the trucking schedules back us up."

"But that's why we need the records."

"I know but we can still work around that, for now. I'll get in touch with the local forces and see if we can't at least get the names of the trucking companies, and hopefully the drivers, who were involved in each of the moves."

"And the helpers."

"But this Tanner guy's a driver, isn't he?"

"Yes, but the drivers apparently go out and help each other. They trade off their own labour instead of hiring someone locally. At least they do some of the time, and they're more likely to do it when they're away from home and just hanging around the moving companies or the truck-stops."

"So his name might not be on the paperwork but he could still be on the move?"

"Right. The Bill of Lading gives the driver's name only."

"But that should be enough to start with. If I can place Tanner at several of the locations then I think I'll be able to take that information and get a warrant to look at his employer's records. I know I have it in my notes but what's the name of his company?"

"Big Sky Moving, affiliated with Dominion Van Lines. Big Sky is in Edmonton but the van lines has branches in every province. The Big Sky drivers have coast-to-coast running rights. All of their drivers are licensed out of Alberta. Alberta has the least red tape and no sales tax so it's very business-friendly. No matter what city they actually live in, their records are in the Edmonton office because that's where their pay statements are made up."

"Okay. We've got somewhere to go with this. I'll get back to the office and contact the Halifax, Toronto, and Edmonton police. The Montreal murder isn't going to help us tie him in and that'll probably end up being one of those unsolved crimes, even if we're sure he did it. I think you're right about needing to go to Edmonton. I'll head back and get started."

"Well it's lunch time here so I'm going to the Queen's for a bite and will be back in the office within the hour."

"You'll actually have lunch there?"

"Why not? if the truckers eat here the food must be good, right?"

Chapter Fifty-Two

Summer 2015

"You know what? I've been reading about murderers." said Jake. "There's some pretty gross stuff on the Internet but I mostly ignore that because it probably isn't factual. Anyhow, I wrote down what I learned and here it is." He pulled out a small lined notebook and read: "Most murders are committed for financial gain (but back in 1980 those women weren't robbed); some murders are committed to cover up another crime (but again that didn't happen with our murders); and sometimes one killing 'awakens a blood lust for more'. That's usually what happens in gory movies about werewolves and monsters, which I like, so do you think that's what happened? Or do you think it was a Dr Jekyll and Mr Hyde kinda thing? where the crazed killer doesn't even know he's got an uncontrollable urge to kill again and again."

"You're enjoying this, aren't you kid? You're even doing research and taking notes, wow. I'm not sure if it's healthy but on the other hand I watched plenty of scary movies in my day so I guess it's par for the course with young guys. I remember the Jekyll and Hyde movie, it was based on a book but I never read the book."

"I read that one in a comic. Actually most of the stuff I'm learning comes from crime shows like 'Law and Order', CSI, NCIS – stuff like that. I'm mostly watching re-runs so it's pretty old but still really good."

"Huh. Which CSI do you like the best?"

"I like the main guy in CSI New York but I think my favourite is Miami."

"I've seen a few of those episodes but when I watch TV it's usually sports. Anyhow, what else did you find out?"

"There were other serial killers operating at the same time: there was The Yorkshire Ripper, called Peter Sutcliffe, in England; and there was Wayne Williams, responsible for at least 20 of the 29 Atlanta Child Murders; and of course the most famous one was Ted Bundy. The Trans-Canada Killer wasn't very famous except maybe in Canada. Anyways, I read that they knew he murdered seven women and maybe more that they don't know about."

"Seven women. It was really big news at the time and now people don't even remember except for the families of the women, I guess. It was shocking then and it's still shocking now. Seven women who were somebody's wife, daughter, sister, mother. You and me are talking about it like it's something in a story but really it's sad when you think about it."

"I know, Grandpa T but I never knew any of the people and I can't help but want to know about it because you were around then and you knew and heard stuff, you maybe even knew the killer, and it's interesting. It doesn't mean I'm bad, does it?"

"No, of course not. You're curious and as you say you don't know any of these people so it doesn't touch you personally. There is something about murder that intrigues people, I guess because it's so unbelievable, the idea of being so angry or wanting something so much that you'd actually kill. I mean, we read about it in the papers but it's never more than just an item in the news. But how did you get started on all this? How did you find out about the case?"

"Well it was like this: I was looking for the colour comics in the weekend paper and there's always lots of sections, you know like Real Estate, and one page had this big heading 'True Crime'. It was a flashback to 'The Moving Murders' from thirty-five years before and it was so interesting. The writer really put down the cops saying if they'd only worked together there would have been less women killed.

And he said that the story never came out until it was all over and even then they weren't sure just how many murders there were because Kingston and Montreal and Edmonton and.. oh yeah, Vancouver didn't really fit the profile. That's what he said."

"I kinda think I'd like to read that article for myself because talking to you about that time has really brought back a lot of memories. But then again, the killings aren't really something I want to think about. Much better to just leave it as a story that happened way back when, just some headlines in the newspaper."

"Except that it was more than that for you back then, right?"

"Oh yes. I was a lot closer to a police investigation then I ever wanted to be, believe you me."

Chapter Fifty-Three

Thursday March 06 – Friday March 07, 1980

Tom used his rear-view mirror to check on his son in the back-seat and decided he'd better pull over. Jamie wasn't complaining but he was looking sickly and if a bit of fresh air didn't help then at least he'd be out of the car when he threw up.

As a kid Tom had been carsick all the time until a waitress at some roadside diner had suggested to his parents that he shouldn't drink orange juice in the morning. His mother had argued about that, orange juice for breakfast was one of those unwritten rules, but his Dad had said 'give it a try'. He wasn't sick to his stomach that day, and carsickness wasn't a problem after that.

Since then orange juice had only made him sick when, as a teenager in the stands of a high-school football game, he'd drunk too much of it with gin. Even then the problem was that they hadn't diluted the juice, figuring they didn't need water when they had gin, and the strong taste of orange concentrate after vomiting had turned him off screwdrivers – and Tang – for life. He smiled at the memory of himself in younger days and mused over what lessons his own son would be learning.

In the meantime he'd pull the car over. It was a quiet part of the road with a wide verge where they wouldn't be disturbed and the car would be safe if they left it to walk a ways.

Janice looked at him questioningly when he slowed down and then turned to look at their boy. She gave Jamie a smile but said nothing, she and Tom had decided it was best not make a fuss. Tom had told her the orange juice story so they were careful about that but orange juice didn't seem to be Jamie's problem - it was the motion of the car.

When they stopped she said she'd stay in the car. She had a magazine story she wanted to read and found she couldn't do so while the car was moving. As she said that she realized that Jamie's queasy stomach was inherited from her.

"Besides, I know what you guys are like. You just want to go pee against a tree, don't you?"

"Lucky guess! And you're just jealous 'cause you can't."

Jamie managed a weak smile and followed his father down the little pathway that led into the woods.

Janice knew they wouldn't be long knowing Tom wouldn't take their boy far, but as her eyes followed them she felt a little uneasy. There were so many weirdos on the road these days. You heard about so many terrible things. Her mind wandered along these thoughts for a minute or two. She hadn't opened her magazine and had managed to set her nerves on edge so she was thankful when they returned quite suddenly. There was real relief in her smile but then she saw Tom's face – he was looking worse than Jamie had in the car – and knew something was terribly wrong.

Tom came round to the driver's door and popped the trunk saying: "Find yourself a handi-wipe, kiddo, there's some in the blue bag."

And when Jamie went round to the back of the car Tom whispered to Janice that he'd seen a body, a woman's body, and he was getting out of there right away.

"But... what do you mean? a body? a dead body?"

"Yeah, but Jamie didn't see her and I don't want him to know about it, at least not yet. I'm going to have to call the cops but I want to get away from here first. The kid doesn't need to be part of something like that."

"Are you sure it, you said she – are you sure she's dead? How can you be sure? What happened, exactly?"

"I didn't realize there was anything, we walked in a little ways and I heard a lot of buzzing. I looked for a wasp's nest and there was nothing in the trees so I thought maybe ground wasps – you know what he's like about bees and wasps – and I certainly didn't want either of us stepping in a nest, but it wasn't wasps it was a big cloud of flies. I figured they were on a dead animal and didn't want him to see something like that, not with the way he's feeling, so I turned him around and right then he was sick. Luckily the wind was behind us so there wasn't a strong smell or I'd probably have been sick right along with him because while I waited for him to finish throwing up I was able to get a better look. I could see it was a girl's body, not some animal, and her face was just a mess of dried blood with her head twisted around so I'm certain her neck is broken. He was facing away, which was good, because he didn't see a thing."

"Oh God, Tom that's gross. What a terrible thing and.. oh here you are sport, feeling a bit better now?"

"Of course he is. He just had himself a big burp, didn't you? Well, let's get back on the road, the sooner we leave the sooner we get there, right?"

The family got settled into the car and Tom was already back on the highway before Janice finished buckling her son into the seat. Neither she nor her husband could talk about what was on their minds but both found the silence oppressive, it made them want to cover it up with sound but they couldn't take about it in front of Jamie. Janice pushed a cassette into the tape-deck and they sped on to the closest town listening to The Chipmunks and thinking about serial killers and battered bodies.

Chapter Fifty-Four

Thursday March 06 – Friday March 07, 1980

The phone call found Cam Stillwell attending the retirement party of an officer a few years older than herself. The event had begun to fizzle out anyhow, because after lunch and a drink what more was needed? A few reminisces followed by insincere comments about how lucky the retiree was. Senior officers knew better than to liven up a celebration with hookers or a poker game so that pretty much left drinking too much, which too often led to indiscreet conversation.

Cam wasn't sorry to get called away – she wouldn't have stayed much longer anyhow, attending only because her boss had delegated her on his behalf since he couldn't make it. "Hmm, so he said." she thought while remembering that the Superintendent didn't look at all disappointed to miss the affair.

Unfortunately the call was the notification of Debra-Ann Lynley's murder. She'd sent an "urgent inquiries" alert that had produced some responses but little of use. The majority had no possible connection, but then they'd widened the field considerably: "Any females attacked, injured or killed by a severe beating who were connected in any way to moving, moving companies, truck-drivers, or trucker venues including victims found on or alongside major highways including possible hitchhikers."

So this lead, of Tom Dawes' discovering a young woman's body a little bit off of a lay-by on the Trans-Canada Highway, seemed likely to the Vancouver police who flagged it for the immediate attention of Stillwell, the liaison officer for the RCMP. Cam Stillwell felt certain she'd found another match.

Details of the murder and information on the victim soon followed. Debra-Ann Lynley was a nineteen-year-old "missing person".

The police suspected she had just up and left. Her parents had been quick to report her disappearance but couldn't suggest any reasons why the girl would run. They tried to convince the police in their small town that Debra-Ann had been abducted but interviews with friends of the missing girl revealed that Debra-Ann had been pregnant and had aborted. Her parents had found out and a big blow-up occurred before Debra-Ann stomped out of the house, but it was only natural that they'd been reluctant to say so.

She'd gone to her boyfriend, Blaine, to tell him she was leaving. Blaine had been helpful and willing over the issue of abortion since neither of them wanted to marry or be saddled with raising a baby at their age and they were still close. They enjoyed a couple of hours in the bed of his camper to say goodbye.

Blaine's camper was parked in the backyard of his family's house and he lived there once the weather turned mild enough to sleep in an unheated mobile home. His mother objected that he'd moved into the camper way too early in the year, it was still cold, but it was well-equipped and, most importantly for a teenager, provided a private space to spend time with his friends.

Joanne had never been happy with the arrangement saying to her husband: "God only knows what they get up to out there. Drinking, having sex, smoking drugs.. He's underage, they're all underage, and we're responsible for the welfare of any kid who comes on our property."

"Hon, you're probably right about what they're doing but don't you see, they'd be doing it somewhere and I'd rather have him here where I can keep an eye on him and the people who come here. I don't want him and his buddies going downtown to hang out with a creepy, criminal crowd. That's another thing: I can sleep a lot better knowing Blaine isn't getting in a car with a drunk driver and that his pals can spend the night out there with him or walk to their own homes."

"I get all that, I do, but still what they're doing is illegal – I mean they're just kids – and since we're not doing anything to stop them then well, I think that we're not being very good parents, are we?

"No, we are being good parents because we're being realistic. We're looking out for our kid in the best way we know how considering the environment, the social environment, that kids live in these days. Booze and drugs are available, and sex is too. It all sounds like an adolescent paradise but you and I both know that isn't the case. Teenagers get themselves into scrapes with the law, get kicked out by their parents, fight with their girlfriends and each other. They suffer emotionally and they cry, they fly off the handle, they overindulge, and sometimes they kill themselves. Our back-door is less than 50 feet away if Blaine needs us. I feel good about that."

"Oh you, you just want the kids to think you're a cool parent."

"I am a cool parent – there's no thinking about it, it's fact. And since you're married to the cool parent well I guess you must be pretty cool too, eh?"

Debra-Ann did think Blaine's dad was cool, especially compared to her own parents, but not enough to confide in. She didn't imagine for a minute that he'd be supportive of her plan to hitch-hike to Vancouver, although it wasn't that far away, to get a job waitressing or clerking in a store or anything to get out of the house.

The Lynley's were a liberal-minded, respectable middle-class family and their daughter's pregnancy wasn't so much an occasion of sin as a let-down. Debra-Ann was tired of being made aware how disappointing she'd turned out to be. Frankly she'd have preferred a shouting match with name-calling and tears then some hugs and apologies after everything was said. At least then it would be over and done.

Blaine had been shook up by the news of Debra-Ann's pregnancy and was relieved at her decision to abort and to call it quits between them. He resolved that he'd be much more careful in his future relations. He scraped up some cash to help her on her way, wished her luck, and told her to keep in touch neither expecting, nor hoping, to ever hear from Debra-Ann again.

Debra-Ann had taken a bus to the outskirts of the town and headed off down the highway. She no longer felt weak from her procedure and was making good progress walking. When she heard a vehicle coming up behind she'd turn and stick her thumb out but wasn't too disillusioned by the lack of response. Her only worry was a that a police car would come upon her before a driver willing to offer a lift did.

As it turned out she was hitching less than an hour before she got lucky and picked up a ride. Unluckily, for her, it was with the Trans-Canada killer.

Chapter Fifty-Five

Thursday March 06 – Friday March 07, 1980

"I mean, the very last thing I need in my life right now is a baby, right? But my parents, they just couldn't, or rather wouldn't, understand. They said they'd look after it. Yeah, right like they looked after me. I mean, seriously, can you imagine me with a baby? Why the fuck would I want to saddle myself with a kid now?"

That's what she'd said to him. He looked over to the empty passenger seat and seemed to see her still there. Debra-Ann, teen queen, bitch-in-the-making, entitled, spoiled, destructive.

He usually didn't pick up hitch-hikers. Unlike many of his trucker contemporaries he didn't relish company on the road. He enjoyed the solitude of his own thoughts and wasn't enthusiastic about hearing the tales of woe the flotsam of the highways spewed out.

Grievances, complaints, running to a better life or running from a bad life. Or not running at all, just drifting. No plan, no goal, no money, and no ambition to earn any. For the most part. Sometimes they were young kids and those he'd pick up. Not to try to talk them into going back home, Hell he didn't know what kind of home they came out of, but simply to move them a little further along their way in safety.

Debra-Ann Lynley was a young girl but she elicited no sympathy from him. Her clothes, though tacky, weren't cheap. He could smell the perfume of her shampoo when she scooped back handfuls of the long blonde hair to throw over her shoulder. Thick, healthy-looking, shiny hair. Someone had cherished her and done their best to take care of her. This girl had been pampered in her home.

She liked being noticed, expected to be the centre of attention. She threw her hair around a lot, her hands always moving. To emphasize a point she'd slam her body back in the seat and sulk, slouched, legs pushed straight out. The ugly, clumsy-looking shoes were expensive.

"You see my parents would take over the baby, just the way they've always tried to run my life, and I'd be stuck there with them and with it. Sidelined, and right when my own life is just about to start. I can just see them with the blender brought out of storage and dusted off so they could puree vegetables into home-made baby food. Designer clothes and "oh isn't it darling it's from Oshkosh B'Gosh", educational pre-school toys, Montessori day-care, they'd probably even buy a new car with an integrated baby-seat.

Like I was really going to put myself through that. They nag me about smoking now, can you imagine how much they'd be on my case if I was smoking and pregnant? and drinking would be another no-no. If they want another baby they can just have their own. She thinks she's so young, let her go ahead and do it all over again. Maybe this time they'll have the son they always wanted. Aw to Hell with them and their stupid lives."

That girl was nothing but trash: swearing and smoking and flinging her hair about in his truck. Nothing but bitching and complaining. Sex education in her school system, birth-control available from her doctor, yet she'd been stupid enough to get herself knocked up. And selfish enough to get rid of the baby. No gratitude for the privileged middle-class life her parents had provided.

To kill the baby because it didn't fit in with her time-table, her ideas about herself and what she deserved, and what she was going to do. Selfishness. Putting their own concerns and their own wants before the needs of their children. Bitches, killer-bitches. Baby-killers.

The killer's thoughts drifted off for awhile. Away from words and into feelings. He drove another twenty miles before saying out loud: "Yeah, she deserved to die."

Chapter Fifty-Six

Thursday March 06 – Friday March 07, 1980

Karima, a coworker on Superintendent Petersen's task force, brought a file over to Cam's desk saying: "Here's a file referencing a murder that occurred in Kingston, Ontario. It actually happened on February 20th but the OPP didn't notify us until they received our second request for information. Based on that request they think this murder is connected to our inquiries."

"Are they right?"

"Yes, I believe so. The victim's battered body was found off the Trans-Canada highway and she had very recently moved into the area."

"Oh yes, that does sound like our man. Let me see, Kingston on the 20th of last month would be the first killing – first that we've heard of, anyhow – right? Have we plotted a timeline?"

"Yes, I've updated your notes with a diagram. It's all happening very quickly, isn't it?" She opened the file to show the sketch. "Here, have a look."

"Is this to scale?"

"I copied a map from the atlas and traced over it to mark our route."

"I see. Hmm, based on the information we have the sequence of murders is Kingston, Halifax, Montreal, Toronto, Winnipeg, Edmonton, and Vancouver. That's clear so far but we could easily be missing killings in between and even before these dates. For example, why were the women of Saskatchewan safe from our man?"

"I believe it only takes about seven hours to drive across Saskatchewan on the Trans-Canada meaning he wouldn't have had to stop so perhaps that's the reason?"

"Or nobody's notified us if there has been a death."

"Would you like me to follow up with the RCMP detachments? and are there local police forces as well?"

"Just in Saskatoon and Regina. RCMP covers the rest of the province. Yes, I think maybe we'd better check further. He could have killed before he got to Kingston or on the return trip to Edmonton. From the look of things the dates won't be too far apart."

"No, it's like this man is on a rampage of some sort."

"But it's unusual that the dates aren't getting closer together. I think that regular? normal? serials kill to an exact timeline (full moon, every x number of days) or else the gap between killings closes as their compulsion grows stronger. That's not what's happening here. Let's see, from first to second murder is two days, from second to third it's three days, but only one day from third to fourth, then three days again, four days, and two.

So it seems like he's keeping himself well enough in control to wait for the right victim or he's okay until some woman does or says something that sets him off?"

"Perhaps. Yes, it's possible. Will we ever know what triggered him off? No point speculating. We need to get ahead of this problem now. Right now I have to square things with the police in Edmonton before Inspector Lund shows up there to step on toes."

Chapter Fifty-Seven

Summer 2015

"You know what's really weird, Granpa T?

"What's that, Jake?"

"Well how come nobody noticed anything? In that newspaper story I read they mentioned that there were no witnesses. Or any people who were around just didn't see anything. That doesn't make sense."

"Too bad there were no curious kids like you around, eh? If you'd been there you would have spotted plenty and told the police all about it."

"No, I'm not so sure I'll tell the cops anything. You know they're always hassling me and my friends, all the school kids actually, when we're at the mall or the swimming pool or anywhere. They ask our names and to see our ID – as if we have ID! – and then they tell us we can't hang around and to go home. I mean it's supposed to be a free country but seems like the cops hate kids."

"As someone who has spent a lifetime travelling the highways I sure hate to see speed traps. I mean, as a professional driver hauling a payload in a very expensive piece of equipment I own I'm pretty sure I can safely judge what's a safe speed for me to be driving and don't need anybody writing me a ticket... where was I? Oh yeah, but I have major respect for the job those guys do when dealing with car smash-ups. Some of the stuff they see in these traffic accidents is just... well there are no words."

"Yeah, that part of the job sure would suck. But what you said before about me being a good witness well you got that right. But if the cops back then are anything like the cops are now they probably didn't even talk to any of the kids on the street. Probably just shooed them away. Nobody notices kids."

"Well don't expect that to change much when you become an adult out doing his job. Nobody notices the moving crew. When folks are moving out all the neighbours want to know is 'Where are you going?', 'How much did you sell for?', and 'Who did you sell to?'. And when we're delivering into a new location it's the opposite questions: 'How much did you pay for this place?', 'Where did you move from?', and 'Why did you move here?'. They like to look at the furniture going in or out of the truck, and they want to get a good look at the family but they sure don't want to look at us.

In fact, the people we move usually don't even remember our names even though it was policy at Big Sky that all drivers introduce themselves and their helpers. Also, we had to wear a uniform shirt and tie (just a clip-on, thank God), to look professional. If it got really hot – and moving furniture is hard, heavy work – then we could take off our shirts but only if we were wearing a t-shirt underneath. A plain t-shirt with no slogans or bright colours. Yeah they didn't want any good-looking bare-chested guys offending the neighbours." He grinned when Jake rolled his eyes at that remark.

"Teacher read us a story in school about a mailman committing a crime but nobody mentioned him because he was supposed to be there so he wasn't noticed."

"Yeah, same kind of thing. People see the truck, and worry that we're going to block their driveway, but they don't really see us so that's why no witnesses came forward with any evidence."

Chapter Fifty-Eight

Saturday March 08 – Sunday March 09, 1980

Pamela awoke shortly before her alarm rang. She turned the switch off and grabbed a cigarette and her lighter in one unthinking action. She needed the toilet but wasn't ready to get out from under the warm covers yet.

With a sigh she sat up reminding herself not to smoke while lying down in bed. It would be such a cliché death and she could hear her mother saying to the police: "I told her – over and over again I told her – don't ever, ever smoke in bed but she won't be told. Stubborn, that's what she is. I never even smoke in the bedroom never mind in the bed because I know what can happen but she's smarter than everybody and she just can't take a telling."

If Pamela's mother didn't smoke in bed it would only be because Dad wouldn't allow it. The two of them had quit smoking years before but Beverley kept picking up the habit again.

When she was smoking she'd only use one ashtray which she'd carry about from room to room. Pamela never knew if this was because her Dad didn't want to see dirty ashtrays everywhere or if her mother was afraid she'd leave a cigarette burning unattended. She did have a thing about fire and she had repeatedly told Pamela to never smoke in bed.

Since her bladder was now demanding immediate attention Pamela carried her cigarette into the bathroom. She had an ashtray in there, along with another lighter and a few cigarettes. If she stumbled through half-asleep in the middle of the night to pee she knew she'd want to light up.

Pamela never bothered to turn the lights on, telling herself "by now I know where all my parts are" and the flare from her lighter was always blinding. She thought it was possible what wakened her wasn't a call of nature but nicotine receptors screaming in her brain. No way she'd ever tell her mother about that!

During one of Beverley's non-smoking stints she'd suggested Pamela figure out how much money she was spending on cigarettes every month but Pamela flatly refused.

"I don't want to know that. I'm sure it's a really a large amount of money but I'm not going to quit so why would I make myself miserable?"

"But darling don't think of it as how much you spend, think of how much you could save, cash in hand, to buy yourself something really nice. Have a goal to work towards."

"Look Mum, some day I hope to light a cigarette and say 'ugh, that tastes terrible' and that's the day I'll quit smoking. If arguments about saving my health aren't enough to stop me then arguments about saving me money certainly won't. I like smoking and I'm hooked and that's not going to change anytime soon. In fact just having this conversation makes me crave a smoke."

"You're already smoking, I can hear you inhale."

"Now you're just being silly and I can't talk to you when you're like this. I'm trying to do my job as your mother to warn you, to give you good advice from my own experience that you should quit now because the longer you wait the harder it will be."

"I'm sure you're right but what can I say? Right now I'm not going to quit because I don't want to. I'm really enjoying this cigarette and the next one is going to taste just as good. Someday ... but not today. Thanks for trying Mum and I do love that you care."

"Of course I care, I'm your mother. I love you too."

When Beverley was back smoking again Pamela never taunted her. Although she'd never tried quitting herself she knew how difficult it could be.

"So not turning on lights in the dark could be the third thing that happens when you live alone," she mused. Recalling a previous conversation she'd had with Arnie when they'd been having lunch out and he'd caught her eating with her fingers she'd told him that losing your table manners was the second thing that happened when you lived in alone. Of course he'd asked what was the first? "The first thing is closing the bathroom door. One day you look up at the closed bathroom door and think 'why did I bother?' and that's it – you just stop closing doors after that."

"My wife does that now but only because she doesn't want to stop the conversation so she goes into the bathroom and just talks louder."

"Arnie you're always making cracks like that. Your poor wife.."

"Hey, you know what I'm talking about because I've seen you when she gets you on the phone and you're just going 'oh yeah? Yeah, uh-huh' while she's talking your ear off."

"OK I admit your wife is a talker, some women – and some men, too – love to yak on the phone. But the way you're going on anyone would think Kelly never shuts up!"

"She even talks in her sleep."

"Stop it" Pamela laughed. Looking heavenwards with his hand over his heart Arnie added: "Non-stop, I swear to God."

Remembering this conversation made Pamela smile all over again. She liked working with Arnie very much, He was an even-tempered man. She knew he had a tough streak but he never seemed to lose his cool even when straightening out some mouthy smart-aleck. He'd just say "Keep talking" and if the guy was dumb enough to do so it wouldn't be for long.

Since it was Saturday she didn't have to go in to work but knew Arnie would be at the warehouse for a while and thought about going in for a chat. She was positive that policeman was ready to arrest Gerry and she knew he was making a big mistake.

She felt she had to do something more than having yet another conversation about this. Both guys were heading to Calgary and she was off work until Monday. She decided to drive down and meet them to talk it over face-to-face. It was only about a three-hour drive, highway all the way, and the car could use a fast run to clean out any build up.

Chapter Fifty-Nine

Saturday March 08 – Sunday March 09, 1980

A late winter snowstorm was coming. Driving a tractor-trailer through the mountains took care and attention but Gerry had hustled to get through ahead of the bad weather and any highway shutdowns. A 20-hour wait at the side of the road was frustrating on a summer's day but mind-numbingly miserable in freezing rain.

Now that he was in Calgary he was anxious to see Pamela. He still couldn't believe she was driving down to meet him and agreed to stay with him at the motel. It didn't sound like she had a romantic rendezvous in mind but Gerry was always willing to go with the flow.

She was upset about something but wouldn't say what, just that something had happened and she had to see him face-to-face. When he'd told her where he'd be staying she'd said "Sure, I'll meet you there sometime tomorrow, I guess it'll be right after lunch".

Gerry wasn't the planning type, he was more of a "go with the flow" kind of guy who was up for pretty much anything and would enjoy a quiet night in bed or a crazy night at the bar. He'd wait until he met up with Pam before trying to figure out what was going on.

He was hoping to catch a least some of tomorrow night's hockey game, sure it it would a good one against Pittsburgh. The Edmonton Oilers had joined the NHL and they had a 19-year-old rookie called Wayne Gretzky who was something else. Gerry remembered talking about him with a few other drivers in Winnipeg and was looking forward to seeing the kid in action.

"I wonder if it's something to do with Dale?" he wondered. He'd tried to raise him on the CB to get a heads-up on what was going on but they hadn't connected. They'd both been on the Trans-Canada heading to Calgary but having only played phone-tag in Vancouver Gerry didn't know whether Dale was ahead of him or behind.

He'd heard chatter that Ray Frank had run into trouble and needed to hand off a buckshee job and Gerry would have helped him out but he'd already passed by.

He figured Dale must be behind him and if so Dale would help Ray, he'd already interlined one of his shipments a couple of weeks ago and if Ray was in trouble again Dale wouldn't hesitate. Ray was a good guy but he had health issues and staying on the road was a struggle. Everyone figured this would be his last summer and they'd all be helping him out as much as they could.

Of course when he did finally get to talk to Dale he wouldn't say anything about Pam coming to his motel, he didn't want to mess up his friendship with either of them.

Chapter Sixty

Saturday March 08 – Sunday March 09, 1980

Pamela drove around the building to the back doors of the warehouse where she knew she'd find Arnie. He greeted her arrival saying "Don't you have a home to go to?"

"Huh! Look who's talking"

"Yeah I do have a home to go to and that's why I'm here and if you lived in my home you'd understand." He had his jacket on but was sitting comfortably in an old recliner with a cooler of beer beside him. He had a bottle on the go and took a long swig before adding: "It's quiet and peaceful here."

Pamela sat down on an upright chair and asked "Where is everybody? I know we don't have any jobs on but there's usually one or two messing around with their trucks or else you've got them cleaning up or something."

"I told everybody to take the weekend off. There's nothing urgent and the forecast isn't good. So did you come by to talk about the cops being here yesterday?"

"Sorta. I'm actually on my way to Calgary and I've got to pick up some driver logs first."

"Why are you going to Calgary? You know there's a snowstorm warning out for the whole province, right? And I thought the cops took all the logs and stuff?"

"Yes, they did but I remembered that I've got copies in my Accounts Payable folder. For once I'm glad Hirsch is such a twerp: you know how he won't let me submit cheque requisitions in advance, right?

I think he's afraid he'll lose them or something. Anyhow, because of that I've got all the Fuel Reports sitting in a file waiting until the 10th, Monday, before I hand them in so he can get May to process them for the due date of the 15th. Anyhow, I keep a photocopy of that month's logs in the file so I've got the February logs and Gerry and Dale still have their March logs in their trucks."

"So what suddenly you're Nancy Drew and you're going to track down clues or something? Don't you think that's what the cops are doing already?"

"They're only looking for incriminating stuff and I..."

"Wait a minute, Pamela." Arnie interrupted. He was agitated and seemed determined to talk her out of making the trip. "Look I can't believe Dale or Gerry are involved in these murders but what if? Huh? What if the cops are right, what then?"

"They're not. C'mon, Arnie – we know these guys and we know they couldn't do anything like this. It's just not possible and I'll never believe it."

"That's what everybody says about other killers when the newspapers interview family and colleagues."

"Neither of these guys is a killer."

"I agree, I don't think so either, BUT what if we're wrong? You're just going to let yourself become another victim?"

"That's never going to happen – not in a million years!"

"You don't know that, Pam. You can't actually know that for sure."

"But Arnie I can, I do, I know these guys. I won't be in any danger."

"I think you're being naïve, I really do. You don't know how guys think, guys are... well, they have nasty thoughts. They can be looking right in your face and smiling and being pleasant and all the time they're thinking of doing dirty stuff to you. They don't do it but they think about it and they probably would do it if they thought they could get away with it."

"Arnie, that's icky. Look, I know you guys think differently I mean you still think it's funny that when Jack Baxter had jury duty I wrote "Jack off" for 5 days in the day-timer."

Arnie couldn't hold back an escaping chuckle.

"See! You still think it's funny. When you were trying to explain at the time why you were laughing so hard I honestly thought you were having a heart attack. Your face got all red and you were wheezing, couldn't catch a breath, but all the time you were laughing and news flash it really wasn't that funny, you know."

"Oh God! it was hilarious. You should have heard us before you got into the office. No on second thought it's way better that you didn't hear what we were saying. Ha ha ha. I'm still laughing about it."

"You guys are idiots."

"But seriously Pamela that's what I mean about you being kind of naïve some times and this idea of driving to Calgary, in a snowstorm yet, to meet up with a couple of guys who the cops think one is a serial killer well, that's just crazy."

"And the cops only think it's Gerry, not Dale. Sure, they've talked to Dale a few times but I can tell that they think Gerry's the guy. Anyhow, you're not going to change my mind and, obviously, I'm not going to change yours, so I'm just going to grab the file and then I'm heading out."

"But the forecast.."

"I'm hours ahead of the storm which might just blow right through anyhow. and with that Pamela walked through the warehouse to the office. She stopped at the door to call back: "Besides, I wouldn't object to being snowed in at Cowtown for a long weekend!"

Chapter Sixty-One

Saturday March 08 – Sunday March 09, 1980

Dale was getting close to Calgary when he spotted a stranded motorist up ahead. The road conditions weren't that bad, not like they were going to be if the forecast was accurate, but nevertheless the little Honda Civic had managed to end up in the ditch.

Pamela drove a Honda Civic, gold-coloured. There weren't too many on the roads out West but he'd seen quite a few when his trips took him to Toronto and Ottawa. Of course gas was more expensive back east.

He wasn't going to try to haul the car out but he'd offer a lift into the city where the driver could arrange a tow-truck, or maybe Calgary was home and he could get help from friends.

He'd started to slow down before he recognized the car and decided he wasn't going to stop. That same car had gone racing past him a few miles back, driving way too fast even if the road had been bone dry which it sure wasn't. As a man who earned his living on the highway he had no sympathy for reckless driving.

However, it was very cold and getting dark and there were no other vehicle lights coming up behind so it was down to him. He unlatched his briefcase and slipped his gun into his pocket, just to be on the safe side. Then he saw that there was only one person in the car and it was a woman.

The headache that always hovered under his consciousness flared up. He stopped his truck.

Chapter Sixty-Two

Saturday March 08 – Sunday March 09, 1980

Pamela was speeding down Highway 2 but with her mind on the meeting ahead she wasn't aware of how fast she was driving. Until she saw the flashing lights of a police car up ahead. Some other driver's luck had run out while, fortunately, she had plenty of time to drop back down to the speed limit.

She was in no mood to talk to any more cops anyhow.

Maybe what she was doing was stupid, even dangerous, but she couldn't believe that. It couldn't be Gerry, no way, ever, uh-uh, that was impossible. She had to meet with him before he got arrested. She didn't imagine her phone would be bugged or anything but she felt that if she could see him in person she'd know for sure.

"No," she spoke out loud, "I already do know. I know he's innocent of this. I just need to get his log-book out of his truck and I'll be able to work it all out, trace through his route and find the proof of his innocence."

Gerry a killer? No way. There was no way she could be so wrong about somebody. Sure, she'd made poor judgement calls before but she'd been fooled, well no even fooled: the love of her life hadn't cheated on her, he hadn't valued her for herself. She thought she'd meant the world to him and for awhile she did – so long as she came gift-wrapped with babies and a white picket fence.

"Ugh, stop thinking about him and about that." she told herself. "This is what matters now. Gerry and I well we're never going to be an item but... he's my friend and he's a really nice man. He's probably horrible to have as a husband well no probably about that but he's a gentle person and he loves women and it just isn't possible that he's a killer."

Pamela wished she could have spoken to Dale before she left but he was on the road himself and they'd all meet up eventually. It would be good to see them both and she felt sure they'd get everything sorted out with an airtight alibi for Gerry all wrapped up and ready to present to the police.

If the storm blowing up from Montana was as bad as predicted they might even get snowed in. Pamela lit up yet another cigarette thinking how attractive that prospect would have been under very different circumstances.

Chapter Sixty-Three

Pamela spotted Gerry's truck as she approached Motel Row and swung into the parking lot of the Rite-Price. She got out of the car and stretched muscles stiff from the long drive and the tension she was feeling.

Gerry came out of the lobby door uncertain of Pamela's mood but when he saw the worried look on her face he pulled her into a tight embrace saying: "Hey now, whatever it is it's going to be OK, baby."

Pamela allowed herself a moment's comfort in his arms before stepping back and telling him not to call her 'baby'.

"We need to talk, I need coffee or a drink or maybe both, and I really need to find a Ladies room."

"The motel's got a restaurant..." Gerry began but Pamela interrupted saying: "No, I can't be dealing with you flirting with the hostess and the waitress and chatting to every other diner in the place – I need somewhere private and impersonal. I can see the Golden Arches so let's head over there."

"Are you sure? it'll be full of noisy kids. At least let's go the Country Style it's just a bit further on. Here, I'll drive. You look worn out." Pamela handed him the keys and walked round to the passenger seat. Gerry was pushing the seat back as far as it would go when the first snowflakes started to fall.

"So I was really happy when you said you wanted to come here but seeing you now I don't think I can look forward to a dirty weekend, can I? What did you want to see me about?"

"Let's wait till we're settled in the doughnut shop, it's going to be a long conversation."

They decided to get their orders to go when they arrived and found the restaurant three-quarters full. While Gerry paid Pamela went to the washroom.

In the mirror she saw her worried look and forced herself to relax. She splashed water on her face and gave her hair a good brushing. She realized she did know that Gerry was innocent and resolved to help him clear his name.

Back in the car they drove to the far corner of the parking-lot and had complete privacy for their discussion. Pamela came right to the point.

"When did you last talk to the police about these highway murders, Gerry?"

"What murders? I talked to the police in Winnipeg about Denise but that's the only murder I knew about ... oh wait, you told me about that customer in Edmonton who got killed but there's she was a battered wife and it was her husband, right?"

"Oh Gerry, there's been a whole bunch of murders – all women, all beaten to death, and all in places where you've been so the police think you're the killer."

"What?!?"

"I know it wasn't you, that's why I'm here. Well, no I wasn't 100 percent sure until I saw you but only because the way the police talked they had me thinking crazy thoughts. Anyhow, we've got a head start..."

"Head start on what? I'm not going anywhere I need to get this sorted."

"Exactly, I didn't mean you should run. I meant we can backtrack, like I always have to do when I'm trying to make sense of your logs, and we can get the proof that you couldn't have done this."

"My logs, God they're a mess – as always."

"And, as always, I'll be able to clean them up. Piecing together your receipts is like doing a jigsaw puzzle. Especially since you always have so many gas receipts."

"No choice. I have to stay under the threshold where they phone to get authorization for the credit card."

Pamela smiled and then started to laugh, actually more of a giggle and a little high-pitched but she felt the tension start to ease away.

"I suppose we better go back and get started. Is everything in the truck?"

"No, I already checked in so I've got most my stuff in the room because I really was going to do some work on my logs before you came. As it happened I ran into a couple of guys at the front desk and we got talking and you know how it is so I didn't actually get anything done."

"Wow what a surprise. OK, we'll do this in the room but Gerry there better be twin beds."

"Two doubles as a matter of fact but seriously Pamela this is some crazy shit you're talking about. I mean, no way the cops can think I killed anybody. I talked to that plainclothes cop in Winnipeg and got everything squared away. What makes you think they think it's got anything to do with me?"

"Gerry they had a warrant and they took all kinds of stuff out of dispatch and they specifically asked questions about your trip."

"What about Dale? Wait I don't mean he has anything to do with this but do you mean they only asked about me?"

"No, they asked for Dale's paperwork as well. I don't know if that was to be thorough, or if they don't really know, or if it was to cover their interest in you because Gerry that one cop asked lots of questions about you and he was really interested in you. I was really worried."

Chapter Sixty-Four

Saturday March 08 – Sunday March 09, 1980

"Thank you, thank you so much for stopping. Thank God. I've been worried sick. I knew it was foolish to even think about walking but I was starting to wonder if anyone was every going to come along" said the woman as she grabbed a shoulder bag and purse and the keys from her car.

She was young, no more than late twenties, and her cold-pinched face was very pretty despite red-rimmed eyes and sniffles from crying. She was hugging an infant to her chest.

"I've been able to keep him warm so far but who knows for how long? So you really are a life-saver. Bless you. Thank you again and God bless." Dale opened his passenger door and helped her to climb up.

He saw that she'd taken off her scarf and wrapped it around the baby before tucking him inside her coat. The hand that grasped his was freezing cold and when she settled into the warmth of the cab she sighed loudly with relief.

"He's just got over being sick with a bad cough and fever and when I heard on the radio about the storm coming I just panicked and drove too fast because I didn't want him to out in the car in bad weather and then I did the worst possible thing and crashed. And to think I came this way because I thought it would be quicker."

"This is the quickest way to Calgary." said Dale.

"Oh we're not going to Calgary, we live at Ghost Lake."

"I thought that was just a summer town."

"It is but me and my boyfriend got taken on as caretakers at the new lodge so we're there year-round."

"That's north of here though, right? Sorry but I've got a schedule. I can take you into Calgary or you can wait for the next vehicle that comes along."

"Oh no, oh please it's really not that much out of the way. We can cut through on the Morley Road, the exit is just up ahead, and it will only be an extra 15-20 minutes tops. And no one else is coming, look there's nobody on the road, and it's almost dark. Please? Can't you please help us out?"

Dale looked at the baby and then into the young mother's pleading face. Thinking how could he abandon this woman and her child and knowing he couldn't.

"I know that road goes through the reservation but where does it come out?"

"On Bow Valley Trail which is really 1A, a good road, and then straight into Ghost Lake. You can stay on 1A and come into Calgary from the northwest or go south on 22 to get back to the Trans-Canada. Really, it's easy."

"OK, OK let me just think for a minute." Dale suddenly felt woozy with the pain pounding in his temples and spots sparking before his eyes. He took a deep breath and said to his passenger: "I'll take you two to Ghost Lake but I've got a brutal headache, maybe a migraine, and I can't talk and I can't listen right now. Sorry, but please don't talk, OK?"

The young mother looked closely at him and said in a quiet voice: "Are you sure you can drive?"

"Yes, yes no problem there. I can drive. I can always drive. I just need quiet so I can concentrate."

She nodded, conscious of the need to keep very quiet and very inconspicuous.

They drove on in silence while Dale struggled to clear his mind to concentrate on his driving and not the pain and not the mish-mash of thoughts crowding in.

Chapter Sixty-Five

Saturday March 08 – Sunday March 09, 1980

Gerry watched appreciatively as Pamela stretched. Despite the very real risk of a wrongful arrest Gerry was also very much aware of her sitting on his bed and his mind travelled that familiar path. He'd always been successful with the ladies and seduction came as natural as breathing.

"Phew, I think we've finally got it worked out. I don't know the exact dates of all the murders but I do know the sequence and I know where they happened: Kingston – you drove through there; Halifax – you delivered there; Toronto – you delivered and loaded there; Winnipeg – you were at the hotel; and Edmonton – you were going to be at that move but the night before the lady was murdered by her husband. So it's all coincidence except that the Kingston job wasn't your shipment so you had no reason to stop there. You filled out in Cold Lake picking up your load for Halifax. Although the Kingston job originated in Edmonton it didn't leave on any of our trucks."

"This is great. You're a sweetheart for getting my logs straightened out and my fuel receipts and hotel receipts prove where I was and when. I know I didn't kill anybody and now I can show this to the police and once they check it out they'll know it too."

Pamela flopped back on the bed saying: "I'm beat. I was feeling pretty stressed when I drove down here, worrying about all of this stuff, and now that it's sorted I just want to flake out."

Gerry moved beside her and gave her shoulders a massage, pressing his fingers down hard. Pamela groaned with pleasure feeling the kinks release. He pushed her hair over one shoulder and bending his head to her neck lightly kissed her.

"Feels good Gerry but it feels too good if you know what I mean."

"I do know because I am very good at making women feel good."

"So I've heard" she said, twisting away from him but he pulled her close and gently licked around her ear. His breath was hot but it gave her shivers.

"Gerry, stop. Really. I don't want to do this."

"Of course you do. Look, no more kidding okay? I've been with hundreds of women and believe me I know what I'm doing, I know how to please a woman, and I definitely know I can please you. I love my life and I don't want to settle down so what I offer is a lot of fun with no strings attached. I realize I'm not the guy you think you want but I'm for sure the guy you need. And I can make you want me, too."

"Gerry that's just, just so.."

"Pushy? Arrogant? I know but Pam I also know that yeah, I am that good. And everyone can do with some good loving."

She studied his face and saw that he was sincere. A night of letting go to his skilful hands and lips was very, very tempting but Pamela knew it wasn't her way.

"Am I tempted? Absolutely! But am I going to give in? absolutely not. I'm flattered and yes, I'm certain you could give me a night to remember as they say but thanks, no thanks. I think we just met at the wrong time, Gerry."

"Well I can at least give you one of my nationally famous stress-busting back rubs, eh?"

"I'll have to say no to that one as well but maybe a rain check?"

"Deal. Now let's go get a drink, I'm sure the bar will have Hockey Night in Canada on the TV." Gerry shovelled his paperwork back into his briefcase and Pamela gathered up her things too.

"Oh, yes. The Oilers are playing tonight."

"Did you hear Calgary's probably going to get an NHL team for the upcoming season?"

"I heard something about them doing a deal with Atlanta?"

"Can you imagine? if it happens the Stanley Cup will never leave Alberta!"

Pamela had her purse and files and grabbed her overnight bag.

"Just leave your stuff here."

"No, I'm going to get my own room while you're ordering the drinks..."

Gerry angrily said: "Well make sure you don't pay because Dale can settle the bill tomorrow morning."

"Gerry, that's a cheap shot."

"But true, right?"

"Actually no, you're totally off-base."

"Is it?"

"Yeah, what the hell's wrong with you? I'm here trying to help you and you're making these wisecracks about my personal life? That's really lousy."

"Oh I'm sorry, Pammy. That's just my frustration talking."

"Look you and I both know that you'll probably – no, make that 99.9% definitely – have company to entertain tonight so I'm just giving you your privacy."

"You don't have to," he grinned and gave a Groucho Marx eyebrow wiggle, "I'm happy to share."

Pamela laughed far harder than the joke warranted but felt she'd luckily sidestepped what could have been a situation.

When she met up with him again at the bar a short while later there was no awkwardness between them.

"Before we grab a table let's have a dance, sweetheart."

"Oh Gerry you know I'm not a fan of this country stuff and I can't line-dance anyhow." said Pamela over her shoulder as she led the way to a table. They'd just gotten seated when a slow ballad began playing and Gerry took her hand saying:

"You gotta love JD Souther, right? I mean 'When You're Only Lonely' is a classic. C'mon, on your feet."

"OK, I do know this song and it is a nice one so we'll have one dance."

They headed onto the floor and Gerry pulled her close. He smelled good and he danced well but Pamela pulled back a little thinking it was wise to keep her distance. He noticed and tightened his grip while he smiled: "Sure I can't change your mind? Maybe they'll play Bellamy Brothers next – you know the one 'If I Said You Had a Beautiful Body Would You Hold It Against Me'?"

"God every trucker uses that line. Now I know why you're such a fan of Country. But listen, aren't you worried that by dancing with me the single ladies are going to think you're taken?"

He threw back his head and gave a loud laugh. A surefire trick to get the attention of everybody within hearing distance.

"The most attractive aspect of a man is whether or not he's got a woman on his arm. Dancing with you makes me instantly more interesting then if I was just standing by my lonesome at the bar. Women like the challenge of catching a man's eye and drawing it away from whoever's keeping him company."

"No they don't. Women aren't attracted to someone because he's taken."

"Uh-uh, you mean nice women aren't. But darlin' I'm not looking for a nice woman tonight." He pulled her close again to whisper in her ear "There's nothing like a bit of 'strange stuff' Pammy, admit it hon, you're interested."

She tilted her head back, narrowed her eyes, and bit at her lower lip saying "Well let's hope some hot-to-trot female is looking at us eyeballing each other right now and thinking she'd like some of your action." With that Pamela stepped away leaving Gerry looking hopeful.

Chapter Sixty-Six

Saturday March 08 – Sunday March 09, 1980

Dale swung his truck onto the exit and his headlights lit up an area empty of traffic or even signs of habitation.

"I'm really not sure about this, the reserve is private land.." he began but the woman interrupted saying: "It's a highway, it's 133x and that's a provincial highway so we have every right to be here. Just keep going, it really is the fastest way."

So they carried on in the growing dark. Occasionally, in the distance, they'd spot the lights of a home set a ways off the road. To some this would be a lonely, isolated spot but others would find it satisfyingly peaceful. Dale figured that on a clear night, not one heavy with snow clouds, the sky must look fantastic, a great big sky – like the name on the side of his truck – with millions of stars visible.

As soon as they crossed over the Bow River she instructed him to turn left but he pointed out the sign saying they should stay on the main road heading northeast to Ghost Lake.

"No, turn right up there, see? It's quicker."

"I can't go on that dirt road, I might get stuck, we'll just have to continue.. aarrggghh!" he cried out in shock and pain. He'd been stabbed! The woman had pulled a knife from her bag and stabbed his upper leg. The pain was enormous, throbbing and insistent, he grabbed for the handle but her words stopped him: "I've probably cut the femoral artery but even if I've just nicked it you better leave that knife just exactly where or you'll bleed out in two minutes. So turn onto that road now."

Dale had no choice but to obey.

As soon as he pulled on to the road a car switched on its headlights. Dale figured out he was being hijacked as his door opened and a man was yelling at him to hand over the keys so he could unlock the trailer but the woman called out that there was no need.

"The shipment's here in his bunk. I recognized the name on the boxes, there's just a couple of them, so move him out of the way and I'll hand them to you."

She placed the baby, which hadn't uttered a sound during all of this yelling, down on the floor. Dale knew it was a real baby because he could still hear its loud breathing and wondered if that meant the infant had been drugged or was still sick from the cold the mother claimed he'd had.

As he was dragged out of the cab and dumped on the ground he had time to think "Drugs, of course." That buckshee shipment he'd picked up from Ray Frank. Lightweight boxes. Drugs from British Columbia, in from the port having originated in the Far East, because there wasn't enough weight to be a payload of homegrown BC Bud.

From start to finish the heist had taken less than five minutes but Dale was in a great deal of pain from his aching thigh. He was doing his best to hold the knife in place but he felt consciousness slipping away. When would anyone find him here? way off the Trans-Canada with no one having heard from him for hours. What were his chances?

Both the man and woman were standing over him but they were just dark shapes standing in front of the car's headlights. He knew they weren't going to help.

Looking down the man said "Did this guy grab you or anything?" and even though the woman shook her head "No" the man gave Dale a vicious kick anyway.

"No, he's not a groper or a rapist he's a knight-in-shining-armour. Rescuer of poor women at the roadside. You've learned a really good lesson here so it's just too bad you won't live long enough to profit from it. Sorry Dude, but my fingerprints are on file." She said as she bent down and yanked the knife out of Dale's leg. The pain was intense and it drove him deeper into the blackness in his mind.

That darkness was a familiar place but this time Dale couldn't surrender to it. Ironically the pain was his lifeline and he was shocked into awareness and suffering. He had to focus on his wound. The depth of pain made him relive the car crash that happened shortly before Christmas, less than four months ago.

That bitch of a woman. The roads were bad and she was drunk and it doesn't take bad driving conditions to make a bad driver in those circumstances. So typical that she walked away unhurt. It was her children who'd felt the pain of the crash. Two little kids in the back-seat of the car, no seat-belts, no protection from the impact, and no protection from a mother who drove drunk. They'd almost made it to their home and if she'd been able to stop, if she hadn't skidded, if she'd kept driving, if, if, if...

He could remember every detail of it. The blow to his head hadn't destroyed that memory, although he wished to God it had. He'd had to fight to keep the truck in line after the crash. He could feel the imbalance when the trailer started sliding round before striking the back-end of the car where the boy and girl were sitting.

He didn't know if he heard their scream, or their mother's, or his own.

Someone screamed, maybe all of them screamed. The screams, the crash, more screams, then silence. His mind was dazed with the shock but his body was already moving, jumping out of the cab to run round to the car even as his brain was saying "You don't want to see what you're going to see there."

During his hospital stay he'd managed to repress those thoughts and the vicious violence of his rage. The worst moment of his life. When Sissy died his heart was wrenched apart and the sadness he felt changed him but killing those two children destroyed him. Only the knowledge that he had done nothing wrong – that he wasn't under the influence of tiredness, distraction, drink or drugs – that he as an experienced professional driver kept him sane.

Other thoughts tried to push up into consciousness but he felt his mind skittering away from those memories. And even now the anger surged within, black vengeful vitriol and blood-red spatters ... he needed to escape these thoughts ... he didn't want his last memory to be ... that horrible scene ... other horrible violent scenes ... thoughts? or memories? He was slipping into shock and forced himself to concentrate on what was happening now.

Suddenly he felt so cold, bone-deep cold. He couldn't feel the snowflakes falling on his face. His life's blood drained away into the gravel and dirt of a road that would soon be covered with snow from the incoming storm.

Traffic on the Trans-Canada Highway was sparse due to the slippery driving conditions brought on by the bad weather but the road, a vital national artery, stayed open and the vehicles kept moving along.

Dale knew the RCMP would be patrolling for stranded motorists and car accidents. He pulled the gun from his pocket and fired.

Sound travels far in the quiet roads outside the city so he was pretty sure someone would hear but would it be too late?

Chapter Sixty-Seven

Saturday March 08 – Sunday March 09, 1980

Comfortably seated at a high-top table in the bar Gerry had already, as he put it, 'scoped the talent' and found it favourable. After a satisfying swallow of beer he said: "Dale was in all of those places, too."

"What?" Pamela was rummaging in her purse for a new pack of cigarettes and missed his smirk.

"Where the killings occurred, Dale was there at the right time. Just like me."

"Yes, but he's in the clear because the same reasoning that applies to you applies to him – he didn't take the load from Edmonton to Kingston."

"No, but he interlined a load to Kingston in Regina."

"What? From who? Whom."

"Ray Frank, you know I don't think he's going to get through this season. He's having trouble keeping up now and we're not even busy yet."

"What's wrong with Ray?"

"He isn't saying but I know for a fact he's been coughing up blood because I saw it happen."

"Oh God, that probably means, well, cancer, right?"

"That's what we all think but nobody's saying anything. Insurance premiums are really high when you're self-employed and if the insurance companies get even a hint of something wrong the bastards will cut you off."

"So you're saying Ray might have loaded the Edmonton shipment but got sick or something in Regina so Dale took the load on to Kingston for him?"

"Yeah, Dale definitely delivered Ray's load in Kingston and then he went on to Halifax. I met him there. We met up again in Toronto and in Winnipeg and in Edmonton."

"So if the police suspected you because of where you were they'll probably suspect Dale now too."

"Yeah but we both know Dale couldn't murder anybody. His logs are probably perfect so he won't even need your help to prove where he was and when."

"He is a good record-keeper, but I wish he was here now so we could check everything over." Pamela was thinking she'd narrowly missed making a big mistake. Gerry was so attractive and so persuasive and she'd almost succumbed to his charm.

She was having a reaction to the stress of the past couple of days but nevertheless... the last thing she needed was a one-night stand with the room-mate of the man she was interested in. And she realized that with Gerry it would have to be nothing more than a one-time thing.

"We'll just have to wait for Dale to get in."

"Yes, we both know he can't possibly be the killer but I'll definitely feel better once he's here and we've talked to him. But since the Kingston woman wasn't killed in her home then just being there doesn't have to mean anything, after all Gerry you were there too, you phoned and told me about it."

"Yeah that's right. The traffic was backed up for miles and everybody was bitching about it on their radios. Funny there was no chatter about the Vancouver body."

"What Vancouver body?"

"I only just heard about it. Apparently a young girl, probably a hitchhiker, was found dead in some bush by the highway round about Abbottsford on Friday or Saturday. No one knows anything too specific but again the RCMP are chasing down truckers with questions. I guess the cops do think there's a connection."

"Don't you? Christ, women are dropping like flies along the Trans-Canada. It must be connected and it must be connected to truckers."

"Well in Kingston there were a fair number of moving trucks so yeah, it could have been anyone. I mean if it really was a household mover then the killer is almost definitely someone we know. But not me, I love the ladies."

"That's for sure! Just convince the cops and you're free and clear."

"I think you got that wrong, you know? Because when I talked to the cops it was all good, no problemo ... hey, what the fuck is buddy doing over there?" exclaimed Gerry jumping to his feet.

Pam turned, looking at the pool tables situated behind her chair, and saw a player swinging his cue wildly while several voices yelled at once and two gunshots rang out.

Chapter Sixty-Eight

Saturday March 08 – Sunday March 09, 1980

Pamela hadn't planned on spending her Saturday night at the Foothills Hospital but here she was, and had been for hours. She'd be sure to tell Gerry that 'he really knew how to show a girl a good time' once she got to talk to him.

Of course he'd been in the middle of things when the fight broke out in the bar and caught a bullet in his shoulder. The surgery was a success and now she was waiting for him to come out of recovery. She'd been terrified at the amount of blood he'd shed but the doctors assured her all was well.

Now she could relax enough to be pissed at him. "The guy is just a magnet for trouble." she thought to herself. "He'll probably say it's my fault for not hopping in to bed with him when he asked. Just the kind of thing he would say. Jerk."

The hospital was very busy with both the smoking and non-smoking visitor lounges packed full. Pamela headed outside thinking the air would be chilly but at least it would be fresh and free of antiseptic hospital smells. She'd have a cigarette or two and then head back upstairs. She wanted to see Gerry for herself to know he was going to be okay. Then she'd head back to the hotel. She imagined the police would be there and wanting to talk to her.

She made her way through the crowd just as a medical team hurried to the doors to meet an ambulance crew rushing in. The urgency of the crew with this new casualty was striking, even if the midst of all the trauma and suffering in the Emergency waiting area. Pamela hurried out of the way but not before taking a peek at the stretcher thinking "That poor person... is it a woman? no, it's a man ... it's - oh my God - it's Dale!"

Chapter Sixty-Nine

Summer 2015

Jake's eyes grew huge and his mouth dropped open in surprise. "You mean that was true about the police actually questioning you at the time?"

"They did but you know what buddy? We gotta get going or Grammy-Pammy will be gettin' on our case, eh?"

"No she won't, she'll be busy visiting with the man who's coming."

"What? Who's coming over?"

"I don't know his name, some guy who is visiting. Someone from way back who is in town."

"When did she tell you this? and why didn't she tell me?"

"You were already in the truck – remember she made me come back to get this jacket and bring it? And she just hung up the phone and said a surprise visitor was dropping by."

"An old friend?"

"Actually, she said 'an old rival' but I don't know what she meant. Anyhow, you can still tell me about being grilled by the cops – I heard them say that on TV. Did they have you in a jail cell or just an interview room? And were you there for long?"

"For ages, it felt like. I was 'helping with their inquiries'..."

"That means you were a suspect!!!" squealed Jake.

"I was, but I wasn't the only one. You see Smokey decided that the killer had to be a long-distance trucker. I don't know all the ins and outs of it but from what I can figure the cops found clues to indicate he worked for a moving company. So, there were plenty of us on the road at the time even though it was still the pre-season, and they interviewed us all."

"At the police station? In one of those rooms with the two-way glass and everything?"

"No, as it turned out we did go to the police station but first we got interviewed in a room at the Queen's Hotel in Winnipeg. That's where one of the murders occurred you know."

"Denise Drake, the dancer." He dropped his voice to whisper: "She danced without any clothes on."

"Oh her. Well, I'd forgotten her name but yeah, that sounds familiar. You do know your stuff, don't you? You've got it all down pat. Anyhow, they interviewed us all, one at a time of course, and told us to come by the police station next morning to sign our statements before we left town.

Now it isn't easy getting around streets in a tractor-trailer so when somebody suggested a few of us grab a cab and go together to sign I thought that was a really good idea since it saved me the hassle of unhooking. I was heading out right away, see."

"So then what happened?"

"I drove to Edmonton, probably straight through since that's what I usually did when I was heading home."

"No, I mean you had your interview, then signed your statement, but that wasn't the end of the murders so didn't the police ever talk to you again?"

"Well yeah, they did in Edmonton. There was another killing, in fact our company was supposed to be moving that poor woman, so I talked to the police then but it was different police and they already had a suspect."

"I thought they made a connection between that killing – and the next one too – with all the rest?"

"They did, or rather the RCMP did, but not then. Although they were probably putting it together then, I mean they're not stupid."

"So it was just Winnipeg police and then Edmonton police that you talked to, right?"

"Let's think, mmm yeah, that's right. After I talked to the Edmonton police I went to Vancouver to deliver. Had a quick turnaround back to Alberta."

"Didn't the RCMP ever talk to you?"

"Probably, but I don't remember anything else because that's when I was back in hospital in Calgary with my injured leg and I was out of it most of the time. They told me afterwards I was lucky I survived. Hospitalized twice in just a few months! It was awful."

"Aww, you probably actually knew the killer, eh? I mean you told me that the household movers were friendly, helped each other out on the road, stuff like that so it's practically for sure that you knew the guy, but you can't remember." Jake couldn't keep the disappointment from his voice.

"Well, I gotta say, Jake, that he wouldn't a been the kinda guy I'd really want to know, right? Not being a killer and all."

"I guess not."

"I mean, if he thought I knew who he was he mighta killed me too."

"Naw, you're a man and he only killed women."

"That we know of, I mean he could have committed other murders that never got connected to him, after all they never caught the guy."

"But they would never give up looking, right? Not when he killed a bunch of women."

The old man eyes lost focus while he pondered and after a long pause he said: "Well, I'm thinking the killer would have to be pretty old by now, in fact everybody involved would be old – look at me! – or maybe even dead after all this time. But you're right, the case can always be reopened if there's any new evidence."

"That because there's no Statue of Limits on murder, least that's what they said on 'Rockford Files'"

"First of all it's Statute of Limitations: not Statue and not Limits, and secondly while Jim Rockford is a good guy, and it's a great show, it's not Canadian and neither is the Statute. We don't have that here, there's no time limit on prosecuting crimes. That's an American thing which you've learned about, sorta, because all the TV shows you watch come from the US. Well and from Britain, like 'Benny Hill' – are you allowed to watch that?"

"Aww, they don't care what I do so I can watch what I want and yeah, I like Benny Hill and we get 'On the Buses', too."

"Oh I like that one, that's a good laugh. And in this old world Jake you find your laughs when and where you can."

"Yeah I guess... but I'm still interested in the Trans-Canada Killer. Did they ever wonder if maybe he was a woman?"

"A woman! I never heard a hint of anything like that. Hmmph, I suppose it's possible.."

"The victims weren't found naked or nothing so you see it wasn't one of those sex crimes."

"Ah, well then I guess it could have been a woman but no, the cops were pretty sure it was a trucker."

"So? There's women who drive trucks."

"Not back then they didn't. I mean, I never once met a lady furniture mover. Women did the packing and unpacking, and lots of drivers' wives rode with them and some, like your grandmother, would do a bit of driving when it was just miles of plain highway, but that was it. No women ran their own trucks. Oh I suppose maybe some freight haulers. I mean, they just hook up to a loaded trailer and drive and then at destination they drop the trailer for someone else to unload and hook up for a return trip. There's no real labour involved. But the cops were sure the killer was a mover, not a freight hauler. Moving was the connection."

"That's right. All of the victims had moved, or were just about to move or something, and that's how they met him and let him into their homes but that's about all they know. Nobody knows much of anything about him, I mean like why did he kill those women? what started him off? and why did he suddenly stop?"

"Maybe he didn't stop. Maybe he moved to the States or even another country and no one ever made any connections so he didn't have to stop."

"Geez, you think that's what happened?"

"I don't know what happened, I'm just speculating and wonderin' and hey, maybe he just didn't feel the need any more."

Jake rubbed his lips, a gesture he used when he was thinking about something, smearing blueberry juice across his mouth. "What need, a need to kill you mean?"

"I don't know what I mean we're just talking here, throwing out ideas, right?"

"Yeah but do you mean maybe the need to kill was like a sickness and he got better?"

The old man paused to consider Jake's question. "Hmm, that seems... somehow familiar."

"Or some people think he must have died."

"Maybe he did. We just have to be thankful that he did stop. For whatever reason. And I'm also thankful that if it was somebody I knew that I never actually knew it, get what I mean?"

Jake smiled and started to say how cool that would have been when he interrupted himself to announce: "There's Granma with the guy."

Grandpa T squinted to make out the visitor's face. He felt his mouth form a huge grin as he hollered: "Well, hey! If it isn't old reprobate Gerry Tanner!"

Gerry smiled back and shaking his head replied: "I can't believe Pammy's put up with you all these years, Dale!"

WHAT HAPPENED
NEXT

a novella

Lynda French

What Happened Next

Lynda French

Published by Lynda French, 2023

Chapter One

"God, I really wish you were dead," thought Pamela looking through the window at Gerry.

Dale must have said something funny because the two of them exploded into laughter. Seeing Gerry throw his head back to let out his trademark laugh brought a rush of emotion: affection for the man she once knew, anger for what he meant to her now, and fear of what he represented.

The big pine tree covered half the window in shade so she saw her own reflection side-by-side with her view of the two men. The three of them had aged considerably.

"After all it has been decades," she reminded herself. "But Gerry looks the worst even though Dale is the oldest."

This afternoon when she saw Gerry getting out of his rental car he'd looked the same: tall, sandy-haired, clean-shaven. A big solid man whereas Dale was rangier in build.

Gerry was dressed the same as always with his shirt tucked into tight blue jeans to show off a Peterbilt belt buckle, and well-worn cowboy boots. But as he drew closer, and she had a better look at him, the changes in his appearance shocked her. She couldn't help but wonder if he was thinking the same thing about her.

Gerry hadn't gotten fat, but he was wider. "I guess I mean thickened: thicker waist, chest, face, even," she thought. And his face also bore a million wrinkles – particularly around his eyes which were still the light blue colour she remembered so well. The wrinkles showed his age but didn't detract from his good looks. They crinkled as he smiled saying:

"Well, you've stared long enough so what's the verdict?"

"Another example proving life isn't fair. Men age so much better than women do."

He took his time looking her up and down while drawling, "Oh darlin' I wouldn't say that."

Pam burst out laughing and gave him a big hug.

"You've always been great for my ego – so long as there are no other women around for me to realize you say the exact same things and act the exact same way with all of us!

No, what I was thinking about was a woman I knew years ago, Heather, who was an avid golfer. Out in all weathers because she was addicted to the game but of course that usually meant she was out in the sunshine and what a mess it made of her face! She was old when I met her but from a distance she looked and moved like a tanned twenty-something. However, up close her face was an awful roadmap of lines. She didn't care, she just laughed at how men would run up behind her and then gasp when they got a look at her face on."

"Well, that's certainly not your problem – you always had a nice complexion. In fact you look great: older but not old."

"I'm 'only' sixty, much younger than an old codger like you."

"Hmmph, I'm many things but never a 'codger'! I'm glad to see you don't dye your hair although I have to say there isn't very much gray in it anyhow."

"Feel free to flatter and compliment me as much as you like, Gerry! Do you think we can make Dale jealous?"

"Huh, would we know it if he was? He was always the best at keeping his feelings to himself, unless he's changed?"

"No, he still pretty much keeps it all inside, but you will find that he's mellowed some. Our son's boy has been staying with us this summer and it's been fun. Jake's at a great age and Dale's really enjoying being a grandpa."

"I look forward to catching up with all your news."

* *

Pam had sent Gerry off to find Dale and her grandson Jake. Now the three of them had arrived back home.

Pamela immediately sent the boy off, telling him he owed his parents a phone call. He went away to his room to make it while she offered to bring the guys a beer if they'd stay out of her kitchen. They were happy to agree.

She could use a drink herself!

Instead, she only grabbed two of the long-neck Budweisers stored in the fridge-door. She and Dale had stopped drinking twenty years ago but on occasion he enjoyed a cold one. He never had a drinking problem – but she did – and he had quit to keep her company. Just like she quit smoking when that chest x-ray he had gave them both such a scare.

But she wasn't going to think about that now. She couldn't. Her thoughts were darting all over the place like a squirrel dithering on the road in the face of an oncoming car. She needed to concentrate on finding out what was going on. Why is Gerry here? Is it a chance visit? or does he want something?

All the while she was thinking these thoughts Pamela was busily preparing a meal. She pulled steaks out of the freezer for Dale to barbeque frozen. Gathering up the cooking implements and condiments on a tray she then added plates, cutlery, and napkins. Filling the sink with water she tossed in half-a-dozen corn-on-the-cob to soak through the husk. Next, she sliced up a big plate's worth of tomato and cucumber. Scrubbed baking potatoes she then wrapped in tinfoil completed the menu.

A few deep breaths to steady herself and she was ready to take everything outside and socialize.

Jake walked in the room saying, "Dad says 'hi', Mom wasn't there."

"That was a quick call."

"Yeah, well that's 'cause Mom wasn't home, and Dad never has much to say."

"True. He was like that as a boy, too. Not like you, eh?" she smiled so Jake knew this wasn't a criticism. "No, your Dad never was much of a talker or a reader. He didn't like to sit still for very long – not even to watch TV – and that used to get him in trouble at school."

"Did he have that ADHD?"

"The school nurse said so but we never agreed to medicating him. Back then parents still had some rights when it came to deciding what was best for their kids. And I guess your Dad outgrew it - if he even had it, that is - because he managed his schoolwork just fine in high-school."

"There are kids in my school who get their medicine in a little paper cup, every day."

"Hmm. They probably just need more PE and recess playtime. See I always figured that what helped your Dad was playing high-school sports. He was on the football and hockey teams, and he did Track and Field, too. In my opinion it's important for boys, and girls too of course, to have an outlet for all the energy they get while growing."

A loud chorus of "Oh Pammyyyyyyy" was shouted from the backyard so grandmother and grandson headed outside with her saying:

"Don't call me Pammy."

Chapter Two

Gerry and Dale sat at the picnic table where Pam unloaded her tray. She fired up the barbeque saying, "Hope you've got enough propane in this tank."

Jake came out with an armload of dripping wet corn which Dale took charge of. He took up his position by the grill and started cooking.

"So, you two got married after all," said Gerry with a smile. "Why wasn't I at the wedding?"

"Because you had disappeared. Nobody knew where you'd gone but after quite a long time we heard you were hauling freight for the van lines out of Indiana."

"Yeah well, there was a lot going on then. My girls were acting up because Jan had met somebody she was serious about, and then the cops were always bugging me. That one guy, Lund? he turned out to be a real jerk. He wouldn't leave me alone. And of course Pammy you broke my heart so.."

"As if!" she laughed. "I spent a lot of time at the hospital while Dale was recovering. Eddie was great about me taking the time off from work. He ending up being Dale's best man which was really nice, eh hon? And Suzi, God you must remember her? she covered my job until I got back and could finish training her properly."

"Huh, I remember Miss Suzi, alright. Great figure, ball-busting attitude... oops, sorry Jake."

Jake just smiled. He was good at keeping a low profile so that the adults would forget he was there when they were talking. He learned a lot that way.

"So yeah, we got married and I became his travelling partner, at least until our son came along."

"How did you enjoy 'life on the road'?"

"It was good, different from what I imagined. I thought driving all those miles and miles would bore me to bits, especially when there's no scenery to speak of, but it wasn't that way. We talked a lot and there was the CB to listen to and Dale always bought the latest gadgets so we had air-conditioning and a CD player. Plus I could read or crochet because riding in the truck was smooth enough that I never felt headachey."

Dale interjected here saying, "Don't believe a word she says, she spent most of her time sleeping."

"Oh boy you got me there. I can drive for hours but being a passenger puts me right to sleep!"

"Did you ever drive the big rig?"

"Well, I wasn't licensed or insured but yeah, Dale showed me the basics and on an empty stretch of flat road, like across the Prairies, I'd take a turn at the wheel. He'd never take the opportunity for a nap, though. He always had to keep an eye on things."

"I just loved the sight of you sitting up straight with your hands in the ten-to-two position and so focused on the road ahead."

"Sounds like the two of you made a good team back then and, obviously, still do since you're together after all these years."

"Thirty-four years, to be exact."

"And you have a son – just the one kid?"

"Yeah, and he made me a grandmother before I was fifty! But what about your family, Gerry?"

"Well, I remarried but it was a mistake so that didn't last very long. No kids with Melanie, but my two daughters now have families of their own so yeah, I'm a grandpa now too."

"And still enjoying the bachelor life, no doubt?"

"You know how it is – sometimes it's lonely, sometimes it's fantastic. More good than bad and that's all you can really ask for out of life, am I right?"

"No, you can also ask for some good food which is coming up so Jake why don't you grab Gerry another beer and bring out that jug of lemonade, too," added Dale.

"I'll give you a hand honey, that's a lot to carry with the glasses and ice."

* *

The three adults played catch up with their news. After eating their fill and relaxing in the dusk Gerry said: "Hey, is it okay if I smoke? it's just that neither of you two have lit up since I got here and I seem to remember you were both pretty heavy smokers back in the day. Plus I don't see any ashtrays."

"Oh, go ahead, Gerry. We both quit a few years ago. I'd never tried before but Dale had managed it once or twice for a few years each time. Anyhow, he comes home with the idea of quitting and I thought, 'yeah it's time'. Wasn't easy but, I gotta admit, it wasn't as hard as I thought it would be."

"Yup, third time was a charm as they say. It helped a lot that Pam quit too. I probably would have crumbled if she was still smoking."

"That's because I've never seen anyone enjoy a cigarette as much as Pammy did. Honestly, her whole body would relax with that first inhale. And she always had a lit cigarette in her hand – or at least nearby – it must have been a heck of a shock to your system when you did stop. What programme did you use?"

"We went cold turkey. Tried the gum but only for a day 'cause it made me dizzy."

"I tried the puffers, that's what the pharmacist recommended, and I used them for about a week and then I was OK with nothing."

"We both gained weight – as you can see – and for a while my gums bled every time I brushed my teeth but the dentist said that would stop end and it did. The hygienist was real happy too because getting the nicotine stains out took so long. But hey, fortunately neither of us developed that allergy to smoke that a lot of people get so by all means you go ahead, Gerry."

"Oh sure, now I feel guilty."

"You should!" said Dale, and at the same time Pam replied:

"Don't be silly."

Gerry shook a cigarette out of the pack and flipped it up in the air, catching it between his second and third fingers. Both Pam and Dale laughed in remembrance.

"Some habits never go away, do they?"

"Yeah, and it's pretty bad when your habit has a habit," Dale said with a chuckle. "We all learned that trick decades ago and the big kids said if you couldn't do it then you couldn't smoke. Huh, most of us outgrew it, Gerry."

"Screw you Terry, because I seem to recall you tap-tapping your smoke every time you pulled one out of the pack even after you'd switched to filter tips."

"That's right – you did do that!" exclaimed Pam.

"Mr Tanner can you show me how to do that?" asked Jake.

Gerry and Pam both replied at the same time with him saying: "Call me Gerry," and her telling Jake it wasn't a skill he needed to acquire.

Dale added: "And call him Mister Gerry, OK Jake?"

The boy laughed answering: "Mister Gerry and Mister Terry but really you're Mister Dale." He seemed to find his words hilarious and Pam was delighted to see her grandson so happy and carefree.

They all paused for a few moments, enjoying their memories and each other's company, when Gerry spoiled it by saying:

"So, what about that thing in the Sunday paper for the 35th anniversary of 'The Moving Murders'. What did you guys think about that? in fact, what did you think about the whole trucker/ murderer thing? The so-called 'Trans-Canada Killer'? He was never caught, and the case was never solved, right?"

Chapter Three

Pamela hoped nobody heard her sudden intake of breath but it sounded loud to her. "What does Gerry think he knows?" she thought. She fidgeted in her seat trying to figure out how best to deflect his question.

Dale surprised them all when he said with some enthusiasm: "Jake here has been reading up on all that! He's been interested, and I'll bet you can ask him anything and he'll have the answer."

Pam turned to her grandson with a horrified expression and Jake hurried to say: "I did read that article Mr Gerry mentioned Grammy, and me and Grandpa have been talking about it because he was there at the time. Well, I guess you both were and.."

"But you're way too young to know about terrible stuff like that... Dale! what were you thinking?"

"Well, it was a long, long time ago, Pam, and it's just a story to the boy. He's interested in learning about how things were back then and to tell you the truth I've enjoyed reminiscing. Funny how once you get talking about a thing you find yourself remembering more and more."

"There's nothing funny about it," retorted Pam, seemingly angry but with fear evident in her voice. Dale looked a bit sheepish, Jake was confused, and Gerry was openly curious. "You don't know what it was like when you were being operated on and I didn't know if you'd recover and when you did, thank God, you couldn't remember a thing. You couldn't even remember what you'd been saying – shouting – when the paramedics brought you into the hospital."

"I was there but I missed all the excitement." said Gerry.

"You caused quite enough excitement of your own getting yourself shot in that bar."

"It wasn't by choice," he laughed.

"I know but there you were getting patched up and I was on my way to step out for a breath of fresh air when the doors fly open and they're rushing in this emergency case who just happens to be Dale. And you, you were hollering your head off."

"What was he saying, Grammy?"

"Oh, some nonsense about this time 'he saved the child' and they needed to 'get the bad woman'. It didn't make sense, but he was so loud and so intense it was quite disturbing. No one would tell me anything until I lied and said I was his fiancee and the only family he had."

"That wasn't a lie," Dale said with a smile.

"It was at the time. We hadn't even had our first date yet! and then they were asking me about your blood type! Fortunately, I knew all about your health insurance plan because I took care of that at work."

"So tell us what had happened Grammy."

"We still don't know, Jake. It's all such a blur I mean I don't even know if it was the Sheriffs, or the RCMP, or the Calgary Police, or even the Reservation Police who found you. Whoever it was they responded to gun shots. Turns out you hadn't been shot, you'd been stabbed and had lost a ton of blood. You were delirious."

"Reservation Police?" asked Gerry.

"That's where they found him, on the Morley Reserve."

"With your truck?" Gerry was incredulous.

Pam echoed the sentiment saying: "Yeah, totally illegal. Dale of all people trespassing on the Reserve. To this day we don't how or why but the investigation concluded that he'd been hijacked on Highway 2 and taken there. His trailer was locked up tight but there were signs that the bunk was ransacked so it looked like something was stolen. They wanted to know what that something was, but Dale never did recover his memory of it. Of course, the cops were convinced it was drugs or guns – as if – but since nobody ever had a bad word to say about Dale and his record was clean nothing came of it."

"Sounds like you're a real live miracle, old buddy."

"The doctor told me I was lucky that the temperature dropped so fast because the cold slowed my heart which meant I wasn't pumping out the blood as quickly. So yeah, I guess it was a bit of a miracle."

"We always figured they got the wrong trucker, but to think they were willing to kill him. Anyhow, why are we talking about this? I don't even like to think about it," declared Pam.

She was satisfied that they'd put that subject to bed for this evening, but Gerry was going to stay a couple of days with them, and she worried that he wouldn't let it go. She had to protect Dale but first she needed to find out exactly what Gerry was playing at by bringing up the past - and what was his endgame?

Chapter Four

Pam tried to cover up a jaw-stretching yawn, but Jake noticed and asked why she didn't just go to bed. "He's turned out to be quite a noticing boy," she thought to herself. Out loud she said:

"I'm going to but let's get everyone settled first. Mr Tanner said he'll be fine on the couch in the den and not to put you out of your room so we don't have to move anything. However, that's a pull-out couch and the sheets for it are in one of your dresser drawers."

The Terrys had turned one of their bedrooms into a den which they preferred to the basement when watching TV in the evening. Unless it was hot and humid – then the downstairs was cool; or bitterly cold outside and then they'd light a fire. The rec room in the basement had a wood-burning fireplace. Dale would start it early and the room would be toasty by time Pam came downstairs, usually with popcorn or hot cocoa. All the sofas in the house had wool afghans that Pam had knitted or crocheted over the years.

Jake helped her pull out the sofa-bed and they made it up in no time at all. Pam was longing for her own bed but she didn't want to leave Dale and Gerry alone when they were drinking. She said good night to Jake then headed out to the backyard. Struggling to keep the tiredness out of her voice she commented that the night had turned cool and did anyone want a coffee or were they coming indoors?

Dale said: "Coffee would be great, hon. The breeze is a bit cool but it's keeping the no-see'ums away which makes a nice change."

"I could manage another Bud, Pammy. Coffee at this time of night tends to keep me awake."

"Gerry, seriously, stop calling me Pammy – I'm not twelve! and I could make you decaf but it would be instant because we don't drink it ourselves so I don't have any pods for the Keurig. But we've got plenty of beer so it's your choice."

"I'll take a beer over coffee any day, sweetheart. Is 'sweetheart' better than Pammy?"

"'Sweetheart' is what you call every woman you know – even if you've never met her and it's only a phone call – so yes, it's grand."

Dale chuckled at the exchange saying: "You two have bickered for as long as I've known you. Anyone would think you had some sort of Tracey/Hepburn romantic attraction going on. Should I be jealous?"

"Yes, you should because if I stood the slightest chance I'd take it," said Gerry. "I mean, look at her she's still gorgeous with no wrinkles and the new light hair colour."

"It's the same old brown, Gerry, it's just well-blended with gray now," answered Pam with a smile. "And you are still as much of a flirt as ever but I'm charmed so keep it up and let's make the old man jealous if we can. Him and his black-and-white late night TV movies!"

She went back into the house to make the coffee and fetch Gerry's beer. It was true that drinking coffee didn't keep Dale awake but she was hoping the caffeine would do its usual job for her. She was determined not to go to bed and leave those two talking. Not until she'd figured out what Gerry was after.

When she joined the men they'd continued their earlier conversation of catching up and she heard Gerry asking:

"What about, old Grub. – I can't remember his real name."

"Jim. Jim Grubowski," replied Dale. "You'll never believe it but he and his ex-wife got back together again. And got married again."

"And by now no doubt they've divorced again," added Pam. "He was so possessive of Marie and she seemed to enjoy stringing him along. What a couple!"

"They deserved each other," said Gerry adding: "Marie came on to me something fierce and fierce didn't begin to describe how Jim reacted. I had to do some pretty fast-talking and he was my buddy."

"It was always like that with those two. They'd egg each other into a fight then I guess they'd enjoy make-up sex. Trouble was they involved everybody else in their fights. Truck-stops, bars, in the dispatch office at our company, it's like they loved an audience."

"Well I can't see second-time around lasting long," Dale opined. "After all, each one said lots of nasty things about the other and at some point that must have gotten back to them."

"No doubt that's added fuel to their fights."

"You'll be right about that. Huh! what a pair. Now, on to a more serious subject because I'm sure he must be long dead by now but how did things go with Ray Frank? I mean we all suspected he had lung cancer so..."

"Cancer yes, but not in his lungs. It was his pancreas. Once the diagnosis was confirmed he went super fast. I never saw him again but you did, right Dale?"

"He came and saw me when I was in the hospital in Calgary. I don't know why you missed him?"

"If you were well enough to have visitors I'd probably gone back to Edmonton for a bit to get things sorted out there."

"Yeah, that's what it was. The nurses had been encouraging me to get up and move my leg as much as I could. I remember Ray giving me an arm to lean on and we almost went ass over tea-ketttle. Of course, that made us laugh and then he started coughing. And there was blood and when the nurse came in to see what the noise was about she immediately sat him down and called a doctor to attend to him.

They gave him some oxygen and, well I couldn't help but overhear, he told the doctor he was dying from pancreatic cancer and the blood was because of his chemo treatment. The doctor said that was an unusual side effect of chemotherapy but he had heard of it happening."

"I don't know when he first got sick," said Gerry, "but I do remember seeing him soon after I got back on the road that winter and he complained of stomach pains then. He thought he had an ulcer or gall-stones or something like that."

"Yeah I helped him with a couple of loads because he had to take a break. It was sudden, the onset of his cancer, and after he visited me in the hospital – which was only a month or so later – that was the last time I saw him. Real shame, he sure was a nice guy."

"He had a nice family too," added Pam. "I met them one summer when his wife and two boys joined him for a cross-country run."

"That's right, she was Hindu or Muslim or something wasn't she?"

"I don't know what religion but she was from Indonesia originally."

"I'm pretty sure that's a Muslim country. Hey, so where were you guys on 9/11?"

"Living here by then, but actually in Calgary on the day. We had to go back there for a funeral. I remember sitting in my cousin's house listening to an American radio station... um, Peak something-or-other.. and we were all stunned at the news. We turned on the TV and then started bawling our eyes out. What about you?"

"I was in the States and I saw some shit that was pretty disturbing, vandalism and looting, but also some touching, like heartwarming, stuff. One time I was driving and up ahead I saw somebody dropping their flag to half-mast – you know how so many Americans have flags at their homes, right? Anyhow, the cars ahead of me started slowing down and then someone stopped, and another did, and then people got out of their cars and gathered around this flag in this stranger's front yard and all they did was stand there with their hands over their hearts. Like they do when they play the National Anthem. But nobody sang, I don't think anybody even said anything. Some were crying. I didn't go over but I did stop, it didn't feel right to just drive by so I waited and after a few minutes people went back to their cars and drove away."

"What a touching story," said Pam.

Dale said: "We generally make fun of them but I'm sure the average American isn't all about handguns and bragging. Those ones who took down the other plane killing the terrorists and themselves in the process were real heroes."

"I was so glad we had driven to Calgary. I don't think I could have gotten on a plane right after that," added Pam. "I don't remember if there even were any flights allowed."

"Well I guess it's time we turned in before the talk starts getting maudlin," said Dale as he stood up with his empty mug and reaching for Pam's. Her reply was another big yawn and they all laughed.

Gerry said that he had an overnight bag in the car which he'd grab.

Pam said: "I've got to finish tidying up the kitchen so I'll wait for you and then I can lock up." When Gerry came back in she showed him his bed in the den and asked if he'd like another beer. He said yes and followed her back to the kitchen to get it. Instead of leaving he popped the top off the bottle and leaned against the counter studying her with one eyebrow raised and a half-smile.

Pam decided to jump right in and keeping her voice low said: "What are you really after here, Gerry? I mean, it's been years and we've never heard a word from you. So why now?"

"Now that doesn't sound very welcoming Pammy – I mean, sweetheart."

"Oh cut the crap. It's late, I'm tired, and I want to know what's going on?"

"OK then, it's that damn article in the paper. It's brought up a lot of questions or rather people are asking me a lot of questions. People suspect me! and even the ones who don't, like my youngest, want answers. Jodie's the only one who speaks to me and I want to give her reassurance but after all these years, and the negative stuff she's heard from her sister and her mother, my words don't carry a lot of weight any more."

"You've got nobody to blame for that but yourself. And what on earth do you think we can do about it?"

"You can help me try to figure out the truth about what happened."

"What? You want us to play detective and catch the killer? The famous Trans-Canada Killer? is that it?" her whispering voice rose with incredulity then she noticed Jake in the doorway asking what was wrong.

"It's nothing, honey. Mr Tanner and I are re-hashing an old argument that's it way too late – in every sense of the word - to be having. Sorry we disturbed you. I'll turn out the light now and we'll all go to bed." She walked down the hallway to the boy's room and sensed Gerry passing behind her.

"Are you sure everything's okay, Grammy?"

She heard the door to the den shut and smiled at the boy reassuring him that everything was fine. Then, thankfully, she headed to her own bed.

Chapter Five

Gerry gave a low whistle as he looked around the den, "Damn, I feel like a time-traveller," he said aloud.

The walls were panelled in pine which the tables matched. He recognized those end-tables – and the coffee table – from when he and Dale shared a place back in Edmonton. It was actually Dale's apartment, but he invited Gerry to stay during the separation period of Gerry and Jan's marriage. Gerry became a permanent roommate soon after. Then he ended up in hospital and when he got out Dale had his accident and was hospitalized too.

"So, when exactly was that?" he mused. He took a good swig of his beer and cast his mind back. The fight that almost killed him happened right after Hallowe'en. He remembered some heavy-duty partying with the girls at the peeler bar. They'd been wearing sexy costumes with scary masks – what a combination! So, it was a day or two after that, the very beginning of November.

The doctors kept him under for days and then he had surgery, two surgeries because the pressure on his brain hadn't dropped the way it should have done so fluid had to be drained again. At least that's what they told him afterwards.

He ran his hand over his scalp and recalled that when he found out they'd had to shave away some of his hair he'd been worried that it wouldn't grow back. But it did, although the new growth had a lot of gray hair mixed in.

He'd stayed with Dale. He didn't have much money – he always spent it as soon as he got it – so Dale's offer was a godsend. Luckily Jan had always worked because raising two girls was expensive and while Gerry did his best, he knew he'd fallen short many times.

The electronics company had been very grateful for Gerry's intervention, and he'd received a big cash reward for saving the shipment. Since he wasn't forced to go back to work too soon, he was able to rest and recuperate.

It was years since he'd lived alone, and he discovered he liked it. It meant taking cabs whenever he went out because he'd never bothered to have a car of his own, always using his wife's when he was in town. At least he didn't have to worry about drinking and driving. Of course, that was years before M.A.D.D. formed and people still joked about having 'one for the road and one for the ditch'.

As a professional driver that was a risk Gerry never took. He was always careful to keep out of the driver's seat when drinking. He knew guys who kept a cooler full of beer behind the passenger seat while out on the road, but those guys were employees, not owner-operators, who would only lose their jobs and not their trucks if they lost their license.

Anyhow, here he was surrounded by the same furniture from all those years ago. Hard to believe. Well, almost the same, they'd never had a pull-out sofa back then, so this was a new couch. But there was the same rocking chair, Colonial-style in brown and orange chintz with frilled skirts. The armrests were wood, handy to hold a drink or an ashtray but so uncomfortable! It had been solid stuff and even now, he rocked the coffee-table with his foot to confirm, it was still sturdy. You'd get sick and tired of seeing it before it wore out.

"Dale always was a bit tight with his money," he recalled, but generous when asked for help which was lucky for Gerry.

Looking around he spotted the same standing ashtray – now filled with wrapped candies – which he dumped out on the table. Nobody had said he couldn't smoke inside, and he'd been careful not to ask.

He'd lived his life following the maxim 'it's better to seek forgiveness then be denied permission'.

He lit up and, relaxing with his smoke and his drink, cast his mind back all those years ago. There were quite a lot of gaps from that time, and he was hoping Pam and Dale would be able to fill in some of the blanks.

Dale's accident happened before Christmas, but he was still in hospital well into the New Year. Gerry had been released and wasn't supposed to be alone but Jan wasn't keen to have him back at their place, so he'd stayed at Dale's and his youngest girl had moved in to take care of him for a week or so. She'd always been closer to him than her sister was. In fact, it was a long time since he'd talked to his oldest daughter. She was divorced herself now, and her kids were adults.

Having a beer and a cigarette on his own, surrounded by all the familiar furniture it was easy to imagine time had stood still but, of course, it hadn't.

Chapter Six

Morning came way too soon for Pamela who had slept poorly but it was a lovely day and that brightened her mood. She felt hopeful that she could deal with Gerry.

She started preparing breakfast and one by one the guys came in and sat down to coffee or orange juice. Dale asked their guest: "Want a 'Calgary Red-Eye', Gerry?"

"What's that, Grandpa?"

"Beer and tomato juice – or clamato juice if you're feeling fancy but I don't think we run to fancy, do we Pam?"

"Beer for breakfast?" Jake was astonished.

"Yes, in fact champagne and orange juice is also a popular breakfast drink. If you're rich and famous, that is. Some people call it a 'Mimosa', but I've heard it called an 'Orange Blossom' as well," Pam answered.

"Eeewww." Jake cast a suspicious glance Gerry's way. Yesterday he had liked 'Mr Gerry' but after catching him and his Grandma having a whisper-fight in the kitchen last night he'd changed his mind. Now he found this drinking thing interesting but was leery, nonetheless.

"'Breakfast of Champions', kiddo."

"So what's it to be, Gerry? You never did answer."

"Lots of coffee sounds great. Nothing to eat, thanks. I'm just going to take my cup out in the sunshine and enjoy my first smoke of the day."

"OK but I want to let you know I need to be someplace this morning, probably till about 1:00-1:30 because we'll be staying for lunch. Anyhow, it's a bowling thing for Jake and.."

"Oh you don't have to bother with that when you've got unexpected company, Grandpa," Jake interrupted.

Both Gerry and Dale spoke at the same time saying:

"No, I want to take you to the tournament."

"For sure go do the bowling thing!"

"I'd ask you to join us but I'm one of the scorers so I have to concentrate on that and I won't be able to visit at all. I'm afraid it would be boring for you."

"Well since this tournament is a guys-only thing I'm going to take Gerry out for lunch somewhere, hon."

"Can we have lobster? I mean, we're in the Maritimes."

"Oh, that's a good idea. I never get to have it."

"Really? I thought you'd be eating fresh seafood practically every day."

"No, Dale has a shellfish allergy which includes lobster, and besides it's awfully expensive now."

"I'll pick up the tab."

"No, I didn't mean that. The thing is, the locals can sell lobster for so much more than they themselves would spend on a meal that we've all gotten used to not eating it. Unless we have visitors, that is. No, this will be a real treat for me, Gerry."

"You should go to Finnegan's Fin Shack," said Dale.

"You're right! that's the perfect place to take Gerry. We'll go for an early lunch so we don't have to line-up to get in." Pam turned towards Gerry explaining: "They don't take reservations." Then she turned back to Dale continuing: "That way we'll all be back here between 1:30 and 2:00, right?"

"Sounds like a plan."

After finishing breakfast Dale and Jake got their gear ready and left in Dale's car for the bowling alley. Pam and Gerry would drive in his rental since the restaurant she'd chosen was about twenty minutes away.

"Gerry, you stay outside. I have to put these breakfast things away and then I'll come and join you. We'll hash out whatever we need to get sorted here because I don't want to fight over our meal, it's bad for the digestion," said Pam with a smile.

* *

Jake had a great time bowling in the tournament. His crew won the second-place blue ribbon which was a surprise to everyone, and a delight to the team.

Dale was relieved to be finished with his scoring duties. While on the road he'd always been meticulous in keeping his logs clear and up-to-date. "But numbers have never been my strong suit," he thought to himself. He was happy to hand over the records and relieved that he'd managed to do the job well enough.

The lunch was hotdogs and tacos – suitably messy fare for the enjoyment of pre-teen boys. Jake was uncharacteristically boisterous: shouting and laughing while overstuffing his mouth with potato chips. For a short time, at least, the sombre questioning boy was replaced by a happy hooligan. Dale was glad to see it.

All of a sudden he found himself feeling very angry towards his son and daughter-in-law's selfish behaviour. All marriages have ups and downs, that's what happens when two people are passionate about one another, but you work through it. You don't send your young son across the country for a couple of months to stew and fret over a possible divorce. Jake had felt the effects and suffered from them.

Dale resolved to call Michael tonight when Jake was in bed and speak his mind. He'd make it clear that Michael needed to step up his Dad game. Pam might fuss about it but too bad. Dale had just had a glimpse of how a normal eleven-year-old usually acts and he wanted to see more of that carefree joy.

He signalled to Jake that it was time to get going and gave him a hearty pat on the back for a job well done. Jake's grin was radiant. But a surprised awaited when they stepped outdoors.

An unexpected summer storm had come up with thunder and lightning. Dale led the boy back into the building, he wasn't going to risk crossing the parking-lot during an electrical storm, and decided they could shelter in place until the worst of it was over. The boys were delighted and kept running to the windows to look out only to be shooed away by an anxious parent. The adults wondered if the power would stay on.

Luckily the storm had begun before Gerry and Pam left home so they postponed their lunch out until the next day, Gerry having made it clear that he was staying over until the three of them had the discussion he wanted. Pam agreed with resignation, knowing it was no use to keep on arguing. If he wanted to play games, she had no choice but to go along until she could figure out what was what.

She remembered now that Gerry always had been difficult when he couldn't get his own way. Sometimes it was better to just give in. Of course, sometimes you have to draw that line in the sand, she told herself.

Gerry found a game to watch on TV and Pam had an unaccustomed daytime nap curled up on the couch. The rain lashed at the windows turning the lovely sunny morning into a dark, wet afternoon. When Dale and Jake finally made it home they found two sleepers – one snoring much louder than the other.

Chapter Seven

To a soundtrack of heavy rainfall, with the occasional rumble of thunder, the adults settled down to discuss their mutual past.

"I've got that article in my case," said Gerry, adding that he'd be back in a minute. While he was gone Pam gave her husband a searching look, but Dale was only calmly interested.

The article was lengthy. Gerry spread it out on the coffee-table, and they all leaned in for a look at the photos it contained, some black-and-white and some in colour. They included the faces of the murdered women and, in some cases, current photos of their family members. The dead women looked so young in comparison.

"Jake told me he read this," commented Dale, turning the first page around to read it.

"Did you, Jake? I still think you're too young for these true crime tales because that's what this claims to be: 'A Retrospective Look at Cold Cases," quoted Pam. "It says here that this writer investigates 'unsolved crimes with a fresh perspective from the vantage point of the future'. Hmm, that seems a bit over the top. His name sounds phony too. I suppose he's read by all the armchair detectives, and I bet they send him their theories, too."

Hearing her disparaging tone Dale threw her a quizzical look saying,

"You enjoy puzzles, Pam. I mean I certainly know better than to dare touch the weekend crossword, which I'm no good at anyway. And you read murder mysteries too."

"Yes, but that's fiction, not true crime. I don't want to think about the real stuff, it's depressing and even scary, sometimes," she replied.

"Well let's put some of your detecting skills to work now. First off, you'd both better read this article and then we can talk about it."

"I need to find my reading glasses," said Dale as he stood up.

Gerry commented that it was great to see none of them wearing glasses full-time and Dale responded saying,

"I decided it was because of the driving and having to keep changing focus from the speedometer to the road ahead, I believe doing that exercised our eyes or something. My distance sight is still good but print size seems so small nowadays that up close is a different story. Anyhow, I'll only be a minute so you go ahead and get started, babe."

Pam wasn't going to admit that she'd already read the article. She'd thrown out that paper too, but it seems not quickly enough if Jake had gotten hold of it. With a sigh, she picked up the pages of newsprint and settled back on the couch to read it again. Gerry kept silent the whole time, and a few moments later Dale came back with his reading glasses in hand. Pam passed him the page she'd finished saying,

"Skip the first part, it's only the writer going on about how clever he is. The writer, I mean, not the killer. He, the writer, sure doesn't think much of the police."

"No, you're right. Even when he's saying how difficult things were you can tell he's putting them down like he would have done better," commented Gerry.

"I haven't got there yet," announced Dale.

"Actually Dale, give me that sheet back. There's no point me and Gerry talking about the bits you haven't read yet. I'll read it out loud and we can discuss as we go." She took the page and added it to the others she was holding. Aligning the pile, sitting up and straightening her back, she went into what Dale thought of as Pam's 'teacher mode'.

Gerry tried to suppress a chuckle of reminiscence. He had a clear recollection of sitting in the Dispatch office being lectured about the importance of accurate record-keeping and the sloppiness of his poor efforts. Dale saw the smile and catching his eye acknowledged the shared memory with a grin.

"Don't think I can't see you two fools acting adolescent," huffed Pam.

TRUE CRIME: *A Retrospective Look at Cold Cases*

Join us every week when writer-sleuth Jonathan Phillips-Pryce is on the case, delving into unsolved crimes with a fresh perspective from *the vantage point of the future...*

THIS WEEK WE ASK: "Who was the mass murderer known as *'The Cross-Country Killer',* also *'The Trans-Canada Killer',* **and** *'The Terror of the Trans-Canada'* **for committing what was known as 'The Moving Murders'?"**

Seven women – *that we know of* – savagely beaten to death as their murderer travelled freely from one end of the country to the other, *under the very noses of police* across many jurisdictions.

An exhaustive study of the crimes, including interviews with the victim's families, revealed that the cops need to hang their heads in shame. Read on to learn what we discovered.

Chapter Eight

Victim: STACEY MORIN

The Facts:

Kingston, Ontario: Morin's fully clothed but battered body was discovered on the side of the Trans-Canada Highway on Tuesday, February 19, 1980. Death had occurred sometime on the 18th, which was also the day Morin and her family had moved into their new home. They came from Saskatchewan. Morin was last seen grocery shopping at the IGA near her home.

The Story:

The sad story of "a young mother cruelly forgotten" when those she left behind moved on without her...

"Here we go again," said Pam. She paused to read the next section then told them: "The gist of it is nobody liked this woman too much. She'd moved with her family to Kingston where she and her husband came from and still had ties. Reading between the lines, it sounds like she wasn't happy to be going back. Stacey wasn't very popular but her husband sure was.

Afterwards the widower and his children were warmly welcomed into the neighbourhood. They all settled in his brother's home, and the two families merged into one.

Danny never remarried and soon enough the youngest of his and Stacey's children started calling Dorrie, his sister-in-law, "Mommy" instead of "Auntie". Shortly after the rest of the kids followed suit. It does seem like no one missed Stacey too much and all the cousins grew up together happy and healthy and living productive lives."

* *

When somebody set up Danny Morin on a date he went along with it and usually enjoyed himself but he wasn't bothered about pursuing anyone into a relationship.

Living with Brian and Dorrie meant his creature comforts were attended to and his children were looked after. He only had to be there and contribute his share to the household expenses.

The only thing missing was a sex life but he found that he didn't miss it much. Maybe having to get married when Stacey got pregnant kind of put him off. Marital relations between him and his wife had never been that great.

Danny liked going to the strip club with the guys from work where they'd toss loonies at the dancers and make all kinds of hooting and hollering noise. Watching the show in the camaraderie of his buddies was enough for him.

It was only natural that Brian and Dorrie discussed this. Neither could believe that Danny had loved Stacey so much that he couldn't give his heart to another. They agreed it was far more likely to be a case of 'once bitten, twice shy'.

Chapter Nine

Victim: TAMMY BLUETT

The Facts:

Halifax, Nova Scotia: On Wednesday February 20, 1980 Tammy Bluett was savagely beaten to death in her new home, and her body was discovered less than 24 hours later.

The Story:

"Shakespeare couldn't envision such tragedy!" as that experienced by the Trans-Canada Killer's second (that we know of) victim.

"Hmm, I wouldn't go that far, after all there's that one he wrote about the girl who gets raped and mutilated and then her rapists are killed and cooked in a pie or something and served up to their parents..."

"WHAT?" shouted Jake.

"Oh, never mind. It's not likely you'll ever be studying that Tragedy in school. Anyhow, this victim's story certainly is a sad one.

She was widowed after a house fire killed her husband and their twin daughters. Her closest relative was a sister living in Halifax – Tammy Bluett and her family had lived in Grande Prairie – so she moved across country to be near her sister and she'd only just moved into a place of her own when she was murdered."

"What a sad story!"

"Yeah, and it was the sister who discovered the body."

* *

Christie Baird, aged 77, felt she'd buried far too many people in her life. Her parents, unsurprisingly; but she'd also outlived her husband, Robin; her sister, Tammy; brother-in-law, Roger; and her only nieces Rochelle and Michelle – the twins.

She declined an interview when that newspaper writer had been in touch because she didn't want to live through all those heartbreaking memories again. Not that she ever forgot but as time passed she'd learned to live with the sadness. No point revisiting that terrible time and making the horror fresh once more.

Of course, the story would be written anyhow, after all the facts were out there, but it would have to be told without a first-hand account of her pain.

No doubt she'd see the article because reading her newspaper from cover to cover was something she'd enjoyed doing for years. She'd also read some of these true crime stories before. But she didn't think she would read this one.

* *

"Poor woman. She lived through a terrible thing, " said Pam with a heartfelt sigh.

"What does the article say?" asked Dale.

"Umm, the actual 'news story' is brief because she sister wouldn't give an interview. Of course, this writer fancies it up by talking about 'her grief being too strong still' ugh, I'm betting she couldn't bear the thought of him gloating over her private emotions.

Anyhow, he goes off on one of his tirades against the police. The rental that Tammy Bluett moved into had had some shady characters living there so the police decided it was a case of mistaken identity and that a previous tenant was the actual target."

Chapter Ten

Victim: JASMINE BROWN

The Facts:

Montreal, Quebec: On Monday, February 25, 1980 police received a domestic disturbance call and found the victim bludgeoned to death. Homicide investigators were at the scene within a couple of hours but failed to make an arrest.

The Story:

The victim "lived her life in fear of a nameless dread" that finally, tragically, claimed her.

"My God that writer's getting worse!" exclaimed Dale.

"I know, eh? I'm guessing it's because he doesn't have too much to report about this case. He gives a bit of background here saying that each province uses its own system for handling deaths, it's something that's not federally mandated.

Quebec uses the Coroner system while some other provinces use the Medical Examiner system, and 'too bad that the CCMED' – which he says stands for the Canadian Coroner and Medical Examiner Database – 'wasn't in existence in 1980.'"

"That's the first killing that was discovered right away, so far that is," noted Gerry.

"You're right. The others were discovered next day."

"Okay he goes on to tell us that 'before the year was out' the widower, Alfonso Brown, who was the estranged husband at the time of the murder, and 'their sports-hero son, Antony', were killed in a freak accident. A pup trailer, hooked up to a dump truck, flipped sideways onto their car. The writer says 'it would have seemed like a huge cloud passed overhead, blocking out the sun, before impact killed both the man and his son instantly'.

Wow, I hope he's right about that. I can remember how it felt when my little Honda Civic was boxed in by tractor-trailers on the 401 and it's true, the big vehicles do block out the sun."

"That car of yours was a death-trap."

"Oh please, it's like the most popular car in Canada."

"Not back then it wasn't! It was so small and lightweight. You have to admit it was funny-looking."

"Hey, I loved Goldie—"

"Grammy you named your car?"

"Of course I did, Jake. Now, can you guess what colour she was?" asked Pam with a smile. Jake just rolled his eyes. "She was my first brand-new car. Cost me $4,100 including the Bondeco rustproofing treatment."

"How do you remember stuff like that?"

"My first love, what can I say? I couldn't tell you what I paid for my second car or any of the ones after that.

But you are right about the safety issues because when it came time to renew my insurance the price had gone from just under $100 a year to over $300. When I called the agent, you know thinking they'd made a mistake, I was told that that car had finally been out long enough to compile statistics and there was a huge risk of fatality in a collision. Well, no wonder! it was so tiny compared to everything else on the road. My very first car, an old Pontiac Parisienne, was a tank in comparison!"

"I remember that car. You had it when you first started working at Big Sky Moving. You're right it was humoungus. It was also several colours, or rather it had primer paint on the side panels or something."

"Yeah she wasn't pretty that's for sure. And she was like third-hand when I got her, she was a 1967 model I think. Weighed a ton."

"Huh, more like two tons! And Jake, those are real tons, not metric tonnes."

"What's the difference?"

"Look it up."

"Anyhow, enough about my cars. I know it's my fault we got sidetracked but... back to the article. Hmm, there's not much more. The police at the time suspected it was a drug thing, the writer comes right out and says that's because the family was Black and the cops were profiling and prejudiced. That actually could be true."

"She was the only Black victim," said Dale.

"How did you know that? I don't even remember hearing about this one," replied Gerry.

"I don't remember either – except that I knew she was Black so somebody must have told me. I forget who."

"Anyhow, no arrest was ever made, and with the remaining family dying so soon after it looks like the police closed the file and marked

it 'unsolved' because there was no one else to investigate or even talk
to."

* *

Marie Garbel would have given the reporter good value for his
money – she'd believed that all newspapermen had plenty of cash to
hand out for scoops – but Marie had died, peacefully, decades before
the True Crime article was written. She was already an old woman in
1980 when she called the police to report the disturbance that led to
them discovering her neighbour's murder.

"Yes, I knew your wife," lied Marie when she met Alfonso Brown
at Jasmine's funeral. She reasoned to herself that she could say this
because she'd have made a point of meeting Jasmine sooner rather
than later if the woman hadn't gotten herself killed the very day she
moved in.

All the residents of that particular building knew Marie lay in wait
to corner the unwary whenever someone was using the basement
laundry facilities. She could hear the washing machines and would
time her arrival while the tenant was loading or unloading their
washer or dryer.

Her idea of a conversation was to ask plenty of questions without
respect of or consideration for personal boundaries. If anyone was
rude to her she'd shrug it off saying, "I don't know why you would
mind, but then I have nothing to hide myself."

She attended the funeral and enjoyed having a morning out. There
was no invitation for a bite to eat afterwards but what could you
expect with a man making the arrangements? She, on the other
hand, had arranged a magnificent spread when poor Joseph passed
away a few years later.

Anyhow, Marie decided she'd be glad enough to get back home to change out of her best black dress with its matching jacket. The ensemble had become uncomfortably snug. No one even saw it because she'd had to keep her winter coat on the whole time since the church was that cold. The proximity of the Saint Lawrence River always brought an added chill to the air.

So the elderly woman attended the funeral of a woman she'd never met, only spied on through the peep-hole in her door, and tut-tutted with the rest about the incompetence of the police saying "What could you expect when they only sent a bit of a girl to do the interviewing?"

In the interest of honest, accurate reporting it's a good thing that Jonathan Phillips-Pryce and Marie Garbel never met to concoct a story.

Chapter Eleven

"Hon, I've gotta lie down for a bit," said Dale. "But I don't want to break up the party so you guys go ahead with this and you can catch me up later." He struggled out of the chair and his face creased with pain. He covered it up with a smile, gave his head a shake, and muttered about 'getting old'.

"Actually, a break sounds like a great idea. I'll put together a meal and we'll continue this after."

"No Pam, no need for you to cook. I'll order us something – it's the least I can do since you're putting me up. How about Chinese? you always loved Chinese food."

"I did, but I'm not so keen on it now and Jake doesn't like it at all. No doubt for the same reason it's lost its appeal for me: the Chinese food you get here in the Maritimes isn't the same as we're used to."

"What do you mean?"

"For a start they don't have Ginger Beef!" said Jake with indignation.

"Oh right, yeah. This girl I knew told me that the Chinese food made on the Prairies is unique. She was Chinese herself and she said Chinese people don't call what we get real Chinese food. Instead, she said it's a mix of Western and Chinese from all the Chinese restaurants in every small town. Ginger beef is one thing and sweet-and-sour chicken balls is another, and some other stuff as well. And none of that's available here? Hmm, well then I guess it's pizza."

"Did you know it was a Canadian who invented putting pineapple on pizza?" asked Jake.

"No, but I'd say he's got a lot to answer for," replied Gerry and Jake giggled.

"As a matter of fact we've got a great Italian restaurant here that does take-out and their pizza is excellent but you can order other stuff if you like instead. I'll go get their menu, it's on the fridge, and you can have a look and decide."

"What about Dale?"

"Oh he just needs a bit of a rest. He'll lie down for 30 minutes – 45 tops – and he'll wake up hungry. We're used to this, aren't we Jake?"

"Yeah, Grandpa T will get real tired all of a sudden and then after a nap he's back to normal. It's because he's old," Jake declared, as if sharing a confidence.

"You're right Jake, he is an old guy but I'm not, eh?"

Jake looked at Gerry uncertainly and replied: "Welllll....."

Pam cut in saying: "Deliveries from this restaurant take awhile because everything is freshly cooked so if we order now the timing will work out right. Dale can have a sleep, I can straighten out this room and Gerry you can help yourself to a beer and go have a smoke if you like."

"I guess I could go for a beer, too," Jake said offhandedly, trying to sound casual. The adults laughed and Pam replied:

"No, I need you to give me a hand tidying up then getting the table set for when dinner arrives."

* *

A couple of hours later, after the pizza had been eaten and the kitchen cleaned up, they gathered in the living-room again. Pam picked up the article, ready to continue where they'd left off, but Gerry spoke first saying:

"I don't remember anything about that murder in Montreal, but Dale you knew she was a Black woman."

"Yeah, I did know that but I can't remember who told me. Or I might have read about it at the time, something like that."

"I don't remember reading about any of these killings at the time. Afterwards, yeah, but not when they happened," put in Pam.

"Oh, I'm sure I read stuff – or heard stuff from other drivers – but I don't remember anyone making all these connections."

"That's how he got away with it, Grandpa! Nobody made the connections."

"The writer mentions something about RCMP involvement but, as per usual, he doesn't think much of their efforts. He mentions a woman, who has since passed away and couldn't be interviewed, and says she was a civilian office worker. It sounds like the RCMP treated the reports that came in – and it doesn't say how many came in – as nothing more than clerical filing."

"More like circular filing, if you ask me!"

Chapter Twelve

Victim: ANGELICA POSANI

The Facts:

Toronto, Ontario: Posani's body was discovered in her new home on Wednesday, February 27, 1980. She was killed sometime the day or night before. The Real Estate agent saw her on Tuesday morning, when the movers were there, and he was dropping off keys and a gift of a fire extinguisher. He was also the one who discovered her body and was held for questioning by the police.

The Story:

"Young, beautiful, ambitious" describes Ms Posani whose meteoric rise within the multinational corporation was legendary back in 1980...

"This writing is godawful," complained Pamela.

"Never mind that, just give us the gist of the story."

"OK, let's see... no family left now, back then she'd moved around a lot in her job so no close friends either. All he can do is rehash the "such a tragic loss" quotes from her coworkers and speculate about how wonderful and perfect her life would have been had she only been allowed to live it. The so-called writer's words, not mine."

"Oh hon, he has to be kinda dramatic or people wouldn't buy the paper," said Dale.

Pam rolled her eyes, Jake's presence preventing the verbal response she wanted to give.

She read some more then gave a recap of what was written:

"There's a hint of a scandal but the writer makes it sound like that was put up as an excuse from the Toronto Police. They indicated there was a man, a married man, involved and that's where their suspicions lay. The source was a twenty-year-old payroll clerk who, amazingly enough still works there. I guess she'd be in her mid-fifties now and I'll bet she terrorizes the rest of the staff!

Anyhow she claims to have been questioned about an affair which she very firmly denied happening. Angelica Posani hadn't yet started her new position but she'd been in the office for orientation and made a great impression on this woman when she was a girl.

Police incompetence fits the theme this article wants to endorse."

* *

Steve Allerton had never forgotten Angie, although he thought of her less and less as time passed. In fact, if it hadn't been for that article serialized in the weekend paper it might have been as much as two years since memories of her surfaced. Remembering her was safe now that he was no longer powerless in thrall to her.

Although he was ten years her senior, and her boss, Angie had taken charge from the start. He had never experienced such longing and desire, and the sensations never abated the whole time they were together. He thought they'd be together forever, it's what he wanted more than anything and thought that's what she wanted too. He was devastated when it ended. In fact, he wasn't prepared to let it end.

It wasn't the actual sex – fantastic though that was – it was the constant arousal making him feel like a teenager again. He wanted her all the time and she was happy to oblige, even in the most inappropriate places. It was a miracle they were never caught!

It all happened a very, very long time ago and while he wondered in shame at the behaviour of the man he had been back then he admitted to himself that the whole dreadful experience had had moments of utter... wonder.

Miranda had kicked him out of their home, Angie had dumped him, then his boss gave him the ultimatum and he'd chosen the promotion to Prince Edward Island.

When Angie wouldn't even acknowledge his existence beyond laying a complaint with HR he'd begged Miranda to come with him and start again. She decided that the small province was far enough away from Toronto – where Angie had relocated – and so she'd agreed. After a long time, their broken marriage had healed.

The island provided an easy, slower-paced lifestyle in a beautiful setting. Steve had never strayed again, and they'd raised their family in comfortable companionship. Now that Steve was retired, he and Miranda did a little travelling and a lot of volunteering. They were both grateful and thankful for what they had.

He always ascribed his time with Angie as a period of madness caused by lust and jealousy. Looking back, he found the whole affair unbelievable, like a dream or rather a nightmare. He couldn't get over what an awful risk he'd taken, and how much he had been willing to lose... and then he recalled how she'd made him feel and the memory caused shivers of delight mixed with dread. His recollections had faded over time, and the past was dead and buried, along with the vibrant but dangerous Angelica.

Miranda must have seen the article as well, but she didn't say anything, and Steve decided that was for the best.

* *

"Does it say anything about how this killing got tied in with the rest?" asked Gerry.

"Hmm let's see, yes here at the end it says she had just moved into her place, she didn't know anyone, the only people she'd seen had been the realtor and the movers. Oh, and here it says that the police had found one of our moving pads, stencilled with the Big Sky name, but dismissed it as equipment commonly shared amongst all movers. Which is true so long as Arnie never caught anybody trying to 'borrow' something of ours."

"Whatever happened to him?"

"We lost touch. A shame because he was a great guy."

"I always felt kind of sorry for him with that wife of his," added Dale.

"Yes and no, I mean she could be a bitch but he wouldn't let her know what was going on so of course she'd get mad. He'd stay late working but he wouldn't call to give her a heads-up. I once asked him 'why not?' and he said 'she'll only hang up on me so why bother?' but she sure liked the overtime pay. She always nagged him to ask for more overtime or a raise or even to take over my job but he didn't want any of that."

"I know us drivers always offered to pay him when he opened up early or stayed late for us because if we saved time then he should get something too. But he'd say 'no you can buy me a case of beer next trip' which we were happy to provide. He never bothered much about liquor but he sure did like his beer."

"Helluva drinker and he could hold it too," Dale said. "Arnie's face would get a bit red and if anyone got the slightest bit mouthy he'd be happy to cuff them in the head but that was it, no signs of drunkenness at all."

"He liked his job and he did it well. He also liked having charge of the warehouse so he could keep everything just so. We never failed a DND inspection, we didn't even get a warning."

"Yeah he was a good guy."

"Okay, moving on."

"Ha-ha, Grammy!"

Chapter Thirteen

Victim: DENISE DRAKE

The Facts:

Winnipeg, Manitoba: Last seen on the stage dancing in the very early hours of Sunday, March 2nd. Her half-frozen body was discovered Monday morning.

The Story:

"She was a survivor" is the epitaph given by co-workers. Denise didn't have any other friends because she worked all hours to provide for her son.

"Right, this is the stripper from the Queen's Hotel. I notice that the writer glamourized the 'exotic dancing' bit and turned her into a devoted Mom and not a drug-driven slut."

"Pamela! Jake's listening to every word."

"Oh honey, I'm sorry. The thing is I find it hard to sympathize with this victim. The dancers were bad news to the truckers by causing lots of problems and even committing crimes. And Gerry don't tell me 'Oh, they're not all bad', because of course not all of them were. I'm sure some really were college kids paying their way through school. Huh. Anyhow, back to the article."

Pam read for a couple of minutes then reported that the writer hadn't been able to discover the identity of Denise Drake's son, so no current-day interviews were available.

"Instead, he goes on about a policeman called Warren Lund, who is a very old man now, and his obsession with the killer. This Lund claims he's always known the name – which he won't reveal – of the Trans-Canada Killer but couldn't secure enough evidence for a conviction. It says it's because of libel laws that he won't tell us the name. Ah, he's writing a book which 'might even have to wait for posthumous publication'. Hmmph, an awful lot of words without substance."

"What's posthumous?" queried Jake.

"After death," replied Dale.

"I sure remember Warren Lund," said Gerry. "I used to think he liked me,"

* *

Jonathan Dube couldn't recall a thing about his birth mother and he was okay with that because he loved his adoptive parents very much. They were an older, childless couple who couldn't adopt through regular channels because of their age. They'd come to a financial arrangement with the boy's mother and then they moved out of Winnipeg. None of them ever saw or heard from Denise again and they decided that was for the best.

Jonathan had grown up in a middle-class household full of encouragement, compliments, and laughter. He excelled in school and went on to university graduating into a fulfilling profession. He was still a young man when his parents died within a year of each other. His only regret was that they never got to meet the lovely girl he eventually married or the two children he adored.

Chapter Fourteen

Victim: HEATHER MORRISON

The Facts:

Edmonton, Alberta: Tuesday, March 4, 1980 Morrison's body was found in her home. She'd been viciously beaten to death sometime the night before. The Police learned Ms. Morrison was scheduled to move out of her home that very day without the knowledge of her abusive husband.

The Story:

"Children practically orphaned" when their Dad is wrongly jailed for Mommy's murder...

"Oh, I remember this one very well, of course, because she was our customer. Poor, poor woman, she had an awful life and a terrible death." Pamela shook her head in sad remembrance. Of all the Trans-Canada Killer's victims this one hit closest to home. "I didn't actually know her, in fact I we never even got a chance to speak, but I knew plenty about her."

"You know it's funny, well funny-peculiar not funny ha-ha, but I can't remember what the inside of that house looked like. I mean, the images of blood-spattered rooms with a beaten and battered body should be burned into my memory but there's nothing. The attack and hospitalization in Calgary wiped everything away," commented Dale.

"For which you should be very thankful!" exclaimed Pam.

"Yeah, you're right but you'd think something like that, so shocking, and it's not like I was used to seeing bloody violence... you did say I suffered from bad dreams way back then so do you think I still see it in my dreams?"

"You've haven't had nightmares for a long time now, hon. I hope all this talk about the murders doesn't bring them on again."

Jake, who'd been surprisingly quiet so far, piped up saying: "My teacher told us that keeping everything inside is bad but that's the way people used to be and since you're old Grandpa T maybe you handled it the way you learned how to handle stuff?"

Dale smiled down at his grandson: "You know, you're one smart kid, kiddo."

"Who shouldn't be listening to this but since you've already read all about it I guess any harm it might cause has already happened," huffed Pam, pretending to be angry with the two of them. She turned to Gerry saying: "And as for you... this is all your fault. You brought in this news magazine and God knows why but you're raking it all up again."

"Because I want, no I need, to know what exactly happened. Dale's not the only one whose memory is shaky—"

"No, not shaky but gone in my case," interrupted Dale.

"Okay, so it's different for you but for me I have only very hazy recollections and I want to know the facts. Remember none of this was tied together back then."

"I'm not sure if it's tied together now. I mean, it seems like this reporter is getting 2 + 2 = 5 in order to make up a good story. When you think about it how could the police have gotten it all so wrong?"

"I hear what you're saying but you're thinking with a 2015 mentality and this all happened back in '80. There was no World Wide Web back then—-"

"No, it did exist—"

"No Grammy, not until 1991. You're thinking of the internet that only the government had."

"Well crimes got solved before we ever had an Internet or a Web," she retorted.

"Of course they did but this was a unique situation. This killer-trucker travelled through different jurisdictions and the local police had no reason to think the murder they were investigating was anything but a one-off thing."

"The writer said that the RCMP did get involved but only to liaise with different divisions."

"And the article says they didn't take it too seriously because they put a woman in charge of that."

"Oh no not a woman - horrors! and a civilian, too. Had they no shame?"

"Ha-ha. I still think they could have done better, I agree with the writer that much," commented Dale.

"You're right, they should have done better. The writer interviewed Heather Morrison's daughter. She's a grown woman with a family of her own now and she's still bitter about what happened to her Dad. Here's what's written in the article:

Amelia Jensen, nee Morrison, in a phone interview from Edmonton, admits that her father Hugh was a difficult man: an abusive husband,

and an absent father, but he was never a murderer. However when Heather Morrison, her mother, was brutally killed the police looked no further than Hugh Morrison. In fact, they found Hugh on their own premises – locked up in the drunk tank that very night! Hmm, that is a bit odd.

Anyhow, the article goes on to say that when Amelia, the daughter, looked into her family history, she learned that back in the late seventies he father had been diagnosed with manic depression which we now call bi-polar disorder. That was controllable with medication, but the drugs were strong and interfered with his drinking. Hugh Morrison was an alcoholic who chose to medicate with booze instead of his prescribed pills. The writer is insinuating his own opinion in here, I'm sure!

Amelia is quoted as saying:

'The police should have traced his movements from when he left work that day until he ended up locked up overnight in one of their cells but obviously they didn't or the truth would have come out much sooner than it did. We learned that he didn't even have cut or bruised knuckles which should have set off alarm bells.' The aggrieved daughter continues: 'I realize that it was 100% his own fault that he was a likely suspect because of how he had treated Mom but I'm sorry to say that the police took the easy answer without investigating.' And of course the writer wholeheartedly agrees with that statement.

The story goes on about how Amelia and her brother Ted were raised by their mother's parents and that even though the case against her father collapsed before ever going to trial he never reclaimed ownership of his children. He was welcome to visit and did so on occasion, but in effect the children did lose both their parents."

* *

"Daddy's here!" screamed Amelia. She'd been looking out the window for the past hour waiting for her father's arrival. She ran to the front foyer. Her brother, running down the stairs, shoved Amelia aside to be first at the door. "Teddy..." she wailed, stumbling to keep her balance.

The ten-year-old ignored her as he opened the door calling, "Hi Dad!"

"Teddy, hey guy look at you - you've grown again. Where's Melly? Ah, there's my girl." Hugh Morrison swung his daughter up in his arms, exclaiming that she was way too thin and declaring that the kids needed ice cream. They shrilly voiced agreement while Amelia squirmed to get down. "You've heard about those 31 Flavours at Baskin-Robbins, right?" he asked them. Both children nodded with great enthusiasm.

They ran to get into his car, a 1978 Cougar in two-tone brown/ beige, while he admonished them to sit up straight and not put their shoes on the seat or the dash. At two years younger Amelia was no match for her brother so she was pushed into the backseat while he rode up front. Vying against each other for their father's attention they chattered non-stop during the drive while Hugh, his hands trembling, lit one cigarette off the butt of another.

The children were out the car the moment it stopped. Hugh winced at the slamming of the door and called out to them, but they'd already raced each other into the ice cream shop. There were several people waiting ahead of them in line. A very small child was being coaxed by its mother to 'pick a flavour' and Hugh grew impatient with the delay.

"Look Triple Chocolate, oh and here's Chocolate Mint, and hey, you'll like this pink one it's called Bubblegum–"

"I like this one with orange and black stripes, or how about that purple there... Daddy, can I have two different scoops?"

"Two? No! you're being greedy. It's not like you'll eat it—"

"Yes, I will, I will, I will so!"

"Stop that right now. A skinny little thing you won't even finish one scoop."

"I will, Dad. I can eat two scoops no problem, I bet I can eat three even," declared Teddy.

Amelia started to whine that she could eat two scoops of different flavours and that's when Hugh lost it.

Remembering the incident many, many years later Amelia couldn't, thankfully, recall the exact words her father had used but she easily relived that moment when the room went silent and how scared she became. Her father had rapidly changed into a red-faced, screaming, fearsome monster before her eyes, ranting and raving and oozing anger – she half-expected him to turn into a cartoon character with steam coming out of his ears.

They never did get their ice-cream, but each got a slap as they were pushed out of the store and back to the car. Both children were put in the backseat and told to stop their crying, or he'd give them something to cry about. Amelia struggled to control her sobs after Teddy had punched her hard in the arm.

As an adult she understood that for her father to have to have his in-laws raise his children must have been hard and he was under enormous pressure. She blamed the wrongful arrest for much of that.

Chapter Fifteen

Victim: DEBRA-ANN LYNLEY

The Facts:

Vancouver, British Columbia: Victim is believed to have been killed on Thursday, March 6th, 1980. The body, found in the brush alongside the Trans-Canada a few miles outside of Vancouver, was discovered by a family of tourists.

The Story:

"She had everything and more!" say the parents now divorced after enduring years of pain and loss from the death of their beloved daughter, knowing her killer was still out there.

"This is a sad story but, unfortunately, not all that unusual: A young woman quarrels with her parents and leaves home, hitchhikes and gets murdered. Jake never, ever hitchhike, okay?"

"I'm not a girl, Grammy."

"Sadly, boys and young men can be victims as well. Especially if they've been walking for miles in either freezing cold or sweating hot weather so when a car finally does stop they're so grateful that it's possible their 'spidey sense' isn't working as well as it should."

"Yeah, I know all about not getting into cars with strangers but if someone ever did try to grab me, I'd fight 'em off."

"You can't fight against a taser or chloroform or an injection. The idea is not to let anybody get close enough to grab you and that means never ever hitching a ride!"

"She's right kiddo, so just agree and do what she says."

"Is that the secret to your long and happy marriage, Dale?" laughed Gerry.

"Don't even think about coming up with some smart-alecky remark to that mister," Pam pretended to scowl at her husband.

"The rest of this write-up is about the parents. It looks like the mother became some sort of activist for women's rights, and the father ended up marrying his secretary."

* *

Amanda Lynley was the Queen Bee in her nursing home. Hers was the loudest voice and she used it to broadcast her opinions accompanying the nightly newscast with a running commentary. She stated that her point of view had leaned so far to the left it had toppled over. Amanda was an advocate of anything and anyone who fought against 'the system'.

She especially despised the police who had first of all failed to protect her darling daughter from a serial killer on a rampage, and secondly, failed to apprehend said murderer. She was on the side of anyone who was against the cops. This often put her at odds with her fellow residents – the older folks often being more supportive of law-and-order - but she enjoyed arguing and would shout down even valid points made by her opponents.

At some point over the years Amanda's memory had altered her relationship with Debra-Ann into a loving mother-daughter unit struggling against the oppression of an overbearing workaholic father who'd driven the girl away from her home.

She was an old lady now and entitled to her version of events but on reading through his notes the journalist remembered her as an unsympathetic character and decided against writing up the interview for his article.

Chapter Sixteen

Pam put down the paper and looked between the two men saying:

"Well that was an eye-opener! I had no idea. But why didn't we know about this? We should have because we must have met, and even known, this guy. How could he have killed so many women and gotten away with it?"

"I have a good excuse for not knowing about it all because I was lying unconscious in a hospital bed. And honey, you spent most of your time sitting by my side. Gerry you were injured too, so you weren't back on the road right away either."

"That's 'cause it's a little hard to shift gears with a bullet hole in your shoulder," he replied in a dry tone.

"You didn't have to get involved, that was practically a self-inflicted injury."

"Screw you!" Gerry laughed at her. Jake stifled a giggle.

"But seriously, I never knew seven women were murdered by a serial killer truck driver back in 1980. It's not a case of I knew but then forgot about it, the truth is I never knew about it in the first place. If it did happen that way, that is."

"I didn't realize there were seven. I mean, I remember the Kingston one. Hearing about it brought back the memory of us all been stranded on the Trans-Canada waiting for the O.P.P. to let us go. I remember too that it was brutally cold, we were in the middle of a real cold snap."

"What's the O.P.P?" Jake queried.

"It stands for Ontario Provincial Police, Jake."

"Don't they have Mounties?"

"Um, yeah they might. Probably up in Northern Ontario but I'm not certain."

"They have them in Ottawa for sure," put in Dale.

"That's right, The Musical Ride. Wasn't it a Mountie who got shot at the War Memorial by that terrorist last year?"

"No Pam, he was a soldier. A Cpl. Cirillo, um.. Ethan? no Nathan! Anyhow, an unarmed man gunned down by a cowardly terrorist."

"They say 9/11 was America's wake-up call so I guess this was ours. We've been naive and stupid for too long."

"No Gerry, I would say honest and honourable. Saying it's our fault because our security is too lax is blaming the victim. We didn't used to need all this security we've got now. A mob of bloodthirsty, murderous lunatics can't teach us anything good. I'm sure our security forces have been aware all along but couldn't find politicians with the will to fund appropriate measures, or lawmakers and judges to enact and uphold whatever legislation is required to stop these people."

"Pam, thirty-plus years ago they couldn't stop a lone trucker out there killing women."

"But it's no wonder nobody made a connection between a hitchhiker in Vancouver and a wife and mother in Montreal, for example."

"And who's to say it is a lone trucker? and how many women, really? I mean, this article mentions seven. As Pam said 'was there even a serial killer?' or is it all guesswork by the guy who wrote this? I always thought it was four but then I never knew about the woman in Montreal, and I didn't connect the girl from BC or that woman in Edmonton. Pam, you said you knew her, right?"

"I didn't know her personally, she was our customer, but she was murdered the night before we were scheduled to move her. But it was her husband who killed her, or at least that's what we all thought then. That's what the police thought too."

"From what the daughter said in the article it sounds like he might not have been his wife's killer but there's nothing definite to say he wasn't. Of course after all this time how could they get proof? Especially since all the killings were handled by different jurisdictions who'd all handle their cases differently, too."

"I remember that cop, the one who harassed you Gerry, giving an interview at the time and then it was hushed up or something because he wasn't supposed to speak to the media and he didn't have actual proofs or something? so his allegations could have caused trouble. Again, my memory of that time isn't the best. He must be pretty old now, if he's still alive."

"The writer of the article spoke to him. Of course the writer also blames the police," said Jake.

"Yes, he does but I'm not sure if he's right to do so. I mean a woman is murdered after she moves into a dodgy neighbourhood of Montreal, another woman is killed when she moves into a new home in Halifax where the previous tenants were known criminals, a girl hitchhiking to Vancouver is killed by the roadside. Those aren't unlikely conclusions for the police to make. And how could we expect the police from those three provinces to make a connection?"

"When you add a woman killed in Kingston the day she moved, a woman killed in Edmonton the night before she was moving, a woman killed in Toronto on the day she moved – obviously there's a connection with moving. Since the victims were all in different cities in different provinces it's not the realtors and it's not the moving company staff because the salesmen, packers, helpers, and warehousemen don't travel. No, It had to be a driver. And then there was Denise, a stripper at a trucker hotel."

"Yes, but where's the proof? I mean, sure it sounds likely but lots of things could be possible until you learn the facts."

"Grammy, there weren't seven guys going around killing women who happened to move all in the same week!" exclaimed Jake.

"He's right, hon. All of the murders happened within a day or two of each other. Let's look at the dates and see what we can figure out." Dale gestured towards the pages of the article and Pam sorted them.

"Okay, the order he's listed them in does go by date. Jake can you make a note of this for us? February 18th in Kingston, Ontario then the 20th in Halifax. The next one isn't until the 25th in Montreal. That seems odd except that on the 26th he killed in Toronto and March 2nd in Winnipeg. So he went East and now is on the turnaround trip back out West. March 4 in Edmonton and March 6 in Vancouver."

"I wonder if there were more killings in Nova Scotia or New Brunswick before Montreal?"

"Or even in Ontario. 1980 would have been a leap year so there were five days between the Toronto and the Winnipeg victims and the Northern part of the province has some pretty isolated spots. Eh, Pam? You said you pitied the residents of the occasional home we saw in the midst of the never-ending miles of pine forest. You thought they must be so miserable in the winter."

"Grandpa T. did you remember that 1980 was a leap year or did you just know it?"

"Jake, Jake, Jake. What do they teach you in school nowadays? If a year is divisible by four it's a leap year unless it ends in double-zero and isn't divisible by 400," at Jake's puzzled look Dale continued: "1900 divided by 4 is how much?"

Jake scribbled on the paper a minute before saying: "475."

"And 80 divided by 4 is 20 so 1980 evenly divides by 4 to equal 495, right?"

"Right. But you can't divide 1980 by 400."

"No, but you don't have to. The 400 rule only applies to new centuries. 1900 was not a leap year but 2000 was. So it's every four years unless the year ends with a double-zero."

Jake turned to his grandmother asking: "Did you know about this?"

"Yes, Jake. It's one of those things we had to memorize, but I always have to count it out in my head to double-check. Or nowadays I can look it up on the Internet."

"Jake buddy, even I know that rule and I'm a drop-out," added Gerry.

Jake thought about what they'd said then suddenly the frown left his face as he announced: "I bet Dad doesn't know it. I'll test him when I get home."

Dale chuckled saying: "You do that, boy. But you might be surprised."

Pam returned to their discussion about the series of killings.

"So based on these dates, which only last roughly three weeks, we can see a pattern of travel."

"It's definitely a long-distance truck driver who connects them."

"And a guy moving household goods along the Trans-Canada in 1980 had to be a driver we knew."

"Who? I can't think of anyone," said Pam continuing: "And it's scary, I don't want to think about it. Whoever it was must be dead by now because they stopped."

"But did they? I mean, what if there were more than seven victims but nobody's added them to the list?"

"Or what if there's less," she countered adding: "I agree that there weren't seven killers but we also don't know for sure that it was only one man who killed all seven of these women."

"Maybe the police will re-open the cases because of this story in the paper!" Jake sounded excited but the three adults only looked worried.

Chapter Seventeen

Dale still looked exhausted. Pamela knew he'd enjoyed Jake's bowling tournament very much, but the excitement had taken its toll. Today his face was gray and drawn and he needed to rest.

Pam had made up her mind that she would find out the truth behind Gerry's visit. They would go out for supper in lieu of the lunch they'd postponed and have a good private talk. She needed to have it out with him and get this thing finished once and for all. "But what will I do with Jake?" she wondered.

Overcast skies and a chilly breeze made a day indoors attractive. Pam knew they owned dozens and dozens of videos so she would suggest that Jake enjoy a few hours with popcorn and Star Wars or Mission Impossible or Harry Potter. Or the boy might enjoy some of the older stuff like E.T.? or Indiana Jones? She'd set up the Blu-Ray player and get Jake settled with snacks and a selection of movies. She recalled that some of their older films – like Porky's or Blazing Saddles – wouldn't be appropriate for a tween so she'd weed those ones out first.

Dale wanted to make the most of Jake's visit, especially now that the summer was drawing to a close and their grandson would be heading home soon. He'd want to join in on the movie binge which was great because she knew he'd nod off right away in his old La-Z-Boy chair. Pam would have a quiet word with Jake to ensure he let Grandpa sleep. "We'll only be gone for about two hours, and these two will be fine on their own for that long," she decided.

Everyone agreed to the plan Pam had devised but it took longer than expected for her and Gerry to get going. It seemed they had an awful lot of movies that Jake wanted to watch and he spent quite some time sorting the videos into piles. Finally he chose The Goonies. By that time Dale was fighting to keep his eyes open.

"Sorry you're having to wait so long to eat, Gerry."

"I'm fine. As I said I could have had a sandwich with the guys, we don't need to eat in a restaurant, but you're keen to go so it's all good. Of course, by time we get there I'll probably be starving."

"I know, eh? Who would have thought it would take so long for Jake to pick a movie? He was super excited going through the different titles. Since he's still here for another four days he's got plenty of time to watch more of them, and he can take some home with him if he wants.

Anyhow, supper will be great. The food is super good and you'll enjoy a real Maritime meal."

"I believe you but I have to say I'm surprised you haven't picked up on the Maritimer slang. You still say "super" all the time."

"Whereas 'round here they say some, like 'some excited' or 'some good', yeah I know. We never do use that wording. I think it would make me feel like I was imitating them, or making fun or something, I don't know. I'll just stick to the speech of my youth and say 'super'."

They got into Gerry's rental and Pam gave directions. Now that tourist season was winding down the traffic had noticeably thinned. It was an easy fifteen-minute drive and Pam pointed out various landmarks along the way. When they got to the restaurant the parking lot had emptied of the lunch time crowd. It was beginning to fill with seniors for the early-bird dinner specials and they were all jockeying for the handicap parking spaces.

Within minutes they were seated and reading the menus. Gerry ordered a beer and Pam had a ginger-ale.

"You don't want a–"

"Nope, I don't indulge anymore. I've given up drinking for desserts as I'm sure you've noticed and no," she said with a laugh, "I'm not fishing for a compliment. I am well aware what dress size I wear nowadays and I don't care!"

When the waitress came Gerry flirted like it was second nature to him "and it still is," Pam thought, observing with a smile. The middle-aged woman gave back as good as she got wagging her finger in his face and laughing as she said,

"Oh, I've got your number mister... it's 9-1-1 for Help!"

They got down to a serious discussion about which of the various lobster dishes would be his best choice and he finally settled on grilled lobster tails. Pam selected lobster salad. It was the sort of meal she would never make a home so that made it a real treat.

They enjoyed their feast while continuing to catch up on mutual friends.

Pam explained that their old boss, Eddie Fedani, had sold the trucking company, Blue Sky Moving, and invested in a Swiss Chalet franchise. CARA Foods required its franchisees to be hands-on, not investors only, and fortunately Eddie and his wife had enough siblings, nieces, and nephews to staff the restaurant and then another, and another.

They were no longer in touch, other than exchanging Christmas cards, but Pam was sure someone in the family would have let them know if Eddie, who must be quite an elderly man by now, had taken ill or had passed away.

Pamela insisted on contributing to the bill and Gerry didn't argue too hard. Seafood prices were shockingly high but most of the clientele were tourists and willing to splurge on what was usually a once-in-a-lifetime trip. As they paid Pam asked if it was okay to leave their vehicle in the parking-lot while they took a walk along the cliff.

"I need to work off some of those delicious calories and since walking's the only thing she's willing to go for well..." The cashier was a pretty young woman who shook her head and smiled at Gerry while assuring Pam that the car would be fine for a couple of hours.

"Oh, we won't be that long. We want to take a look at the view and get some fresh sea air."

They took their time walking up the steep path. There was a handrail which both of them made use of. Once they got to the top Pam was surprised that no one else was around. The day was overcast and after yesterday's sudden rainstorm it looked like visitors had chosen indoor entertainment.

Finally, Gerry led them into the conversation Pam had been putting off saying: "When you read out that bit about that cop claiming he knows who the Trans-Canada Killer is I decided that I've had this 'shadow of suspicion' hanging over me long enough. I don't know for sure if he meant me, but enough people have wondered, and it's ruined my life."

Pam replied heatedly saying, "No Gerry, that isn't true. You've always been on a self-destruction course. You're a dissatisfied man always wanting more."

"Huh! I guess I wasn't lucky enough to settle down with the right woman, eh Pammy?"

"Gerry you and Dale are so different. He and I have lived a regular, unexciting life and that's exactly how we wanted it. Because it wasn't boring to us, it was smooth sailing, whereas you – you never wanted that. You wanted a speed boat, you wanted to waterski with one ski, go hang-gliding, paragliding, bungee jumping, zip-lines... you always wanted to be in the middle of the action, you could never have lived on the sidelines."

But Gerry wasn't mollified by Pam's explanation. Narrowed eyes and thinned lips showed his anger. He shook his head saying: "Oh sure, I messed up two marriages and had dozens of affairs, broke some hearts, ran up debts, got some STDs, but don't kid yourself, Pam, I'm not the bad guy. All along it's been Dale, who has everything, who is actually the one – he's the 'Trans-Canada Killer.'"

"He's not! You must be!"

Chapter Eighteen

"That's what you think? That's I'm the one? Are you fucking crazy?" Gerry shouted and Pam snapped back:

"Don't speak to me like that."

"Sorry if I'm offending you Pamela but what the.. you've thought that about me all this time?"

"No, I.. I'm sorry I blurted that out but Gerry yes, I do believe it must have been you because it wasn't Dale. I mean, if it has to be a Blue Sky driver than it has to be you." She reached for his hand, but he stepped away from her.

"So, all these years you were happy to cover up for me. You never said a word to anybody, Miss Perfect Pamela aiding and abetting MURDER, mass murder committed by me. You expect me to believe that?"

"I never thought that way, at least only in my subconscious, I guess. No, not even that because I never believed in a serial killer truck driver.

Listen I'm not the most observant person. I mean for example today, when we get home, Dale will say something like 'it's great sailing weather were there many boats out?' and I won't have a clue. I looked out at the water, if there were boats there, I saw them, but they didn't register...

Gerry interrupted her saying: "What's with you and smooth sailing and sailboats today?"

"It's an example, that's all. God, I'm getting all flustered. Forget the sailboats I only mentioned them to show that I'm not interested in stuff that doesn't concern me."

"No, why would you be when you're happily living in your own little world. You're all nice and secure, right? well guess what? it's time to wake up and smell the coffee."

Pam was practically shouting as she said: "You're twisting everything I say. Listen, you need to understand that I have not spent the last 30-odd years thinking you were a serial killer because I didn't think about it at all."

"I see. So, you're saying that it's not interesting that you've got a guilty secret, a horrifying secret, about a close friend – or at least a coworker who thought he was a close friend of yours – so you buried it deep in your brain. You forgot all about it, got married, raised a family, lived your best life and now, now that we're talking it's all coming to the surface, is that what you're saying? Seriously?"

"Dammit Gerry I can't explain myself. I do have a secret but that's not it. My secret is actually Dale's secret, and I'm trying to protect him."

* *

"Protect Dale from what?" exclaimed Gerry.

"From himself, from his guilt trip, from his nightmares."

"Does he still have those?"

"Not for years and years now. That why I'm afraid that raking things up about the past might cause them to return. He hasn't had one for so long. It was so upsetting to have him suddenly sit up in bed shouting about 'that woman' and 'she's a killer' and 'she should die'. It was horrible."

"I remember, from when we shared a place, and you're right it scared the shit out of me when he'd start yelling. You hear something like that, in the pitch dark, and your heart is pounding a mile a minute. I forgot about those, but Pam the accident was an awfully long time ago."

"But I don't know if he's talking about the drunk driving mother from the accident or the stabbing woman who almost killed him."

"Oh right, when he ended up in hospital in Calgary. Did they ever catch her?"

"Yeah, actually not long after it happened. You know how it is when somebody's not used to climbing up into a big truck – she had her hands all over the door frame and the cops had her fingerprints on file so it didn't take long. She claimed she was coerced into doing it by her boyfriend. You know, the Karla Homolka defence. She also said she didn't know what he took from the truck. Nobody believed her."

"Was she Native?"

"No, the reason they chose the Reservation was because it was quiet there, no lighting, nobody around."

"Dale was lucky he got found in time."

This time when Pam reached for him he didn't pull away. She held his hand in both of hers and said: "I begging you, don't keep going on about all this. It's over, 'let sleeping dogs lie'. Dale went through a terrible time that was rough on me, too. I don't want to go there again and he can't, I mean.. well." She stopped abruptly and Gerry looked at her quizzically. He was no longer raising his voice but she could hear how serious he was when he stated:

"There's still more, isn't there? There's a secret and it's not the fear of nightmares returning. So, tell me what's going on Pam. We're not leaving here until you do."

"OK Gerry, you win," she sighed. "But I'll have to tell him I told you. I shouldn't be saying anything because it's his story to tell but well yeah, you should know."

"Know what?"

She expelled a big breath and confided: "Dale only has a few weeks left to live."

Chapter Nineteen

"No way."

"Unfortunately, yes. He's got lung cancer and there's nothing they can do."

"There must be. People are getting better from cancer all the time. There's all these new treatments and even transplants..."

Pam interrupted saying: "He refused to do anything, and now it's too late."

"What do you mean he refused? Couldn't you make him?" Gerry replied angrily.

"I tried and tried. In fact, when Michael announced they were sending Jake here for the summer I was going to refuse because I didn't need the distraction of an unhappy young boy being around. I was planning to concentrate on convincing Dale, of nagging, crying, yelling – doing whatever I had to do – but from the very start he dug his heels in. You know how stubborn he can be. He said to me 'I've already passed my biblical allotment'—"

"Dale said that?"

"I know, eh? Obviously someone used that term with him and it stuck. Anyhow, he said 'let someone younger get new lungs, I'd rather spend my final days enjoying this time with you and with Jake' and, ultimately, it is his decision."

"Dammit to hell, Pam. Oh, that is crappy news." Gerry pulled her into a hug and Pam felt herself letting the tears fall. Trying to keep a brave face on things takes a real toll, she realized, and the release felt good but she needed to get her emotions under control again. She straightened up and wiped her eyes dry.

"So, you see it's in everyone's best interest to let this go."

"Oh, Pam. Why can't you see what's right in front of you? Those nightmares you're so worried about might not have a thing to do with the accident or the hijacking. Knowing he's running out of time might be bringing stuff to the surface of his mind and Dale might be reliving the murders he committed."

* *

"Stop saying that," she screamed.

Gerry responded furiously as well: "Give your head a shake, it was Dale, and you know it was."

By this time their walk had taken them right to the edge of the cliff. They'd wandered off the path and Pam felt a moment of fear, but she rallied to insist Gerry was lying.

"No, you're the one who had black-outs."

"Mostly from drinking too much but yeah, sometimes from bad headaches. But so did Dale, don't you remember? His head was always hurting."

"You're wrong. You are so wrong. Dale is a very gentle, caring, loving man. He's never raised his voice, never mind his fist, in all the years we've been together. You saw the photos in that article, those women were severely beaten and whoever did that was crazy, blood-lust crazy. Dale could never be that way. He has always been respectful towards women.

In fact, after 9/11 he got very anti-Muslim saying Islam wasn't a real religion because of the way women were treated. He felt very strongly about that. How can you say this same man went out brutalizing strangers?"

"How can you say I did?"

"Oh, not on purpose, Gerry. I know that. You had a terrible head injury and when you got out of hospital you killed those women in a dissociative state. When you got shot you were shocked out of it."

"That's what you've been thinking all these years?"

"No! I didn't realize I even thought that. I haven't been thinking about it at all...I... I guess I forgot about it. I was happy to forget about it."

"That's because in your heart of hearts Pammy you know that everything you've been saying and thinking about me is actually true about Dale. Dale suffered PTSD or a psychotic break or something after that fatal accident. He wasn't himself when he went on a killing spree, he was enraged and violent."

"He's not the Incredible Hulk!"

"Neither am I!"

"But the police back in Edmonton... they were so sure about you."

"Yeah, and that's what's causin' me problems now. What if this article re-opens the investigation? I can't go through that again."

"Well, I can't have Dale upset by your ridiculous accusations."

"Listen, it was a long time ago but I remember you and me in that hotel room going through my logs and you proved I couldn't have done it. You must remember! You never did get a chance to check Dale's logs because he never made it to Calgary that night."

"I don't need to prove it. I know Dale. We've been together for over thirty years and I know him through and through. There is no way he could be the killer."

"Don't you remember you wanted to find out if he delivered in Kingston? That victim was the woman who got killed when she was going to the grocery store. Reading that article gave us all kinds of information we didn't have then. Like the Montreal victim being a Black woman. I never knew that but Dale did.

We also learned the details of that young girl who got murdered outside of Vancouver, on her way to the city. I was already in Vancouver before that even happened. I hustled so I'd get waiting time for my load, remember? I don't remember names or anything, but I do remember that trip. How could I forget? It's what ended everything."

"Dale is not the killer," Pam insisted.

"He is the killer. It's either him or me and sure as shit I know it isn't me. It isn't me, Pamela. Dale is the 'Trans-Canada Killer' and you know it."

Pamela's eyes strayed to the cliff edge again and for one wild moment she wanted to jump over it into nothingness. Gerry's words pierced a hole in her heart, and she wanted to run away from everything. Because she believed what Gerry said was true - and she hated herself for that.

Chapter Twenty

"Okay, if you're so sure then I've got questions for you: why did he start killing? in fact, why did he stop killing? or do you think he's spent the last thirty-five years murdering women whenever he felt like it. Is that what you think?"

Gerry grabbed her by the shoulders and pulled her away from the edge and back onto the path. Pam was yelling and crying, and he wanted to shake some sense into her but knew he had to calm her down. There was nobody else walking up here but that could change at any time.

"I don't have all the answers, and it's not like we can go around asking people – especially Dale! but I've spent a lot of time thinking about this and here's what I've come up with. It's like what you said about me: an injury sent me into some state and the shooting brought me out of it, except it's Dale we're talking about.

It's my belief that when Dale had the accident with the car, where those two kids were killed, it unhinged him temporarily. He must have been full of anger – and rightly so – against the drunk mother but Dale could never get over the fact that he's the one who drove into them even though there wasn't a damn thing he could have done differently. It wasn't his fault, but he took the blame and always felt guilty about it."

"So how did he hide this side of himself so well? how come I never knew?"

"Because even Dale didn't know. He wasn't aware he was doing it! You mentioned that word already, something like disaffected disorder–"

"Dissociative," interrupted Pam.

"Yeah, what we used to call 'Not Guilty by Reason of Insanity'. They call it something else now, and there have been several cases over the past few years. Creepy stuff."

"You mean that 'Not Criminally Responsible' defence, right?"

"Yes, that's it. Remember that boy in Calgary who murdered his roommates? He stabbed them to death."

"I don't think they were roommates, or at least not all of them, there were five altogether and it happened at a house party."

"Right, de Grood. Matthew de Grood. He looks young in the photo the newspapers used but by time he got to court he sure looked like a man."

"Yeah, a lot of people had trouble believing that he wasn't responsible."

"I still don't. Mind, I live in Calgary so I read all the coverage at the time. That's why I remember the case so well. The victims' families aren't accepting this special defence either. They keep fighting against him, or his doctors, claiming he's better. It was the same with that guy from BC who killed his three young children."

"Right, he had a Dutch or German name or something. I can't remember what it was but I do remember feeling so sorry for the children's mother. What a terrible, terrible thing."

"And of course, the guy who beheaded his seatmate on a Greyhound Bus in Manitoba, in Portage."

"Portage La Prairie, right. Tim MacLean was the young man who was killed, and it was such a horrible killing. The killer something-Li got a new name and he's out now. Unbelievable. But yeah, they used that same defence for him."

"That was so shocking. We remember all of these cases because serial killings and savage killings are still rare here in Canada. Sometimes they even use that defence for an attack that doesn't end up as a murder. I have a hazy recollection about a young man and a professor..."

"I never really believed in that defence myself. I mean the courts and the psychiatrists – the experts – accept it so it must be real, but I think once they're 'cured' they should then be tried for their crimes."

"And this is what you think Dale has?"

"Had, not has."

"So how did he get rid of it, hmm? Did he wake up one day and decide the sun was shining just right so miraculously he was all better? If so, why didn't he say something?"

"Well again, I'm only guessing, you know that, but what if when he got hijacked on the way to Calgary–"

Pam interrupted again to say: "When he got stabbed, you mean. Not hit on the head. No brain damage this time."

"Yeah well, what if before he got to the hospital he remembered everything about those past weeks of killing? I mean, he was almost dead from blood loss, right? and they say your life flashes before your eyes, don't they?"

"Mmm that only applies to drowning but okay, say that's what did happen. That Dale suddenly realized he was a cold-blooded, vicious, brutal serial killer – then what?"

"I think he tried to shoot himself."

"What?" cried Pam. She looked so stricken Gerry reached out to pull her close.

"Listen, you and I both know that Dale, our Dale, isn't some Dr Jekyll guy. If he did have this black-out kind of thing happening then when he came to and realized what he'd done he wouldn't be able to live with himself. He'd kill himself."

"Okay, first off you mean Mr. Hyde, he was the bad guy, and sure I could see Dale thinking he'd rather be dead then live with himself knowing what he'd done – if he had done something like that - but he didn't die. He fired that shot to attract attention and it worked."

"No, he was just too weak to hold the gun up properly to aim."

"And after he survived he conveniently forgot what he'd been trying to do because he once again forgot what he'd supposedly done?"

"Look, I know you're being sarcastic because you don't want to believe this but yes, when he got to hospital and was fighting for his life his brain said 'right, screw the shit-thoughts for now and concentrate on healing'. Are you sure about it being Mr. Hyde?"

"Positive. Umm, okay so now you've given me something to think about. I'm not saying I agree with everything, but I guess it is a possible solution."

"It is. Dale had a brain injury in an accident that traumatized him. Something about each of these women triggered him into a murderous rage and he, well, murdered them. That lasted for three weeks and then the craziness left–"

"Oh, right. How likely is that?"

"Well, how about he was forced to face up to what he'd done and that sobered him up, except it was getting back his sanity, and then his mind pushed everything down deep while it dealt with getting him better and it's never resurfaced, so as far as he's concerned it never happened."

"Why hasn't he remembered in all the many, many years since then?"

"Because of you, Pamela. Because of the love you two have for each other. You brought him comfort and calm and, I guess, reassurance or something like that. The bad thoughts stayed buried deep inside his head and he had no reason to remember. You've kept him safe." Gerry teared up as he said this, and Pam felt her eyes watering and then the tears spilling over.

"So, I harboured a killer, covered up for him and protected him and basically hid him."

"You never knew that's what you were doing but yeah, that's pretty much my theory about it all. And he said he stopped driving cross-country long ago so that could also explain why the highway killings stopped."

"I agree that if Dale ever realized exactly what he'd done – assuming he was the Trans-Canada Killer, that is – then yeah, I do believe he would have killed himself, or tried to. But I'm not sure if I buy the idea that he couldn't have known, I mean, that's pretty messed up."

"It's like a subconscious thing, I guess. And hey, do you think that struggle going on in his brain might be why he had nightmares?"

"Oh Gerry, I wish to hell you had stayed away from us."

* *

It was still light out when they got back home even though they'd stopped on the way so Gerry could pick up a case of beer. Dale and Jake were outside with Dale stretched out on the chaise-longue while Jake played a jumping game involving the bench of the picnic-table.

Pam felt wrung-out but managed to put a good face on things by answering Dale's questions about their meal brightly. As soon as she could manage it she suggested Jake come indoors and pick out the DVDs he wanted to watch before he left.

Dale saw something in the faces of his wife and his friend – despite their attempted cover-up – and said:

"C'mon Gerry, let's go for a ride, I'll drive."

He led the way to his pick-up and neither man said anything until they were on the road.

Chapter Twenty-One

"You and me are used to doing our thinking behind the wheel and there's something about driving along that makes it easy to talk. Now, I'm guessing from the long faces that Pam told you my news?"

"She did."

"Thought so. Having to pretend everything's okay around Jake has started to wear on her and I'm sure she appreciated having someone she could talk to."

"Well..."

"And I appreciate it. I am so very glad to have seen you again. I always owed you a lot for the friendship we knew way back when and still now."

"You don't owe me anything, I relied on you."

"Huh. I have to admit that I always envied you your easy manner with women and men too, and how relaxed and casual you were about everyday things. Stuff like paying bills and returning phone calls, stuff that would weigh on me if I didn't take care of it right away."

Gerry laughed saying: "Like I always told you: don't sweat the small stuff."

"Yeah, and I hated hearing that. I didn't want to be irresponsible like you, but I did admire the way you handled things with no stress. You always had an open friendly interest in life and in other people. You could start up a conversation with anyone and you'd enjoy it, too."

"You mean I'm a nosy prick, eh?"

Both men chuckled and continued for a few miles in silence. Then Gerry said:

"Why didn't you fight it? What if something could have been done?"

"To tell the truth Gerry, I've had enough of hospitals and I've seen too many people struggling from one operation to another, and all the time they're hoping and then getting disappointed all over again. I couldn't face that."

"But a cancer diagnosis doesn't have to be a death sentence nowadays. I mean sure, it used to be that the Big C meant the end and people suffered a lot in order to gain a few more months but they've come such a long way since those days."

"Naw, it happened fast with me. By time I saw the doctor he was using words like aggressive and radical treatment, and I thought to myself 'uh-uh, no thanks'. I don't remember if you ever knew that I'd been married before Pam?"

"Oh right, yeah I did. Oh yeah, she died of cancer too, right?"

"Yeah, Sissy, she was so young and she was in so much pain. I guess part of me never got over seeing that. You know, if we'd known what she was going to go through I would willingly have put a pillow over her face and spared her all the agony. And I'd have owned up to it too because it would have been the right thing to do. She suffered horribly.

Now they're talking about 'assisted suicide' and let me tell you I'm all for it. Nobody should suffer like that in this day and age. I'm sure as hell not going to."

"Well you're being pretty calm about it all."

"Couple reasons for that. First off, I've had some time to come to terms with things. I've had a good life. I married a wonderful woman who I raised a son with, and now we've got a grandson who's a great kid. I've been lucky and I've had a good run."

"But you've had some pretty bad times. You mentioned your first wife dying so young, and then there was, well, the accident that took you down, and then getting stabbed and almost dying. Shit, you haven't been all that lucky, Dale."

"But I got through it all and yeah, sometimes life sucks but we find the strength to get through. Pam has given me so much strength. That's my other reason for accepting what's happened, it's actually somebody else's story but it hit home with me.

In town there's a bakery run by a woman called Jasmine. She's Muslim and I don't like Muslims. I never thought one way or the other about them until all that shit started happening in the eighties in Iran. You're just about my age, you must remember when we used to call it Persia and we used to spell it Moslem? Anyhow, when I learned these people wanted to destroy us well I wanted nothing to do with them. So long as they stayed in their part of the world they could kill each other all day long for all I cared."

"Yeah, I agree, and then there was 9/11."

"9/11 and more. So anyhow I'm at this bakery and boy, bakeries sure smell good, eh? They've added a couple of tables and chairs and sell coffee and a pastry, muffin, whatever. No doughnuts, though. So me with my sweet tooth of course I sit down and get talking to the lady. She's a good listener and very calm, very self-assured – like she knows all the answers – but not bossy or anything. She's actually very relaxing to be around. Pam loves talking to her and, of course, she got the woman's story.

Jasmine's husband was killed in Syria or someplace like it, and she came to Canada with their two girls as refugees. I knew they were Middle Eastern or East Indian but I didn't know about their religion because they don't wear those headscarves so I couldn't tell.

She explained about there being different sects – same as Christianity – and how her beliefs don't include things like wearing hijabs or the other garments. Nevertheless you can tell that her religion is a deep part of her and her life. When you're talking to her you see that she's truly at peace with the world. I mean, sure she complains about stuff like taxes and how cars going racing down the street, shit like that, but I don't know how to explain it... but she's very restful to be around. She's kind and you feel that. The things she's told me have been a real eye-opener."

"You're turning into a convert!" laughed Gerry.

"No, God no. Never that. But I no longer lump them all together as Muslim, now I say 'extremist' for the bad guys."

"Well, I can't say you've convinced me. Sure, she sounds like a nice lady but hey, isn't that part of the plan? the thing about it being Okay to lie to infidels like us?"

"I know what you're saying but it's not like that with Jasmine. Not in a million years."

"If you say so."

"I do, and I've had these kind of things, these positive experiences - happen my whole life. You know what it's like, once you meet someone different your opinion changes. Or doesn't, I mean it depends on the person of course, but once you see folks as individuals it's hard to make blanket judgements. You know what I mean, right?

"Yeah, I guess I know what you're saying. So anyhow, this woman, this Jasmine helped you find your serenity, is that it?"

"Well, what she said and the way she is herself... yeah, she helped. Not that she knows about the cancer, nobody knows. We're gonna have to let some people know closer to the time but we've been hoping to keep it quiet until Jake goes back home in a few days."

"He's a real good-looking boy but then mixed-race kids usually are."

"That's true, and Jake will turn into a heart-breaker for sure, same as his father was.

Pam learned she couldn't have kids back when she was a teenager and she told me like it was a confession of a bad thing or something before we got married – as if that would matter to me! I guess I'd always expected I'd have a family some day but I never planned it in my mind or anything. So I was fine with no kids but after we'd been married a couple of years she asked what I would think about adopting and right away it felt like a great idea.

There was one drawback, though. Child Welfare Services said we couldn't adopt if I was going to be on the road as a long-distance trucker. They said it wouldn't be fair to the child to have an absent parent. Even though that's how it would be if we'd had the kid on our own. I mean, you and I both know plenty of families in that exact situation. Gerry, you were in that situation."

"Yeah, but I'm not the best example, good buddy."

"Ha! you're right. But anyhow, Child Welfare has to do its very best for the children so I agreed to come off the Trans-Canada to haul locally."

"I knew you'd stopped running cross-country but I didn't know why."

"Yeah, it was for Michael's sake, so that Pam and I could make a proper home for him."

"But both you and Pam are Albertans so what made you decide to settle here?"

"Well, we grew up with the mountains and the big skies and yeah, we're Albertans but we both fell in love with the ocean. I bet this'll sound funny to you but to us Banff and the parks have all become so touristy and so crowded."

"No way! Niagara Falls, now that's shockingly commercialized but Banff and Jasper are rustic and scenic with none of that neon shit or loud music blaring out on the street."

"True, but those places became very different from what we knew and grew up with. I've heard other people say the same as what you said, that the parks aren't commercial at all, which is why I said you'll think this is weird but yeah, to us they have. Anyhow, the ocean – now that's something else!"

"As a Newfie I have to confess that the ocean to me is, well it smells and there's dead things washing ashore, it can be very dangerous, and it gets so cold in the wintertime..."

"See? we each turned to something different. Pam came with me on one of my trips to the Maritimes and that's when we fell for the place. Everything was so green. It was a lot cheaper to buy here as well so that worked out great."

"Happy family and a white picket fence, eh?"

"Something like that. We don't see as much of our son as we'd like since, funny enough he moved out West, but it's been terrific having Jake with us for the summer."

"He's a good kid."

"Nooo, he's the nicest and best kid in the world!"

Chapter Twenty-Two

The two men had arrived back home in a good mood, best of friends as always. Everyone had turned in early.

Pam puttered around in the dark of their bedroom, not wanting to wake up Dale. At night his breathing was harsh but not as bad as his snoring had been! It was one of the nurses at the cancer clinic who told her about lifting up the broadloom to help reduce – or even end – the snoring problem. Pam commented that she could do that and put down a few throw rugs but the nurse shook her head saying: "No, no. Leave it as bare floors only. Throw rugs are dangerous accidents waiting to happen."

Dawdling, Pam realized she was putting off going to bed. She was dry-eyed now but afraid the tears would come gushing as soon as the thoughts started racing around in her head. She knew Gerry's coming would mean nothing but bad news, but she had no idea how devastating it would be.

Most of her mind - and all of her heart - refused to believe what he had said about Dale. He was her husband who had loved and cherished her all these years, what Gerry said wasn't possible. Except a smaller part of her accepted that it was.

Dale has suffered from blackouts and he'd had a couple of scans before the doctors okayed him to drive again. He wasn't a big complainer, he kept things inside, but she remembered that he'd had crushing headaches even after he got his Class A back.

She'd always known that the killer was connected to Big Sky Moving because of the moving pad found in one of the victim's homes. That policeman who came to Edmonton from Winnipeg had hammered that point home. She'd explained that anyone could have picked up one of their pads as a mistake or a theft. Arnie, the warehouseman, had even taken the cop out back to show him the pads stacked up in each loading bay, beside the big doors.

But of course, it was everything else too. All circumstantial but when you added it up well... At the time they hadn't added it up because there was a lot they hadn't known. And then what they did know got blown away by subsequent events.

"In truth, Gerry was a more likely candidate," she thought. "He might proclaim himself to be 'a lover of the ladies' but his attitude is pretty demeaning when you think about it."

He romanced plenty of women but once he got what he wanted he dumped them. Pam recalled the many phone messages and even being accused of not passing them on because Gerry hadn't called back. Could his callous treatment have indicated contempt - or worse?

She remembered when she met up with Gerry in Calgary and he'd told her then about Dale delivering in Kingston. She hadn't known about that before. And with what happened later that Saturday night it was no wonder she'd forgotten it along with everything else. But of course that damn article in the paper reawakened memories and brought so much to light.

She understood Gerry's worries about the cases being re-opened. Nowadays social justice warriors were quick to take up causes and choose sides. Hordes of unknown people got involved with their opinions and their anger and shaming and victimizing.

No doubt the author of this 'true crime' article fervently hoped this story would go viral. His ridicule of the cops as incompetent or lazy would go down well with the conspiracy-theory crowd. Those people who make themselves important by believing they've got insider knowledge.

A story about a previously unknown Canadian serial killer would 'spread like wildfire' along with accusations of police corruption or cover-up. Everyone and everything would come under the merciless spotlight of public opinion, ill-informed or otherwise.

Gerry was right. This could mean trouble for all of them. They needed to come up with an alternate solution, a plausible suspect, someone to divert attention from Gerry or Dale.

She slipped under the duvet and Dale immediately turned to wrap an arm around her waist, same as always. He was still sound asleep but since the bed was only a double they always spooned in the night. Pam surprised herself by falling asleep right away.

Chapter Twenty-Three

As usual, Pam's bladder woke her up in the wee hours. When she came back to bed her mind stayed awake with thoughts swirling but not panicky, coalescing into ideas. She considered various scenarios while snuggled under the duvet.

Next morning she woke in a good mood having come to a decision and worked out a plan

Dale was half-humming half-singing in the kitchen as he fried bacon. She stopped in the doorway to enjoy the sound of his pleasant baritone. When he saw her he opened his arms wide and she slipped into his embrace. With the top of her head nestled under his chin she listened to him sing the song's chorus:

♫ I know my past

You were there

In everything I've done

You are the one. ♫

Pam tilted her head back and gave him a smile saying:

"'5 Days in May' is one of my favourites by Blue Rodeo."

"You're my favourite."

"I can't be, you wouldn't give me the moon, remember?"

Dale laughed recalling an old memory of the two of them one night at Bow Falls in Banff. They'd been admiring the full moon and its reflection on the water. He'd told her then that she could have the mountains but he was keeping the moon.

"Such good times, baby."

Pam suddenly buried her head against Dale's chest and gave him a tight bear hug.

"What's this all about?"

"I'm going to miss you so much," she whispered.

Before Dale could reply Jake bounded into the kitchen full of energy announcing he was starving and the bacon smelled soooooo good!

"Are you guys dancing?"

Pam blinked back tears and answered: "I'm afraid Grandpa doesn't dance."

"Really? why didn't you ever teach him?"

"I wanted to but he refused to learn."

"No need to go making a spectacle of myself."

"I've heard of couples who dance in the kitchen and I always thought that sounded like such fun. You can always be a spectacle for me."

"Kitchen dancing sounds like something Gerry would do. I can see him two-steppin' and line-dancing and getting in everybody's way."

"You're right about that. Where is he, outside?"

"No, he's still in bed!"

"You're joking. Look at the time."

"Well, he finished that case of beer he bought so I'm thinking he's not so much sleeping as sleeping it off. Guess he passed out!"

"Ha! I remember those 'bad old days'. Let's make lots of noise and wake him up."

"You already did, Miss Pamela, thanks so much."

Gerry appeared in the kitchen with his hair on end, unshaven, and scowling.

"Just the guy we want to ask: Gerry, did you ever dance with any of your wives in the kitchen?"

"Of course, doesn't everyone?"

"Seeeee," said Pam.

The four of them sat down while Dale poured coffee and Pam gave Jake orange juice.

"Anyone else for juice?" she asked, holding up the container. Gerry shook his head but Dale said he'd take a glass.

Gerry doctored up his coffee with plenty of sugar, took a drink then said he'd finish is outside while he had a smoke.

Dale served up a breakfast of bacon, scrambled eggs, and toast. That represented about the sum total of his cooking ability. All summer Pam had appreciated that most days Dale fixed breakfast for him and Jake, although sometimes it was only cereal, before they headed out for the morning. It gave her some quiet time to herself while she tidied up the place and got ready for the day. They'd meet up again at lunch time and the three of them would do something together, even if it was just playing a game of Uno.

She also knew that Dale placed great value on that time with his grandson, and in the future Jake would remember those mornings as happy times.

"Can I be excused? I want to go ride my bike," Jake asked. He was already standing, hopping actually, and his grandparents waved him away. They'd picked up that bike at a garage sale for an excellent price.

Gerry came back in with his empty cup saying he'd drunk the coffee but still had a brutal headache and thought he'd go back to bed.

"Do you want anything to eat?"

"God, no."

"How about a couple of extra-strength aspirin?"

"No, I... wait, yeah okay, maybe aspirin will help."

Pam fetched the bottle and Gerry shook out the tablets and threw them in his mouth. Dale passed over his glass of orange juice saying:

"They'll work faster if you don't take them dry."

"Really?" Gerry was doubtful but took a sip nevertheless. He didn't look well as he headed back down the hallway to his temporary bedroom in the den.

Dale stacked up some plates then moved them to one side while he reached across to take Pam's hand.

"You know I hate to think of leaving you on your own. It's the waiting, the not knowing 'when' that's getting to me." She didn't reply, knowing there was more to come.

"I want to get this assisted suicide arranged while I'm still well enough to make decisions."

"Oh no, Dale!"

"Hear me out. I never talk much about Sissy, it's so long ago that I was married to her, but lately I've been thinking a lot about her death. I was talking to Gerry about it. Remembering her pain and my anger that there was nothing I could do to fix it. She begged the doctor to give her something but it wasn't legal then–"

"It's not legal now," Pam interrupted. "Sure, the Supreme Court ruled in favour a few months back but the law hasn't been done up yet. You can't get it."

"Actually I can. I've looked into it..." he stopped at the hurt look on her face and reached for her other hand. Holding both tightly he continued saying: "This matters to me a lot. I spoke to Dr. Robertson who can't do anything himself but he mentioned that doctor who's been in the news for helping people out now, ahead of the new law being enacted. Dr. Robertson knows her and will refer me. He said she's confident none of the charges against her will come to court until after the law has passed which her lawyer says means they'll be dropped. I don't care about any of that but I'll be her guinea pig if she'll do the deed."

"But I don't want to lose you a moment sooner than I have to!" cried Pam.

"Honey, I can't go through what Sissy went through, and I'm not going to have you feel what I felt. I felt helpless and hurting and... ashamed isn't the right word but I kind of felt embarrassed for Sissy. To let other people see her naked pain it was so... I don't know, I can't describe it but I sure know I don't want it."

"When Dad died I remember Mom telling me that a nurse said something to her about 'seeing their pain makes it easier for us to let them go, because we want their pain to end'. Well, I don't want to see you in pain, and I can understand that you don't want to waste away in a hospice, but Dale, honey, I.. I..." she started crying but noticed Jake hovering in the doorway.

"Oh come on in Jake, don't mind me. Grandma's a teary old fool." She hastily wiped her eyes and sent Dale a 'to be continued' look but his face was set and immediately she knew he'd made up his mind.

"Are you sick or something Grandpa T?" asked the boy.

"Well you know Jake I have been feeling pretty tired a lot lately so it might be that I've caught a bug or something."

"You should go to the doctor then."

"Buddy, that's a good idea. I'll take your advice and make an appointment. But not until after you leave because I don't want to be sitting around in a doctor's waiting room when you and me have only got a few more days together. What a waste that would be, eh?"

Chapter Twenty-Four

"Gerry's leaving today so I'm going to drag him out for a walk and a final chat before he goes. Jake, why don't you and Grandpa watch another movie while I'm gone?"

The boy ran to the living-room to choose a DVD while Pam headed down the hall. She knocked loudly on the door to the den saying:

"Rise and shine, Gerry. Some fresh air and exercise will cure what ails you."

A muffled voice called back: "Pretty sure that's the cure for jet lag, woman, not a hangover. I'll be out in a minute, let me get dressed in peace."

Pam checked on Dale and Jake. Satisfied that they were comfortable – Dale's eyelids were already drooping – she waved goodbye and went outside to wait for Gerry. When he appeared she noticed he still hadn't shaved and realized if he grew a beard it would be solid white.

They wandered down the road towards a hilly area covered in blueberries. Pam told Gerry that she'd decided to say and do nothing.

"If I tell Dale what you think, what you've figured out, I know he'll turn himself in. Even if his memory doesn't come back he'll say if he committed those crimes the police will have to investigate. He'll insist on accepting responsibility, even if it all happened in some fugue or dissociated state."

"He wouldn't exactly be confessing, he can't if he doesn't actually remember it. I don't think they'd arrest him. They might even think he got carried away after reading the article and was making it all up. I heard some people do shit like that, to get attention or to be punished or something."

"True, but even if you're right and the police don't believe him he would suffer terribly over it. He'd feel guilty, and then he'd start worrying about what other bad things he might have done and forgotten. You know, he always said he couldn't understand how some people couldn't figure out what was right or wrong. Dale always said it's an easy answer because the right thing to do is whichever choice is hardest."

"Yeah, he always saw things, moral things at least, in black and white. I could sense him disapproving of me way back when when we were rooming together. So how are you going to cope with this, Pammy?"

"Since you forced this truth on me now you have to share the burden of secrecy. We both have to learn how to live with the knowledge and keep it locked away inside. I won't have Dale upset when he has so little time left. And I won't have him remembered as a killer either," she spoke fiercely.

Gerry was nodding along as she spoke. He said in his own way he loves Dale too. Everything would always be kept as a secret between them, so long as he wasn't arrested for the murders.

"You won't be arrested, we all know it had to have been that American driver. It's what we all said at the time. The guy with the super strong Southern accent."

"What guy? I don't remember him."

"Sure you do, he travelled alongside you and Dale. Every time you arrived at a new place he'd already be there or would arrive shortly after. I remember both of you commenting on it. I can't remember the guy's name but he was from the South and he was around for a few weeks. I only met him the one time – when you two were in Edmonton – and as best as I can recall he wasn't a tall guy – about 5′ 8″ or 9″, big though with a pot belly – no doubt it was a beer belly – and a broad chest with big shoulders, big arms. A strong man. His hair and beard, a bushy one, was black and gray but not a salt-and-pepper mix, no he had quite dramatic colouring of solid black streaked with solid gray. Soft-spoken and didn't say much but he was friendly enough. You remember him now, right?"

"No, you know I can't place–"

"Wrack your brains if you have to, because if you value our friendship you will recall him," Pam stared into Gerry's face purposefully. Finally he understood.

"Umm yeah, you know now I do remember. Can't believe I forgot about him. Didn't he have one of those double first names like Billy-Bob, Billy-James, but it wasn't Billy, uh, it was Jimmy-something, right? Jimmy-Mac?"

"Ha-ha no, that's from an old song, an old Sixties song: 'Jimmy Mack when are you coming back?' something like that. But you know Jimmy-something does sound familiar."

"Jimmy-Joe! That's it, Jimmy-Joe from New Orleans. He listened to jazz music instead of country."

"So you remember him now?"

"Clear as day. He was always hanging around and you're right he was a quiet guy, a listener, never joining in the debates or arguing. Hmmph, wonder what ever happened to him?"

"Oh, I expect he went back home when the police got around to questioning drivers about the murders. He might have told people he was up here working illegally but that's not the real reason, he hightailed it back home before his movements could be investigated. He slipped away while the going was good and no one was the wiser."

"You know it makes sense now but back then none of us pieced it all together. We weren't thinking serial killer stuff so nobody mentioned him to the cops."

"Yeah, that's what happened. I don't think I ever even heard the words 'serial killer' back then."

"I do. I remember Grub or somebody telling us all it had to be but he always had an opinion on everything and liked to hear himself talk. Nobody paid him much attention. Do you think Dale will remember that American guy?"

"His memory is pretty sketchy from that time but he'll agree with us if we say the guy was around."

"Yeah, Jimmy-Joe whatever got away scot-free."

"Hmm, somebody like that, once he got a taste for killing, no doubt he kept killing when he got back Stateside. I expect he was caught down there and sent to death row."

"You're right, I'll bet that's what happened."

The two exchanged conspiratorial smiles, happy with the so-called memory they'd managed to create. Each was confident they could share it with the police or the media if they were ever questioned.

"You know Pamela, when it's all over... much later on and when you're ready for company again, I'm going to come back to see you."

Gerry's eyes held a challenge, his charm turned on full force and his mouth curved into his trademark I-know-a-secret smile.

Pamela looked at him hard then, giving her head a slight shake, replied quietly: "No, I don't think that's a good idea."

"Oh Pammy," he laughed: "When did I ever let common sense get in my way?"

"Don't call me Pammy!"

Grateful acknowledgement is made for permission to reprint an excerpt from the following copyrighted work:

"5 Days in May" written by Jim Cuddy and Greg Keelor. Performed by Blue Rodeo. Discovery Records & Warner Music Group © 1993 All rights reserved. Used by permission.

Thank you Susan de Cartier, www.StarfishEntertainment.com

About the Author

Ever since her Grade Two composition was read over the school's PA system Lynda has been passionate about writing.

Her first novel "The Trans-Canada Killer" was published in 2022. Thanks to reader feedback she's written a sequel. The novella "What Happened Next" is not a standalone.

Lynda and her partner live with a tuxedo cat in the sunniest city in Canada, nestled in the foothills of the Rocky Mountains.

Read more at www.lyndafrench.com.

Milton Keynes UK
Ingram Content Group UK Ltd.
UKHW040640050923
428087UK00001B/117